Natasha Mostert grew up in South Africa, and was educated in Johannesburg and New York. Previous jobs include selling shoes, working as a university teacher, a freelance journalist and in the publishing department of a New York television station.

Writing is not Natasha's only passion. She is also an avid kickboxer, and her main sparring partner is her instructor, a former European kickboxing champion. Boxing also helps her with the writing process. In her study hangs a boxer's speedball, which she uses to break the tension of her creative day.

To learn more about Natasha, her novels, and her involvement in the CPAU Fighting for Peace programme, which is teaching Afghan women how to box and feel empowered in their lives, please visit her website: www.natashamostert.co.uk.

D1375888

Also by Natasha Mostert

SEASON OF THE WITCH

and published by Bantam Books

THE KEEPER

Natasha Mostert

OKS

CKLAND • JOHANNESBURG

TRANSWORLD PUBLISHERS
61–63 Uxbridge Road, London W5 5SA
A Random House Group Company
www.rbooks.co.uk

THE KEEPER
A BANTAM BOOK: 9780553818680

First publication in Great Britain
Bantam edition published 2009

Addresses for Random House Group Ltd companies outside the UK
can be found at: www.randomhouse.co.uk
The Random House Group Ltd Reg. No. 954009

The Random House Group Limited supports The Forest Stewardship Council (FSC), the
leading international forest certification organisation. All our titles that are printed on
Greenpeace approved FSC certified paper carry the FSC logo. Our paper procurement
policy can be found at
www.rbooks.co.uk/environment

Typeset in 13/14.5 Fournier by
Falcon Oast Graphic Art Ltd.
Printed in the UK by CPI Cox & Wyman, Reading, RG1 8EX.

2 4 6 8 10 9 7 5 3 1

AUTHOR'S NOTE

I make use of both Chinese and Japanese martial-arts terms and for ease of reference I have used the term *ideogram* for graphic symbols that are genuine ideograms, i.e., characters representing ideas, as well as for *logograms*, where the characters represent morphemes or words.

I dedicate this book to Isabella and Tatyana:
two little Keepers in the making

THE KEEPER

LIGHT

There's no prayer like desire

Tom Waits, as quoted in Mark Epstein, *Open to Desire*

PROLOGUE

Rosalia came into his life during his gap year. He had just finished school and hiking through Europe on his own felt like a great adventure. He was surrounded by beauty: soaring cathedrals, museums like jewel boxes, ethereal frescos, heroic sculpture. He was happy. It was a year in which time was suspended and reality kept at bay.

But after ten months he was running out of money. Soon he would have to return to England and decide what he wanted to do with the rest of his life. He had no idea what this decision would be, and the knowledge that such a defining moment awaited him made him feel emotionally exhausted.

Palermo was to be the last stop on this journey. He arrived late in the afternoon but still in time to visit the city's most famous tourist attraction.

He drew his tongue over his dry lips; he was thirsty. On his way to the catacombs he had become lost. He did not speak Italian and had difficulty following the broken English of the shop owners he asked for direction. It all felt slightly nightmarish as he walked through Palermo's alleyways, his legs becoming ever more tired and heavy.

He looked straight up at the far sky above him and it was a glazed, parched blue. There was no relief from the heat even though the tall houses on either side almost touched each other and threw deep shadows.

In here it was cooler and very quiet. The tourist buses had all left. Even the hooded Capuchin monk who had taken his donation with listless fingers had disappeared. He was on his own: all alone with eight thousand mummies.

The most surprising thing was that the bodies did not smell – there was no odour except for dust. He wondered if they had ever smelt. Perhaps when they were first placed inside their strainers and left to dry there would have been a stench of rotting flesh. Even the porous limescale would not have been able to dampen down completely the fruity smell of human ooze. But after an eight-month stay in darkness, these corpses would have been taken from their cells, washed with vinegar and lime and exposed to open air: fresh as a housewife's laundry.

He looked down at the guidebook in his hands.

In 1599, Capuchin monks discovered a way to preserve the dead, and Sicilians from all walks of life flocked to be buried here in the Catacombe dei Cappucini. The deceased often specified the clothes in which they wished to enter the afterlife and many stipulated that their garments were to be changed over time.

His eyes travelled up the twenty-foot wall until it

reached the vaulted ceiling. The mummies lined the wall in rows: monks, lawyers, shopkeepers, matrons and maids. Virgins with steel bands encircling their heads to indicate their untouched state. All were dressed, and many were standing, some with hands folded across their stomachs and a jolly slant to their heads. Others screamed silently with open mouths. Many had lost ears, or were missing jaws and hands, while others had defied the passage of time with more success: the caramel flesh truly mummified and the eyes cradled within dusty sockets. There were even mummies with ropes round their necks, but another glance at the guidebook told him that these were not the corpses of criminals but the remains of pious men. The ropes were not nooses, but symbols of penance, worn by the monks during their lifetime and carried with them into death.

Death. As he walked slowly down the long, death-choked corridors he wondered at the ambiguity of this word. When did death take place? Did death come when the brain stopped? His father, a doctor, had told him the brain sometimes continued its electric dance for up to ten minutes after the heart had ceased to supply it with blood. 'The master switch' was what his father called the brain. The conductor. The commander-in-chief.

But he remembered his grandmother's death. His father had given permission for her organs to be harvested and she was to become what was known as a 'beating heart cadaver'. On the day she was pronounced no longer alive, he remembered leaning kiss-close and marvelling at the colour of her skin. Her brain had flatlined, but she was hooked up to a respirator and her heart was beating. Inside her liver was a pulse. Her hands were warm and she would bleed if she were cut. This was his grandmother. They told him she was dead, but she looked alive.

The practice of mummification was outlawed in 1881. But in 1920 an exception was made for three-year-old Rosalia Lombardo, nicknamed 'Sleeping Beauty'. Her father, stricken with grief, begged a certain Dr Salofia to keep his daughter alive for ever. Remarkably, Dr Salofia managed to defeat the process of decay. Rosalia is a marvel and looks like a pretty sleeping doll who might awaken at any moment. Dr Salofia's secret died with him: no one knows the method he used to preserve the little girl.

She was lying in a glass coffin in the chapel and her face was innocence itself: the nose pert, the mouth sweet, the cheeks infant plump. Her ears were tiny shells, and long lashes feathered her closed eyelids. The soft pink bow on top of her head made her look vulnerable, as did the wispy tendrils of hair tumbling over her forehead.

He stared at her, not quite believing how perfect she was.

How could her father have borne it to leave her here? Why preserve a three-year-old child and leave her to sleep under the gaze of a thousand leering scarecrows?

A beam of late-afternoon sunlight fell through the tiny, leaded window and made it look as though a sheen of sweat was on her brow. And in that instant he suddenly had a clear understanding of how his future must look. Life-defining moments sometimes happened serendipitously. In that one moment – in that most unlikely of places – the course of his life was set.

Rosalia was not about preserving the dead. Rosalia was about making a wish. A wish to stop time – a wish, in fact, for eternal life.

Keep her alive for ever. A father's desperate plea. And clever, busy Dr Salofia with his chemicals and fluids and overreaching genius had gone to work. But he was not a healer, he was a preserver. He had succeeded in keeping intact a perfect shell, but in the end that was all she was: a shell. The brain dead. The heart dead.

Maybe the master switch was neither the brain nor the heart. Maybe the answer to life lay elsewhere . . .

When he arrived back in England he enrolled in university to study medicine. His father was convinced he had played the deciding role in helping his son decide on a profession, but that was not the truth. It was not his father who had been key, but a little girl with a pink bow in her hair.

And now, every night before closing his eyes, he would think of darkness coming to the chapel of the Catacombe dei Cappucini and tiny Rosalia sleeping in her glass case, a thousand mummified bodies pressed close around her like an army of the dead. And it would remind him that the strongest desire of all was to live. To live *for ever*.

THE KEEPER

I think that when you tattoo somebody, something can happen. Not always. But something extreme can happen . . . You are physically opening up the body . . . And if you're opening a person up, you're letting something in. You can put information in.

Alex Binnie, as quoted in Chris Wroblewski,
Skin Shows: The Tattoo Bible

CHAPTER ONE

The net curtains inside the window lifted and the night air that entered the room was scented with the smell of exhaust fumes, chips fried in old oil, warm pavements and, incongruously, the perfume of roses.

The man sitting in the deep armchair glanced out of the window as the curtain fluttered again. In the darkness outside, he could just see the rosebush drooping against the windowsill and the sight of the creamy petals made him smile. Amy had worked hard in their small garden and it was beginning to show. The only thing left was to fix the crumbling brickwork of the outer wall. He had promised ages ago he'd take care of it, but for the past eight weeks every free moment he had was spent at the gym. But hadn't it been worth it? Besides, now that the fight was behind him, he would have loads of time to tackle the outstanding chores round the house.

He shifted in his chair, trying to ease himself into a position that would cause him the least amount of discomfort. His entire body was sore. The muscles of his shoulders ached as though he had carried around bags of cement. Even after three days, his left leg still throbbed where Burke had kicked him in the thigh. Burke was a tough bastard. And sneaky – the referee had had to step in twice. But what a fight: he knew he would never have another one like it again.

From the direction of the kitchen came the voices of Amy and Tom-Tom. It was long past Tom's bedtime, but he and Amy were going easy on the little fellow: they were all feeling festive this week. He could hear his son's voice as he excitedly described something he had seen in the park earlier in the day. Amy was laughing, and then came the sound of running water and the clatter of dishes.

He smiled again. He usually did the washing-up but Amy was giving him the week off as a reward. 'Just this week, mind,' she had warned. 'Don't get too comfortable in that chair, O Victorious One.'

'I think a win like that deserves two weeks of downtime, at least.'

She pulled a face. 'You defended yourself like a Muppet in the fourth. Dropped your hands. No reward for that.'

'True. So how about rewarding me for being sexy and handsome?'

'One week,' she said firmly.

So he had four more days of the easy life left; better make the most of it. He stretched out his hand for the television remote control. Amy had taped the fight and he wanted to watch it again. It would be about the hundredth time, but what the hell, they didn't make them any better than this.

The tape was already loaded in the VCR. As he pointed

the remote at the set, something descended in front of his eye – a shadow blurring his vision. He barely had time to register it, when it disappeared. But then a few moments later, there it was again – a darkness. He blinked and his vision cleared once more. Odd.

A sound at the door made him turn his head. His son was waddling into the room, a fluffy green toy clutched to his chest.

'Hey, little one. You want to watch the fight with Daddy?'

But Tom was having none of it. 'No.' Without further ado, he pressed a small fat finger on the VCR's eject button. 'Tubbies.'

'OK.' He knew better than to argue. He watched as Tom substituted his *Tellytubbies* tape for the fight tape, the pudgy little hands switching cassettes in a no-nonsense way he had to admire. The kid knew what he wanted.

The screen filled with singing Tubbies. Truth to tell, he found the creatures bloody creepy. The identical pinched faces, the small, fixed smiles, the round eyes ... ugh.

As he reached out to pull Thomas on to his lap, a blackness moved across his eye again. It was the same shadow as before, but this time it lingered longer, as though a disc were slid across his eyeball. It caught him by surprise.

He touched his eyebrow. He blinked slowly, deliberately. When he opened his eye again the disc had slid back to where it had come from and his vision was once more unimpaired. Weird. And scary. He did not like this.

Thomas snuggled against him and after a while he felt

himself relax. His son was growing up fast but he still had that baby smell coming from the back of his head. God certainly knew what he was about when he created that smell. One sniff and you were pretty much at the mercy of the little tykes.

The red Tubby was giving a flower to the Tubby with the antenna on his head. The yellow Tubby was skipping from one leg to the other. The purple Tubby ... He couldn't see the purple Tubby because the disc was moving across his eye again like an eclipse, blocking out the light.

At the same time his body was suddenly gripped by a colossal energy drain. The drain seemed to emanate from his abdomen, as though all the energy in his body were sucked from a spot just below his navel. His breath left his lips in a surprised ooph. Every organ in his body sagged. He tried to lift his arm but he did not have the strength. He tried to move his head but it was too heavy.

At that moment he knew he was about to die. He did not see any tunnel. No bright lights in the distance. No heavenly voices beckoning. Just the terrible sense of vitality and life and power rushing from his body, as though there was a hole in his stomach with his life force gushing out of it like a blindingly bright geyser. He looked down as though he might actually be able to see the energy flowing from his body in an incandescent stream: white and fierce.

'Aaah.' His lips moved but the sound was tiny. His eyelids fluttered; the black sun was moving across his eyeball once more. And from far away he heard Thomas saying, 'Daddy? Night-night?'

At that exact moment, two hundred miles away, a woman was asleep and dreaming. Her bedroom was filled with shadows but outside her open window the night sky was stained with the orange haze of city lights.

The hinges of the window creaked. A breeze was blowing: it carried with it a wild, primordial smell from the vast river that flowed strong and cold somewhere out there in the darkness. Of all these things the woman was unaware. She had already walked deep, deep into her dream.

A voice was urgently calling her name: it was her mother's voice and it came from far away. She kept following the voice, her heart beating anxiously.

In the distance was a pool of light. The light was weak – the kind of light you encountered in monasteries and old libraries – and indeed, when she reached it, she found herself in a room where the walls were covered with books. Suddenly it was deadly quiet. She could no longer hear her mother's voice.

So many books. But only one book that mattered. It was tucked away on a high shelf and she had to stand on her toes and tip it towards her with one finger. The book was large and she marvelled at the elegance of the binding and how soft the tooled leather felt inside her palm. The title was stamped in gilt and even though the lettering was faded she could still read it well. *The Book of Light and Dust*. She had never seen this book before but the feeling it evoked in her was one of awe and dread. Slowly, she opened the cover but as her finger touched the first, creamy white page, her eyes went blind.

She dropped the book and brought her fingers to her unseeing eyes. In the inexplicable way of dreams she lifted her head to look into a mirror and her face stared back at her, true in every detail except for the eye sockets that were withered and empty.

Her mouth contorted in horror and she screamed.

CHAPTER TWO

Nick sensed her presence at his elbow a split second before he felt the slap on his bum.

'Come on, Nicky. Get a move on. Keep up with me – come on, come on.' Another admonishing pat and Mia accelerated past him.

Nick stared at her bitterly. She looked as fresh as a daisy. There might have been a little sweat at her hairline and her T-shirt showed a couple of damp patches but her breath was flowing easily and there was a spring to her footsteps. He, on the other hand, was dragging his feet like an old man and from his throat came an odd, very unattractive wheeze.

She was now running backwards, beckoning him like a mischievous siren. 'Catch me! Come on, you can do it!'

He gave a despairing gurgle and made an attempt to increase his speed, but he just didn't have it in him. He was only one week into his training, which meant he was nowhere near fit and also needed to lose another thir-teen pounds.

Mia was now sprinting effortlessly down the tree-lined avenue. The woman was indefatigable. Under normal

circumstances he would have enjoyed watching her graceful figure as she moved away from him: the shapely legs,
the strong, beautiful V of her back, the delicate but
rounded hips. But just at this moment, she made him feel
like a decrepit old dog.

He stopped and drew his hand across his forehead. His
chest burned. His legs wobbled. He felt like seven pounds
of crap pushed into a two-pound bag.

Why the hell was he doing this to himself? He could be
drinking a latte at Caruso's right now. Reading the paper.
Eating a pastry. One of those little cannoli with the thick
cream filling and the crumbly sweet crust ... served to
him by the cute waitress with the cute lisp who said she
liked his curly hair.

He closed his eyes briefly. Shape up, Duffy. Be a man.
No pastries for you: oat bran and skimmed milk. And no
pretty waitresses either. Eleven weeks to go before the
fight.

Eleven weeks. Shit.

Doggedly, he started running again. Mia had already
reached the gate and was about to leave the park. She
cupped her hands round her mouth. 'I'm heading out! I'll
get the coffee ready!'

He perked up. Coffee. Yes, he could do with some
coffee.

She gestured at the steel monkey bars to her left.
'Thirty pull-ups. OK, Nicky? Three sets. No cheating!'

He sighed, lifted a hand in acknowledgement.

But he managed to do only two sets of pull-ups before

his shoulders gave out on him and he decided enough was enough. He had another gruelling training session lined up in the gym tonight – it made sense to conserve energy. As he left the park, the temptation to hail a taxi was almost irresistible but he didn't have the guts. Mia would give him no end of hell if he didn't run – or at least jog – the distance to her place.

It was only seven in the morning but the heat had already settled on London like a steaming dishcloth. Summer was his favourite season, but the city hadn't seen rain in weeks and pollutants in the air were creating a haze the colour of lemon squash. As he jogged past irritable pedestrians, his lungs sucked up the exhaust fumes of the cars and he coughed like a refugee from a cigarette factory. Bloody hell. This couldn't be healthy.

He turned off the traffic-congested high street into a relatively quiet side street. Straight ahead of him, at the end of the terrace, was the green and gold sign of the Mystic Ink Body Art Studio.

The place had made the leap from tattoo parlour to studio a few years ago after Mia had embarked on a ruthless renovation process, ripping out the Gothic interior and replacing it with dazzling white paint and pale wooden floors. A big improvement, Nick was the first to admit, but he was sometimes nostalgic for the old place.

Before the makeover it was your typical old-fashioned tattoo parlour. Fearsome pieces of machinery lurked in the corner. Taped against the walls were 'flash' art depicting coiled pythons and big-breasted women. When you entered, you pushed your way through a beaded curtain that continued to whisper long after you had passed through. In those days it was known simply as Molly's Place.

Molly Lockhart. Blue eyes, blonde hair. Skin straight from the fjords. Mia's mum had been a stunner, no argument. But there was something unknowable about her. You would look into her eyes and get the impression they were focused on something only she was able to see. A wild bird, that one: no wonder she had died a wild death.

Nick always wondered what it must have been like for Mia to grow up with Molly as a mother. Body artist, Reiki practitioner, stargazer: many people round here had called Molly wacky. Others were true believers – his own mother, for one. She used to consult Molly on a regular basis and for many years Nick's birth chart had hung above his mother's bed: stars and constellations and secret significations beautifully mapped in Indian ink by Molly Lockhart only a few days after his birth. That chart now hung in his own flat – not because he set any store in its celestial predictions, but because it represented such a strong link with his childhood.

And with Mia. Her own birth chart had been plotted by Molly alongside his. In a strange twist of fate, the two of them were born on the same day – he, a puny preemie; she, a lusty, bawling Amazon weighing in at almost ten pounds. And not only were they born on the same day, they were born only an hour apart.

His mother was fascinated by this coincidence. 'That is important, yes?' she would ask in her Greek-accented English. 'Nicholas and Mia. Their future – destiny – it is linked, yes?'

If only, Mum. But it takes two to tango.

He could smell the coffee as he walked down the steep steps that led down from street level to Mia's tiny court-yard. The door on the other side stood open and he could see straight into the kitchen. Just like her mother before her, Mia both lived and conducted business in this narrow, terraced house. On the top floor were her bedroom, bath-room and the single room she used as an office. On the raised ground floor was the Mystic Ink tattoo studio with its separate entrance. In the basement was the kitchen and a surprisingly spacious living room extending a full twenty feet to the back.

She must have arrived only a few minutes before him. The coffee was still dripping into the pot.

She looked over her shoulder as he entered. 'Taxi?'

'Of course not.'

'Just checking. You're so lazy, Nicky.'

'Yes, dear.'

'I mean it.' An exasperated glance. 'If only you applied yourself a little more . . .'

'Stop bullying me, woman. Just because you're older than I am doesn't mean you can kick me around.'

She smiled unwillingly and gestured at a chair. 'Sit yourself down. Just watch out you don't squish Sweetpea.'

Sweetpea was Mia's pet chameleon. It was perched on the back of the seat and rolled a solemn eye at Nick as he gently placed his thumb against her belly. For a moment he thought she was going to act coy, but then she daintily hooked her prong-like toes on to his finger and allowed him to deposit her on the far corner of the table. Mia had a thing for chameleons. This was her third such pet and Nick still remembered the day she introduced the first one – also named Sweetpea – to her friends at school all of fifteen years ago. The teacher was unimpressed but Mia had instantly rendered herself the coolest kid in the neighbourhood.

And she was still cool, Mia Lockhart Cortez: as quirky and unusual as her name. He sat down on the chair and watched as she took two mugs from the cupboard.

She had a fascinating face. God had done a terrific job blending Molly's fairness with the dark good looks of Juan, Mia's Spanish father. Mia's eyes were black and her brows and lashes brushed with soot, but her hair was blonde; the colour of thick, dark honey. The surprisingly square jaw belonged to Juan. The rosebud mouth was Molly's. But it was her nose, slightly crooked and flat – the result of a childhood accident – that Nick loved most about her. It gave her an air of rakishness; a kind of jaunty insolence.

Unusual for a tattooist, Mia was not a walking advertisement for body art. On her right shoulder was inked the symbol for chi and round one ankle was twined a fragile garland of flowers. The Usui Reiki symbols – the symbols for healing – were tattooed on her wrists. He supposed she could be sporting other body art as well, but if she did – sadly – he had never been afforded the privilege of a private viewing.

She was looking a little pale this morning, he thought. He hadn't noticed it in the park, probably because he had been so caught up in his own misery. She also had shadows under her eyes.

'Are you all right?' He took the mug of coffee from her.

'I didn't sleep well, that's all.'

'Are you sure?'

'It was just a bad dream.' She placed her own mug on to the table with a firm little bump that made it clear the subject was closed. 'By the way, Nicky. I wanted to ask you if I could place an advertisement on Kime.'

'Of course. Send me the copy. I'll make sure you get a good spot.'

Nick was proud of Kime. If not exactly MySpace, Kime was still a bona fide success story. Launching your own social networking site on the Internet was a gamble – and an expensive one – but eighteen months ago Nick had decided to give it a try. After five years of working himself into burn-out on the trading floor, he felt he had earned the right to kick back and play a little. He had the money, so why not? But what was supposed to be a hobby had taken off in a big way. Nick had envisaged a modest site – a small, cosy forum catering to fighters and fight aficionados – but over the course of two years Kime's membership had grown by quantum leaps. The constantly rising number of contributors meant Nick was able to sell advertising space on the site at an ever increasing rate.

Mia's lips twitched. 'How's Rick doing these days?'

Nick shrugged, slightly embarrassed. She was referring to the fictional hero he brought to life on Kime every two weeks. Along with the profile pages and the communal discussion board, the site also played host to the adventures of Rick Cobra: ruthless ninja assassin with a heart of gold. Swift as a panther, strong as steel. Wrote poetry and made love to his cello with the same skill he made love to his women. The discussion board was still the big draw but it was gratifying to know that a growing number of fans were logging on specifically to read about his hero's exploits.

'Rick's doing fine. He has finally tracked down the gunrunner with the ruby tooth.'

She wrinkled her nose. 'I hope he's dumped that whiny redhead. What's her name again, Brunhilda?'

'Broselinda.'

'Right. That woman's no good for him.'

'She's misunderstood.'

Mia snorted. 'So how much do I owe you for the ad?'

'It's on the house, Mia.'

'No, no.' She stood up. 'Let me get my chequebook. It's in my office.'

While he waited for her to return, Nick idly opened a sketch pad that was lying on the table. The pad held a single charcoal drawing on the very first page.

He stared at the sketch, perturbed. It showed a woman's face, the features delicate but the mouth twisted in torment. And the eyes ... there was something very wrong with the eyes – they seemed hollowed out. That's when he realized: this was Mia. It was a self-portrait.

A movement at the door made him look up. Mia had re-entered the room.

He gestured at the sketch pad. 'This is . . . interesting.'

An odd expression flitted across her face. She closed the sketch pad and pushed it away from him – almost hitting Sweetpea in the process.

'What do I owe you?' She did not respond to the enquiring expression on his face and he knew better than to push.

He gave her a hefty discount, being careful not to alert her to the fact, and she signed the cheque with a flourish.

'Great. Thanks.'

'Will you be at Scorpio tonight?'

She nodded. 'I'll be doing Chilli's eight o'clock class.'

Chilli was Mia's teacher; her sensei. Mia was not a fighter, but she trained in martial arts. Combat was not her goal, but perfection of technique and a strengthening of the mind. Which did not mean that what she did in training was easy: Mia was able to break a board with the blade of her bare foot doing a spinning back kick. She could probably take him out easily if she felt like it.

Nick leaned over to give her a goodbye kiss on the cheek. She smelt of flowers, warm grass and a hint of sun-baked sweat.

'Remember' – she looked at him sternly – 'train hard . . .'

'Fight easy. Yeah, yeah. I know.' He hesitated. 'Are you sure you're OK, sweetheart?'

'Don't worry, Nicky. I'm fine.' She smiled. 'Now go on, get going.'

He crossed the tiny courtyard with its tubs of glowing pink and orange geraniums. As he was about to climb the steps that would take him to street level, he glanced back over his shoulder.

Mia was still standing at the table, looking down. The sketch pad in front of her lay open once more. Her body seemed relaxed, but it was the expression on her face that made him pause.

She looked apprehensive. No, she looked *scared*.

CHAPTER THREE

The Book of Light and Dust
For Rosalia
I

Once more I find myself lost in a void: the wind blowing through a clearing in the woods, a pool of dark water. Mysterious words and ancient memories are whispered in my ear. This is a place filled with many questions but only one answer.

The body wears out and we are old. Colours are not as bright; smells are not as sharp. We do not weep as easily. We sleep less and we dream less. Light is turning to dust.

But what if you become a thief? What if you steal the light and change what cannot be changed?

Imagine grasping the essence of life in your hand: the great energy. As fierce as a slashed throat. As terrible as a vast, glittering desert. White powder addictive.

Natasha Mostert

Imagine being able to live for ever.

THE WAY: BLOOD TIDE
BLACKLIGHT: DIR: K5 SP3, FRC: 3, TIME: 2, SUs: LU3
Whitelight: mas. TW5

38

CHAPTER FOUR

There was nothing like a bad dream to ruin your day.

Mia turned off the tap in the shower. For a few seconds she stood still, listening to the gurgle of water as it drained.

She was starting to feel better. Not great, mind you. Not 'hey-life-here-I-come' good, but better. She probably had Nick to thank for it; he always managed to make her smile.

As she reached for her bath towel she caught sight of her reflection in the mirror. With her arm outstretched, she was able to see in its entirety the large tattoo that covered the left side of her body, starting at her breast and stretching over her rib cage, her hip and her upper thigh.

It was a lovely piece of art. Her mother had inked it into her skin on the day Mia turned eighteen and was legally of an age to receive a tattoo. Ever since, this beautiful figure with the elegant limbs and fairy hair had flowed in shades of blue ink down the one side of her body.

The Keeper: her other self.

The Keeper's features were fine and the tattooed contours of her body as delicate as those of a Rackham water-baby. But it was her eyes that held your gaze. Long-lidded, set under eyebrows that swooped upwards like a startled bird in flight, they had been inked with such skill, they appeared alive. Deep in one eye was a circle with three lines entering it at an angle. It was an arresting tattoo and Molly had carried an identical figure on the left side of her own body – a tangible link between mother and daughter.

Mia turned away from the mirror and shrugged into her dressing gown. As she opened the bathroom door and stepped into her bedroom, a rush of steam followed her.

The room was full of light. There were flowers on the dressing table and a bumblebee hummed against the window. The leaves of the creeper peeking over the sill threw a perfect shadow pattern on the wall. Everything was calm; everything was serene.

Unlike last night. Last night this room had been dark with dread: the remnants of a bad dream carried into wakefulness. She recalled a book with a strange name: *The Book of Light and Dust* . . . a book that had the power to turn her blind. It had been a terrible dream and she had woken up in tears. She still recalled how alien the room had felt and how heavy her heart, how desperately sad.

As a little girl she had been prone to nightmares. She would leave her bed in darkness and make her way to her parents' bedroom, where she'd stand on the threshold to look at their sleeping forms. She never woke them: listening to their breathing would be enough to calm her and after a while she'd simply pad back to her room and go to sleep. But she was not used to nightmares any more and her parents' bedroom was no longer a safe haven waiting at the end of the passage.

Mia turned her eyes to the photograph next to her bed. It was the only picture she had of her parents together and one of the very few she had of her father, who had disliked having his photograph taken.

Her mother was relaxing into the strong crook of her father's arms and his eyes were hooded as he looked down at the woman whose head rested on his chest. Molly's gaze was fixed on a spot somewhere behind the photographer's shoulder and there was a small smile on her lips. It was a smile that said, *I am beautiful and I am adored.*

The voice in last night's dream had belonged to Molly, and because her mother was the one calling her, Mia had followed. Why would her mother make her walk into a nightmare?

As Mia looked at Molly's smiling face, a sudden thought entered her head and she felt cold.

Why hadn't she thought of it before?

Because it wasn't possible, that's why. None of her guys was about to enter the danger zone. Valentine had retired after his wife had the baby. Jeff wasn't due to fight for another three weeks. And Okie had an injury and wasn't even allowed to train.

But now that the thought had entered her head, she knew she wouldn't be able to relax until she had talked to the men, heard their voices and made sure they were OK.

She glanced at her watch. A little early still, maybe too

early? Fighters were a superstitious bunch at the best of times. They insisted on wearing their lucky trunks for a fight, carrying around a lucky penny, following exactly the same pre-fight rituals. If she told them she was calling because of a bad dream, they would be spooked. She was going to have to play it cool. Lifting the receiver, she started to dial.

Jeff answered on the first ring. Everything was fine. He had already made his weight, his training was going great guns. 'Everything is good, Mia. No problems, no injuries.'

'The fight is still scheduled for two weeks from Saturday?'

'Yes. So remember to do your thing the Friday night before.'

'I will. And, Jeff, you call me if the date changes. Promise?'

'Will do.'

'And say hi to Bonnie.'

She could sense him grin on the other end of the line. 'Are you serious?'

Bonnie was Jeff's wife. She had never liked Mia. She knew there was no romantic relationship between Mia and Jeff, but she didn't like the closeness.

It was the same with Amy, Valentine's wife. She really, really didn't like Mia. In fact, Mia was convinced Amy had made Valentine move from London to Liverpool just so she could get him as far away from her as possible.

Okie had no partner, so no static to contend with there,

thankfully. She caught him just as he was about to leave for work.

Okie was feeling sorry for himself. No, things were terrible. The rib hurt. JC wouldn't allow him back into the gym until it was fully healed. Life was hard. Life was – in fact – hardly worth living.

'Okie, hang on. You're basically fine, right?'

He sighed. 'Yeah, I suppose so.'

'Nothing seriously wrong?'

Another deep sigh. 'No.'

That left Valentine. Of the three, she was the least concerned about him. He was fully out of the danger zone. When Amy fell pregnant with Tom three years ago, he had retired from the ring and since then they had kept in touch only sporadically. She couldn't remember when the last time was they had actually spoken to each other. A year? Longer?

In fact, she thought as she called Valentine's mobile number, it was time she found someone to take his place. Nick was the obvious choice. Since his return to the neighbourhood eighteen months ago, she had pondered the idea more than once. But there were problems with this scenario: problems she did not want to deal with right now.

Valentine wasn't picking up. All she could do was leave a message on his voice mail to call her.

So that was that. And she couldn't sit around moping for ever: she had a full day ahead of her.

As if to confirm this thought, she heard the door to the

studio slam. Lisa was here. She'd better get moving.

Quickly Mia dried her hair and pulled on a cotton dress. As she was about to leave the room her eye fell on the sketch pad, which she had brought with her to the bedroom after saying goodbye to Nick.

She opened the pad and stared at the face with the withered eyes.

'Mia? Are you there?' Lisa's voice floated up the stairs.

Mia ripped out the page, crumpled the paper into a tight wad and lobbed it into the bin.

So much for bad dreams.

When Mia walked into the studio, it was to find Lisa peering into a mirror. Lisa was always in grooming mode, constantly checking to see if there was a blemish in need of attention.

'There you are.' Lisa lifted an eyebrow. 'I was wondering if you were in.'

'Sorry. I went running with Nick this morning.'

'Ah. How is the cutie?'

'Overweight. Unfit.'

'As long as he has those blue eyes and curly hair, it doesn't matter. And a guy has to have a little flesh on him.' Lisa nodded emphatically. 'It's a sign he's into the good things in life. Good food, good sex . . .'

'Nick won't be making love in the ring. He'll be up against an ugly stranger who's trying to knock his block off.'

'Oh, man.' Lisa sighed. 'I love all this fight-talk

stuff. It's so *primal*.' She turned back to the mirror and started applying lipstick in an eye-popping shade of red.

Lisa liked bold colours. In fact, there was nothing shy about Lisa. Six feet tall, sloe-eyed and with Queen of Sheba hair, she looked like a close relative of both Kat Von D and Xena, Warrior Princess. Embedded in one nostril was a tiny diamond. Nose jewellery was not Lisa's only body jewellery: she was pierced in just about every body location you wanted to think of. Or not wanted to think of, as the case may be.

They had met a year ago when Mia was advertising for someone to take Izzy's place. She had inherited the old man from her mother and he had partnered her for six years until a bad fall finally forced him to retire. Lisa was much prettier than Izzy and inspired less apprehension in customers – Izzy with a tattoo-gun in hand had been an unnerving sight. Lisa also didn't have the hacking cough. But Mia missed the old boy.

Lisa was now starting to prepare a tray, meticulously setting out petroleum jelly, ink caps, surgical gauze, tape and a disposable razor. The 'sharps' – needles – were in a covered sterilized container. Angelique, Mia's favourite machine, was autoclaved and ready to go. Mia walked over to the washbasin and began scrubbing her hands. As she pulled on her latex gloves she heard someone at the door and looked over her shoulder. Her client had arrived. It was colour-me-crazy time.

For the next three hours she had no thought of

anything else as she worked on the final stages of inking an elaborately designed giant carp on to the back of her client – a woman by the name of Una. Usually her clients explained to her the significance of the tattoo of their choice, but not this one. It was her third visit and Mia still did not know anything about the woman except her name and that she must like big fish. Unlike most of her clients, Una did not expect Mia to keep up a conversation while working. In fact, Mia thought, it almost looked as though Una had gone to sleep, which was pretty amazing considering that needles were constantly plunging into her skin at the rate of about three thousand punctures per minute. Receiving a tattoo on the back rarely made anyone scream out loud – it was the tattoos on the sensitive, private areas and the bony parts of the body that required you to grit your teeth – but, still, a three-hour session was not for sissies.

It was past noon when Mia finally finished and gestured to Lisa to clean the skin with a water and alcohol solution in preparation for the dressing.

She moved her head slowly from side to side, trying to get rid of the knot in her neck. Tonight at the gym she would need to do some serious stretching.

The thought reminded her of something else and she frowned. Valentine. He had not called back.

Mia picked up the receiver and called his mobile-phone number once again. But again she was directed to his voice mail.

She supposed she could try him at home. She dialled

the number, all the while hoping Amy would not be the one picking up.

There was no answer at the Scott household. Slowly she replaced the receiver back in its cradle.

Valentine. Where are you?

CHAPTER FIVE

The Book of Light and Dust
For Rosalia
V

How to meet death.

The light will be terrible, warns the Tibetan Book of the Dead. The light will make your spirit cringe, you shall avert your eyes, your terror will be great and consciousness will leave your mind.

This is one way. This is the way chosen by the faint of heart. The experience of dying so dreadful, you cannot bear to look it in the face. Choose this way and you will be plunged back into the river of reincarnation: the journey to be repeated once more.

But the Bardo speaks of a second way. Turn towards the light consciously. Stare into the sun and let it burn through your retina. Take the terror to your heart, look into the light without flinching.

This is the way of the courageous heart. It leads to enlightenment and you are given a choice: to be born yet again; to be born never again.

There is a third way. The Way of the Dragonfly. Do not meet death. Steal light. Live for ever.

THE WAY: FALLEN EYEBROW

BLACKLIGHT: DIR: GB2 K4, FRC: 9 TIME: 9, SUs: LU2 PC1

Whitelight: K3 GV14

CHAPTER SIX

He loved this neighbourhood. As Nick walked the few hundred yards from his flat to his office, he realized again how pleased he was to be back. These days he could afford to live in a much swankier part of town but he never even considered it. This was home.

The houses round here all looked as though they could do with a coat of paint. The shops were small with dusty windows. There were a few signs of creeping gentrification – one or two chichi coffee bars, a shiny yummy-mummy gym, which had recently opened its doors close to Scorpio – but this area of south London was still a neighbourhood in the purest sense of the word with people knowing one another well. When he made the move back eighteen months ago, he had been surprised by how many of the families who had lived here when he and Mia were kids were still around.

Nick's mother remarried just before his sixteenth birthday and Nick's new stepfather took his bride and her son with him to his home in Scotland. At the time Nick was heartbroken to leave London, but had he stayed, his life would have turned out very differently.

In Scotland, Nick entered a far more affluent world than the one in which he grew up. His stepfather was a banker and Nick suddenly found himself in one of Edinburgh's finest schools, where discipline was strict and expectations high. Never a particularly enthusiastic student, Nick discovered – much to his surprise – that he had an aptitude for numbers and an appetite for risk. Even at that early age, his stepfather taught him to play the market and gave him a sizeable account with which to experiment. Nick relished the rush. He had found something besides fighting that he was good at.

After high school came St Andrews, but academia did not excite him and after eighteen months he dropped out and headed for New York and five exhausting, exhilarating years of trading on the floor. But his heart remained right here in London, which was why he had returned, giving lie to the cliché that you can never go back.

During his twelve-year absence he had visited only twice: both times to see Mia. The first time was a year after his mother's marriage and their subsequent move to Edinburgh.

It was not a successful visit. Everything felt wrong. His mother was perfectly groomed and dressed in a Chanel suit and he was in flannels and a blue blazer. The two of them looked hopelessly out of place in Molly's haphazard kitchen. Molly herself, still beautiful but so thin, was in one of her distracted moods. Mia hardly said a word.

The second time was six years later, at Molly and Juan's double funeral. Mia had changed. There she was – all grown up – no longer the little girl with the wild hair and gangly limbs who used to roam the streets at his side. Her face was tight with grief and her eyes shadowed, but she still had the ability to make his heart flip over. She was happy to see him and grateful he had made the trip, but if her own heart was doing aerobics she did an excellent job of keeping it to herself.

Still, he kept up the relationship over the years that followed, unwilling to allow her to disappear from his life. Even during the years abroad, he stayed in touch. Christmas cards, birthday wishes, sporadic e-mails – he made sure to keep the link intact. And then came the decision to return to London. He was making excellent money in New York but he was tired. Life was short: it was time to go full-out for what he really wanted. But in this he had to admit to being only partially successful. He was now a part of Mia's life again, but it was astounding – and exasperating – how easily they had slipped back into their roles of childhood friends.

In front of him was the building where he rented an office and which he shared with Flash, his partner who was responsible for the technical wizardry that kept the Kime online community rolling. On the face of it, Kime was a two-man operation but this was deceptive: Flash commanded an army of techies who operated from places as far afield as Israel, India and Croatia. A global village in one room.

Nick had expected his partner to be at his desk, but as he entered the office Flash was nowhere to be seen. But he couldn't be far: there were telltale signs that he was in the vicinity. An unopened can of Coke – Flash's engine fuel – and a half-eaten tray of Jaffa Cakes sat on top of a stack of papers. And Flash's iPod was docked. Flash rarely moved anywhere without it.

Nick had the desk at the window; Flash, the one behind the door. Flash did not like sunlight. As if to confirm this peculiar aversion, there was a gigantic poster on the wall behind his chair showing a vampiric-looking female clutching a bunch of gerber daisies in one hand and a bloody heart in the other. Nick had never been able to fathom the symbolism, but then, Flash's world was pretty much outside his ken. Flash was also involved with some other social networking sites that were rather esoteric in their interests. The poster on the wall was the logo for Night Tramps. Nick had browsed their site only once, before deciding he was still not grown-up enough for certain things.

He dropped his bag on the floor and sat down behind his computer. As he logged on to Kime, he felt that familiar flutter in his stomach. He was still excited by the entire project. And how could he not be? He was no Mark Zuckerberg, but Kime was drawing serious investment money and had the potential to become huge. What had started life as nothing more than his own private blog – a Post-it note with random observations about fighters and the fighting world – had turned into an ambitious social networking site and the premier forum for fighters and fight aficionados of all persuasions: boxing, martial arts, kickboxing, Muay Thai, and MMA, with its rock-star fighters and obsessive fans – the fastest-growing American spectator sport. Kime allowed members to post profile pages with personal information, and encouraged them to take part in whatever discussion was taking place on the communal discussion board. And because Kime provided a flexible environment, allowing members to add applications to their pages, there were even members running small businesses via the Kime platform.

The name of the site was unusual and he had Mia to thank for it. Kime was a Japanese word and a martial-arts term. Truth to tell, Nick had never been one for all that martial-arts window dressing of spirit shouts and chi and searching for the path. He was a kickboxer: he liked to punch and he liked to kick and was not expecting spiritual enlightenment as a perk. But Mia had explained to him that 'kime' referred to the unique physical and mental focus required of a warrior. He liked that.

'Hey, tough guy.'

Nick looked up. Flash was lounging against the door. Tall, ultra thin and with permanent shadows under his eyes, he looked like a cartoon character from a Tim Burton film. He was nineteen. He made Nick feel old.

Flash slid into his seat and reached for his Coke. 'Have you checked out the board yet?'

'I've just got in.'

'Some guy died. Some fighter.'

'In the ring? I haven't heard anything.' Nick was

surprised. Many of the fights covered on Kime were small local bouts, which would not necessarily receive TV attention. But a death in the ring – even in an unimportant fight – would have made the news.

'I don't know.' Flash was adjusting the earpieces of his iPod. 'But there's loads of stuff on the board.'

The shock when he read Valentine's name was like a blow to the stomach. Nick felt himself actually leaning forward. With disbelieving eyes he continued to read the death notice, which someone had posted on the Kime communal board:

Valentine Scott had never won a championship belt and his name will be unfamiliar to people who do not follow combat sports. He was merely one of the thousands of weekend fighters who fight in small local bouts in unglamorous locations for very little money. But he possessed something that no amount of training or natural talent can give you. Valentine had heart. Knock him down — and in his career he had suffered quite a few of those — and he will stand up again. Hurt him and he will not back off. Hurt him badly and he still will not quit even though victory is already beyond his reach.

Valentine died in his living room at his home in Liverpool, a few days after his Muay Thai victory against Gerald Burke. This was

```
'the Wolfman's' comeback fight — his first
after a retirement of three years. His death
is a mystery: Valentine had not received any
serious injuries during the fight and was
given a clean bill of health afterwards. Three
days later, his heart simply stopped.
```

Nick leaned back in his chair and rubbed his eyes. He still couldn't believe it.

Valentine Scott. They had lived two houses away from each other, attended the same school and chased the same girls. As kids they had also trained together at Scorpio gym, where they had affectionately beaten the crap out of each other. Despite his sweetheart name, Valentine was a ferocious fighter. Nick was bigger than Valentine, but the guy had punched him to a standstill more times than he could remember. After his mother's marriage and their relocation to Scotland, he and Valentine had lost touch but he remembered Mia telling him that Valentine had moved to Liverpool.

Mia. Shit. She and Valentine had been good friends. He wondered if she knew. He lifted the phone to call her but then decided against it. This was not the kind of news you told someone on the phone. He would break it to her tonight at Scorpio.

He turned his attention back to the screen. The death notice was followed by a long list of tributes posted by other Kime members. They ranged from the heartfelt to the weird.

'Sad day. Miss you, man. Your spirit lives.' Another entry: 'Yo, Wolfman! Have fun in the great dojo in the sky!' And even: 'Sleep softly, great warrior.'

Another entry drew Nick's attention. Compared with the other contributors, the guy who wrote this was Hemingway, but as Nick read through the words he grimaced.

It was the custom among certain warrior tribes in Africa to eat the heart of a vanquished opponent in the hope of making the fallen warrior's courage their own.

Eat his heart and you may capture his life essence. Eat his heart and his energy becomes yours. A grisly tribute, perhaps, but a tribute nevertheless. Only warriors with indomitable spirit would be accorded this honour. Valentine Scott was such a warrior.

Well, this was creepy. Nick did not recognize the call sign of the contributor: Dragonfly. There was no icon, avatar or personal picture of Dragonfly next to his name, and when Nick clicked on the link to go through to the guy's profile page it was completely blank. The join date explained the lack of information: 12 July. Dragonfly had joined Kime only today.

Nick flicked from Dragonfly's page back to the main discussion board and read through the death notice once again. He frowned: something here did not compute.

Valentine had not died in the ring because of injuries, he had died days later. In his living room.

He reached for the phone again and dialled the number of Lee James, a sports journalist with whom he sometimes had a beer.

Lee did not have much to tell him.

'The guy simply dropped, what can I tell you? He was sitting in his armchair and suddenly it was lights out.'

'What was the cause of death?'

'His heart stopped.'

'Yes, Lee.' Nick tried to curb his exasperation. 'Why?'

'Well, that's the big mystery, old son. Autopsy shows no hidden heart problems.'

'There's been an autopsy already?'

'H'mm. The promoters probably wanted to clear their side as soon as possible.'

'And he received no injuries in the ring.'

'Nada. A few bruises, that's all.'

'Will you be writing about it?'

'No, dear boy. The guy was not exactly a household name. And as there is no dramatic ring death . . .'

After he hung up, Nick sat quietly, suddenly at a loss what to do next. On the other side of the room Flash was hunched over his keyboard, his head moving up and down to the beat of the music flowing through his earphones.

Nick looked through the window. The streets were filling up with people and traffic. The manageress of the florist shop on the corner was arranging potted plants on the pavement outside her window, the flowers a vivid splash of colour. It was just a normal day with people doing normal things. The sky was blue. The air was warm.

But in the far distance, Nick noticed a cloud. Just one – a small one – but he suddenly wondered if it might rain.

CHAPTER SEVEN

When Mia brought her bike to a stop outside Scorpio gym, the sky was a purple-red in colour and she noticed a tower of storm clouds building up in the west.

As she rechecked the lock on the Kawasaki – there was a real problem with theft in the area – she felt someone beside her and looked up from where she was squatting next to the front wheel.

Oh, no. Sighing, Mia stood up and nodded at the tall, expensively dressed woman who was watching her critically.

'Hi, Claudine.'

'Mia.' Claudine Normandy flicked Mia an up-and-down glance and Mia sighed again. With that one glance the woman had managed to make her feel unkempt. Claudine spent much of her time in the beauty salon at Harrods and it showed. Mia was suddenly acutely aware that her own boots needed a polish, her fingers were stained with ink and that she had helmet hair.

'I just dropped Andrew off for practice.'

Mia nodded. Andrew was Claudine's brother – a mild-mannered accountant who spent his days working behind a desk – and a surprisingly skilled fighter. A nice guy, you'd never believe he'd have such a piranha of a sister.

But Mia wasn't fooled. Claudine hung around Scorpio not because of Andrew, but because of Nick. The woman was in full hunting mode. Nick, of course, was a man and stupid. His vanity was tickled by the fact that a princess like Claudine fancied him.

'Nick is in there.' Claudine shrugged a graceful shoulder.

'Uh-huh.' Mia tried to edge past her.

'He's looking good. I told him I'll be at the fight, cheering him on.'

'I'm sure he'll like that.'

'You know, I keep saying to myself I should drop in at the studio. Get you to do some work for me.'

Each time Mia saw Claudine, she said exactly the same thing. It would never happen, of course. Claudine with a tat ... the mind boggled. But Claudine knew of her friendship with Nick and this was just another way the woman was trying to wiggle her way into his life.

But as always, Mia nodded and said, 'Of course, stop by anytime.' She made a play of looking at her watch. 'Sorry, I have to run or I'll be late for my class.' Without giving Claudine a chance to respond, she turned away quickly and pushed her way through a revolving door that was liberally stained with the accumulated fingerprints of Scorpio's many members.

Scorpio was located in a large, renovated warehouse. Doubling as both a fighter's gym and a martial-arts school, its members came from all walks of life and ranged from street-smart locals to white-collar City workers like Claudine's brother, who enjoyed the experience of a genuine spit-and-grit.

The gym had few frills. There were no gleaming weight machines, no treadmills or spinning bikes. The floor of the dojo was covered in dark-green mats, which, no matter how often they were washed down, still left students with black dirt clinging to the soles of their feet. A speedball was fixed to the wall and a variety of scuffed heavy bags dangled from chains attached to the ceiling. The air was always thick with boxer's musk – the slightly rancid scent of heated bodies, leather gloves, damp wraps and old sweat.

As Mia entered the dojo she bowed deeply and felt herself relax and become centred. The dojo was her happy place. Outsiders would look at this rectangular space and think it dingy. They did not feel the energy within its walls.

The dojo was roughly divided into two parts. One of these catered to the 'grapple-and-grunts': boxers, kick-boxers and the full-contact martial artists such as the judo and ju-jitsu practitioners. The other half catered to the 'vogues': martial artists who practised choreographed forms – katas – intent only on perfecting their technique. Two very different masters held sway over their respective domains. The grunts were headed by JC, a squat man with salt-and-pepper hair and a pugnacious expression. The vogues were presided over by her own teacher, Chilli, a tall, slender Eurasian.

There was, of course, cross-pollination between the two sides but Mia was well aware that there were die-hard grunts at Scorpio who hummed Madonna's 'Strike a pose there's nothing to it' whenever they watched the vogues perform. They not only scoffed at the discipline required to master the precise and powerful repetition of the katas but were also blind to the deadly intent hidden in the dance. It was fair to say the lack of understanding was mutual. Many of her fellow students poured scorn on the competition aspect of combat in the ring and appeared pained by the meaty smack and thump of the blows and parries coming from the other side of the room.

Mia was a vogue, but she was utterly, irrevocably drawn to the grunts. It was not so much the actual fighting in the ring that attracted her, but watching these men train together filled her with a deep, uncomplicated pleasure.

She liked men. She liked watching them interact: the heavy-handed camaraderie, the often infantile clowning around, the unexpected tenderness with which they hugged each other after a particularly gruelling bout of sparring. And she was fascinated by their body language, which reflected hierarchy and pecking order in a way women could never emulate. Of course, within the walls of Scorpio, a different set of values reigned. In here, social status and discrepancies in income were obliterated in a haze of sweat and effort. If you had to stick your nose into another guy's armpit while he pummelled you, it didn't much matter whether he was a banker or a plumber. It was all about heart. Some guys had it, many more did not.

She spotted Nick in the far corner. He was bathed in sweat and, even though his features were flattened by the protective headgear he was wearing, she could see he looked unhappy. The source of his discomfort wasn't difficult to guess. JC stood at his elbow, his thick hands cutting exclamation marks in the air. She couldn't make out the words but the hectoring tone of his voice was unmistakable.

No one knew what JC stood for. JC himself always told newcomers that his name stood for 'Holy Terror, get it?' JC was not to be messed with. The flesh round his eyes was thickened from all the punches he had weathered over the years.

'Hi, Mia.' She felt a hand on her elbow.

Okie stood behind her, a guilty grin on his face. He was wearing a T-shirt sporting the words 'Bad, Black and Beautiful'. Okie was not known for his modesty.

'Okie! What are you doing here? If JC sees you . . .'

'Yeah, I know.' Okie shook his head, dreadlocks swinging. 'He said he'd thump me if I came back before the rib's properly healed. But I forgot my book in my locker and I want to know the ending.'

Okie was addicted to romance novels. The cover of the book he was clutching in his hand depicted a massively muscled man dressed in a kilt leaning over a woman with a stupendous bosom. To Mia the woman looked astonished but maybe, she thought, she just wasn't very good at distinguishing between surprise and ardour.

She had to smile. Okie picked up a lot of flak for his

taste in literature but he would have picked up even more if it weren't for his wicked left hook.

Okie cocked an eye at her. 'I hear Nick went running with you this morning. How did it go?'

'Painful.'

'Yeah. Our boy is too fond of the pastries. Why the hell doesn't he just keep in shape? Every time he fights it's like he has to start from scratch. What he needs is to practise discipline. Like me,' Okie added virtuously.

Mia punched him on the shoulder. 'Is that halo heavy?' Okie and Nick were good friends but they were both in the same weight division and there was a healthy rivalry between them. Okie was technically more proficient than Nick, but Nick ... Nick was relentless. The laid-back manner, the easy smile – they masked a never-say-die determination that could shatter rock. And Nick was able to take a punch: he had a chin that rivalled Jake LaMotta's. To a fighter, nothing was of greater value.

Okie frowned. 'Seriously, Mia. Nick needs a training buddy for the next three months. Someone who can do his roadwork with him every morning. If my rib was up to it, I'd have been up for it, but as it is . . .'

'Maybe JC will find him someone.'

'Maybe. Anyway, I'm off before JC spots me.' Okie leant over and pecked her on the cheek. 'You look pale, sweetheart.'

'No, I'm fine. A little stressed, maybe, but aren't we all?'

'Chilli will get you chilled.'

'Yes. I'd better go and change. The class starts in five minutes.' But as he began to walk away from her, moving with that loose-limbed, coltish gait peculiar to so many fighters, she said, 'Okie, you really are OK, aren't you? Apart from the rib, I mean.'

He stopped and looked back, surprised. 'You're starting to freak me out, Mia. First this morning's call and now this. What's up?'

'Sorry. I'm just being silly.' He still looked alarmed and she hastily changed the subject. 'Are you coming over for pot luck next week?'

'As long as you shut away that creepy thing you have crawling round your house.'

Okie had issues with Sweetpea. And the animosity was mutual: whenever Okie came near her, Sweetpea would blow up her cheeks and assume a pinkish hue.

Mia shook her head. 'Never fear. I'll keep her upstairs.'

'In that case, count me in.'

'See you Monday, then.'

'Right. In the meantime, sweet dreams.'

Mia sighed. 'I'll try.'

Nick pulled off his gloves and staggered to the corner where his towel and water bottle were. JC had no mercy. Thank God he was finished for the day.

He took a swig of water and looked across the room to where Chilli was teaching his class of vogues.

Many years ago, at the tender age of thirteen, he had joined one of Chilli's classes. It had been a way of trying to get closer to Mia, who had studied with Chilli since the age of six. He had only a vague recollection of Chilli holding forth about 'drawing energy from the golden stove' and 'breathing with power'. What he remembered very well, however, was that he had attacked the breathing exercises with a little too much enthusiasm and had started to hyperventilate, almost passing out in the process. After that embarrassment he had stuck pretty much to the other side of the dojo.

But these vogues didn't fool him. Their air of detachment was just so much puffery. You didn't invest hundreds of hours into perfecting one single kata without your ego becoming involved big time.

But as he watched Chilli's disciples, all dressed in white, practising their austere, elegant moves, he had to admit the vogues were the princes of cool. They certainly didn't have the cauliflower ears like the blokes in front of him who were pounding it out on the mat, straining against locks and choke holds. And the vogues pulled. All they needed to do was mutter a Bruce Lee koan, 'Never take your eyes off an opponent even when you bow,' and the girls would go weak at the knees. It made him sometimes feel quite bitter.

There were only two women in the class: Mia and a girl who was built like Lara Croft. But Mia was the one you watched. She took your breath away. She had a core of steel and her movements showed the kind of integrity you acquire only after many, many years of constant practice. Mia, he knew, really did believe in *do*, 'the way': that fusion of the physical and the spiritual that will lead the martial artist to enlightenment.

'It's mind and body coming together,' she once explained to him, 'through intense physical effort.'

'And what do you gain from it?'

'At the very least, tuning in to your own vital energy – your chi. At best . . . becoming one with the chi of the universe.'

He had shaken his head, unable to follow her into these esoteric realms. But he admired her dedication. And he would never tire of watching her do what she loved best.

Her face was completely serene. Some of the other students had their foreheads scrunched in effort, veins swelling in their necks. Mia showed no obvious tension. She snapped out a kick so fast and powerful, his eye had difficulty registering the entire movement. Concentration. Skill. Grace. A devastating package.

The class was winding down. Chilli was bowing to his students; the students following suit.

Mia saw him watching her and waved. She exchanged a few words with Chilli and then started walking towards him.

He smiled at her and offered a towel.

'Thanks.' She was sweating profusely, her cheekbones and forehead gleaming. But she looked happy and at peace.

He sighed inwardly. Well, better get it over with.

'Mia . . .'

'Hmm?' She dabbed at her face.

'I'm afraid I have bad news.'

She stilled her movements. Her eyes became guarded. 'What?'

'You remember Valentine? Valentine Scott?'

Her face went white. 'He's dead, isn't he?'

He looked at her, taken aback. Before he could respond she asked, 'When?'

'Yesterday. How—'

But she didn't give him time to finish his sentence. Without another word she turned round, the towel slipping from her fingers. And as she walked away from him, he saw her touch the left side of her body in a strange, furtive gesture, as though she were in pain.

CHAPTER EIGHT

THE BOOK OF LIGHT AND DUST
FOR ROSALIA
VX

The great events in our lives are physical. Childbirth. Sex. Combat. Death.

No poetry, or music or the thoughts of great men will flash across the transom of our minds at the moment of dying. We will remember only the moments when we felt the fibres of our body sing. Bloodily. Messily. Ecstatically.

Is not the brain shaped like a pair of boxing gloves?

Many questions but only one answer. To live. To live for ever.

THE WAY: STRIKING HEAVEN

BLACKLIGHT: DIR: LU 3K2, FRC: 3, TIME: 2, SUs: BL3

Whitelight: mas. BL2

CHAPTER NINE

'Hey, Mia, let's have a race.'

If she closed her eyes she could see Valentine before her now: his cheeks smooth but the strong wrists already hinting at the man in waiting. And she, burnt brown as a gypsy, her hair wild, but so happy to be allowed to run with the boys.

They usually hung out in a pack: a bunch of exuberant kids whooping up the neighbourhood. But on that Sunday afternoon there were only the three of them: she and Valentine and drippy-nosed Davie, who lived with his dad above their corner shop.

Valentine had started it. 'Girls can't race as fast as boys.' His easy superiority and dismissive tone had sparked in her a predictable response. It was only when she saw his satisfied smile that she realized she had been caught.

He dropped his head and stared at her slyly through his lashes: 'Sweatpea. If I win, I get Sweetpea.'

Her heart lurched.

'What?' he jeered. 'Are you chicken?' He added one withering word: 'Girls!'

A strong mental offensive required a strong mental response: that was what Chilli had taught her. Before the first blow was struck, the battle was already won or lost. 'Unbalance the chi of your opponent, Mia. Reach out with your mind. *Seme.* If the mind is right, the sword is right.' She was only ten years old when he first taught her that, sitting cross-legged opposite him in the disciplined environment of the dojo. His words had a satisfying heft to them but she did not really understand: they were only words. But out here, in the hot street with Valentine watching her with alert eyes, she suddenly understood completely.

'Sure.' She shrugged, her body language deliberately languid; her eyes meeting the burning energy of his gaze with indifference. 'And if I win, I get the bike.'

Valentine's eyebrows snapped together. The bicycle had been his birthday present. It was a proper racing bike with six gears and Valentine had painted the handlebars in post-box red. On the crossbar he had painted the words 'First luv'.

'OK.' But for the first time there was a slight hesitation to his voice.

Neither she nor Valentine had even considered asking Davie if he wanted to take part in the contest. Not that he had minded. Davie was a gentle soul.

'Twice round the block.' Valentine pointed to the far end of the street. 'Quickest time wins. Davie will keep time. He's neutral.'

'I wouldn't cheat, Valentine.'

'No, but I might.' That cheeky smile of his. He gestured at the bike. 'You ready?'

The saddle had been too high off the ground for her, she remembered that well. And it was hard and painful. The bike wobbled under her hands.

But then she got going and the speed grabbed her like a vice. The first part of the course was downhill. Down, down past the hairdresser, where Nick's mum usually stood with pins in her mouth and a hair dryer in her hands, but the shop now closed on a Sunday. Down, down past Davie's dad's corner shop – open but quiet. Down past the launderette and the post office. Her legs pedalled furiously, ecstatically. The wind rushed past her face. She could do this. She could beat him. But stronger, far stronger, than the driving spur of wanting to win had been the happiness of that moment. Life could not be more intensely lived than this. No thought. Only sensation.

And then came the sharp turn into the next stretch of road and suddenly she was on top of a parked Volvo that was hugging the pavement. She had time to register the Garfield puppet with its suckered feet clinging to the back window of the car, but no time to turn the handles, no time to correct her course. The bike slammed into the rear end of the car and her hands jerked loose from the handlebars. She was catapulting through the air – head over heels – flying – the adrenalin gushing through her body and her brain crystal clear.

Blood. That was what she remembered best. Not the pain, but the blood. How bright red the blood was and how much of it. She had broken her nose and there was blood everywhere.

Valentine's white face. 'Mia, Mia. Are you all right, Mia?' And then Valentine's mother, big Mrs Scott, had arrived on the scene and slapped her son against the head. 'Shame on you, Valentine Scott. What were you thinking? Little boys should protect little girls.'

No, little girls should protect little boys . . .

Why hadn't Valentine told her he was coming out of retirement? He had always been meticulous about telling her of his upcoming fights. Something – or someone – must have stopped him. And now he was dead.

'Mia? Are you all right?'

'What?' Mia looked at Lisa. For a moment she felt intensely disorientated.

'What's wrong, girl?' Lisa looked at her curiously.

'Sorry.' Mia touched her forehead. 'I was thinking of something else.'

The sun was hot. Last night had passed without the threatened thunderstorm but clouds were still amassing on the horizon and the heat was on. She and Lisa were sitting on the steps outside the door of the studio, taking their first break after a hectic morning. Summer was always their busy time. When people were shivering and wearing thermal underwear, body art was not high on their to-do list. But skimpy outfits and exposed skin made them feel sexy and the number of drop-ins at the studio rose dramatically in July and August. In the summer months she and Lisa started at nine, instead of noon, and

Fridays and Saturdays they kept the shop open until midnight.

'That guy' – Lisa jerked her chin in the direction of a group of builders on the opposite side of the street. 'Do you think he knows I'm checking him out?' As Lisa spoke, one of the men, dressed in jeans and a vest, glanced at them before picking up a bag with rather more flexing of muscles than was necessary.

'He's dishy. Looks like he can sling you over his shoulder and drag you to his cave, no problem.' Lisa's fantasies were pretty straightforward. Feminism was not high on her list of priorities either, but she did believe in taking the initiative. 'Maybe I should walk over and say hello. What do you think?'

Mia shook her head. 'Have fun. I'm going inside.'

She needed to finish two designs: a his and hers for two of her regular clients. Tiger for him, lotus flower for her. She pulled out the sketches and looked at her work critically. The flower was just about done, but she wasn't happy with the tiger. She picked up a pencil and started drawing the tiger's stripes.

It was not much cooler inside the studio than outside, despite the efforts of the ceiling fan turning above her head. She sometimes considered replacing the old-fashioned *Casablanca* fan with air conditioning but then always decided against it. Her father had installed that fan with his own hands and she had too many memories of Molly working on hot nights to its soft revolving swish; the shadow blades moving gracefully across the walls.

And that night when Molly told her it was time for her, Mia, to receive her first tattoo, the fan had been moving as well. She had tried to concentrate on the spinning circle above her head as the needles entered her skin and the pain – more intense than she had imagined – made her nerves sing. And she remembered how sharp the light was that came from the long-armed Anglepoise lamp Molly used for night work. It had blotted out the colour of her mother's face, even as it highlighted the tiny beads of sweat pearling along her hairline and the long white fingers gripping Angelique with delicate strength.

The tattoo was Mia's eighteenth-birthday gift. And that was the way Mia always thought of it: a gift. It was the word her mother had used as well, that night when she had inked the delicate figure indelibly into her daughter's skin.

'The lady is a special gift, Mia. She confirms your identity: who you are. I give her to you today, just as my mother gave me my Keeper and her mother hers. And so forth and so forth. A long line of women.' It was then that Mia became scared, in that room filled with brightest light and deepest shadow and the ceiling fan turning above her head like a demented moth.

A special gift . . .

The tip of the pencil broke and a line streaked across the page, marring the outline of the tiger's claw. At that moment there was movement at the door and she looked up quickly. But it was only Lisa, flush from her encounter with her buff builder.

'He's asked me out on a date, tonight. Is that OK, Mia?

I know we decided that I'll do tonight's shift but can we switch?'

'I have a class with Chilli tonight, Lisa.'

'Please, pretty please? You know what I always say: strike while the iron's hot. And tonight is the only night Rufus has free.'

'*Rufus?*'

'Hey, you once went out with a guy called Conan. Come on, girl, be a friend.'

'All right. But you owe me.' Mia reached for her handbag. 'You can start with keeping an eye on the studio. I have to go to the bank.'

Inside the bank it was blessedly cool but the line at the ATM was long. In front of Mia was a man who had a tattoo creeping up from underneath his shirt into his neck. Mia studied it critically as she slowly shuffled towards the cash point. The tattoo was clearly the work of an unskilled scratcher who had exercised poor control of his machine. Some lines were patchy where the gun had skipped, but there were also lines where the gun had bitten too deeply, leaving deep scarring.

She was still looking at the tattoo, her thoughts distracted, when her mind suddenly snapped to alert.

Someone was watching her.

Mia turned her head round slowly, her eyes scanning the line of people behind her, but no one was paying her attention. Neither was anyone in the group of people at the front of the bank where the tellers were. Most of the faces seemed irritable or bored and not particularly focused. But she knew she wasn't wrong. And it wasn't just casual interest she was picking up; someone close by was directing his energy towards her with great intent. She could feel it against her skin: an icy electric current.

One of the goals of martial-arts training was to develop a highly developed sense of your opponent's intentions. It wasn't just a case of reading non-verbal clues — posture, breathing, dilation of pupils — it came from a deeper source. It was the ability to gauge your opponent's chi — his inner vital energy — before the first blow was struck. A highly skilled practitioner could pick up the energy vibrations bleeding off his opponent without that person even being within eyesight. Martial artists called it *haragei*. The average guy who lacked training in chi sensitivity and who did not have a lexicon of fancy Japanese terms at his disposal might talk about feeling the hairs on the back of his neck rise or someone walking over his grave. Whichever way you wished to describe it, it was an actual physical sensation and Mia was feeling it now.

Who was it? Not the youth with the canvas jacket impatiently slapping a rolled-up newspaper against his leg; not the older, distinguished-looking man in a charcoal suit . . . certainly not the woman with the fractious baby, even though she kept throwing glances in Mia's direction . . .

'You're next.' The blonde girl behind her, tired-looking with shadows under her eyes, tapped Mia on the arm and gestured at the ATM beyond.

Mia mumbled an apology. She tried focusing on typing

in her PIN but it was difficult to concentrate. The energy in the room was spiky, disturbed. As she waited for the machine to spit out the money, she looked round her again but could not identify the source.

And then it was gone.

Mia breathed deeply, surprised to find herself feeling slightly light-headed. She waited impatiently for the transaction invoice to print. All she wanted now was to get out of here.

Outside the sun had disappeared. Thick clouds moved across the sky and the wind had sprung up. Mia decided to take a short cut through a deserted garden square that was hemmed in on all sides by looming Victorian buildings. The many trees threw long shadows. The single wooden bench looked uninviting.

A sudden thought made her pause. Had she collected her debit card before storming out of the bank? Better to make sure. At the bench she stopped and placed her handbag on the seat. As her hand rummaged for her wallet, she looked up at the red-brick mansion flats facing her with their many staring windows.

The debit card was where it should be and she breathed a sigh of relief. But as she picked up her handbag, there it was again: the same sense of being watched. It was real and unpleasant. And this time she knew exactly where it was coming from.

She spun round and looked to where a man was standing at the far corner of the square. He was carrying an open umbrella and his face was in deep shadow: she could not even make out the colour of his hair. His body was relaxed, one hand pushed deep into his jacket pocket.

Months later she would look back on this moment and remember. She would remember the way in which a curtain had flapped from one of the windows on the ground floor in a strange, slow-motion movement as though time was winding down. She would remember the sick feeling, which had settled on her chest. She would remember that this was the first time the thought of her own death had come to her mind.

A drop of rain fell on her face. Another. And then the heavens opened and sheets of rain came pouring down. Within seconds she was soaked, her hair plastered to her head. Mia brushed the back of her hand across her eyes and blinked. When she looked again, the figure was no longer there.

CHAPTER TEN

THE BOOK OF LIGHT AND DUST
FOR ROSALIA
XXX

Today I watched you. Stranger, who I know.

I know your faithful heart. I know what moves you; how deeply you can love.

Warrior woman; loyal healer. You hunt, you defend, you carry in the chambers of your mind the songs and legends, the wisdom of your sisters.

I am curious of your ways.

Gifted innocent: you touch the great energy easily, carelessly. You need not steal to hold it in your hand.

Let me come to your window ...

THE WAY: JADE PILLOW

BLACKLIGHT: DIR: CV3 LV8, FRC: 1, TIME: 12, SUs: ST8

Whitelight: GB23

CHAPTER ELEVEN

The window on the top floor was open but the narrow terraced house on the other side of the street showed no light. The heavy downpour of rain that had swept through London earlier in the day had changed to a thin but steady drizzle. The moisture in the air made the glow from the street lights appear as gauzy and mysterious as a picture-book illustration.

The man sheltering in the doorway blinked as a flight of pale moths hovered before his eyes. Then the moths disappeared, ghost-like, into the shadows.

Nothing else stirred. The street was empty and the windows of the houses dark. At the far end of the terrace was the high street: glazed light, the swoosh of wet tyres and the night noises of the city. Here, it was quiet.

He pushed his hand into the inside pocket of his jacket and took out the slip of paper with her name. The words were written in big looping letters and looked self-conscious, as though the writer had been striving to conform to some ideal standard of penmanship.

For a moment he looked at the piece of paper in his hand unseeingly, his mind flashing back to that day, not so long ago, when he had watched Valentine write this note for him.

'Mia Lockhart. The Mystic Ink studio.' Valentine was frowning in concentration, the pen in his hand moving slowly across the paper. 'You go and see Mia and she'll see you right. Best tat artist around, man. Tell her I sent you.' Valentine handed him the piece of paper and smiled, teeth white against the swarthy skin.

He smiled back, all the while knowing the man in front of him had been marked by death. Although at that moment Valentine was looking like someone at the peak of physical fitness. They had just finished a last three-round sparring session together: two rounds of striking and one round of grappling. A light workout because, the day after, Valentine would step into the ring and he needed to be fresh.

Valentine stuffed his gloves and shin-pads into his gym bag and swung it over his shoulder. 'I owe you, man.' Valentine seemed almost emotional. 'You really helped me these past few weeks. You've been a great training buddy.'

'A pleasure. It's been fun.'

'You're coming to my fight, right?'

'I'll be there.'

'Great.' Valentine smiled. 'See you then.'

He watched as Valentine walked out of the door, knowing it would be the last time he would see the man alive. And despite his promise, he never made it to the fight. The fight held no interest for him. His attention had already moved on.

Mia. The Keeper. He would get to know all her secrets.

The memory of Valentine faded from his mind and he slipped the piece of paper back into his pocket. Time to move on. Valentine belonged to the past.

Once more he looked up at the open window on the top floor of the house opposite. He wondered if it was her bedroom. From lying in wait earlier today, he already knew that the windows next to that solid front door led to the studio. They were heavily shuttered. But downstairs, in the basement, the curtains did not quite meet behind the closed windows. He would be able to look inside.

He crossed the street and turned up his collar against the rain. The steps leading down from street to basement level were slick and the soles of his shoes slipped. He grabbed at the railing to steady himself and in the process pushed over a dustbin, unleashing a clatter of rolling metal.

He froze. But the house remained dark and quiet.

Carefully he continued down the steps and crossed the small courtyard. He placed his fingers against the cold pane of glass and peered into the darkness inside.

After a while his eyes could make out shapes and forms. A kitchen table with a checked cloth stood underneath the window. Against the far wall was a stove. Pans and spatulas were hanging from steel hooks set into the wall. Potted plants were arranged on the kitchen sink. There was a dresser too, filled with ornamental plates, and he could make out the rectangular shapes of picture frames. But the images inside the frames had no definition, the gloom inside the room too deep for him to see.

He stepped back, feeling dissatisfied. Looking up at the open window on the top floor, he wondered again: was she inside, sleeping? In his mind's eye he pictured her body against pale sheets; tousled hair, a slender hand resting on the pillow, the palm open and vulnerable.

The idea of her made him short of breath. After following her around earlier today, he now knew the shape of her face, but he was not yet sure of the colour of her eyes. But they had a bond, the two of them. When she had stared at him across that garden square filled with wind and shadows, it had felt as real as the touch of fingers on his skin.

But he would have to be more careful: her sense of *haragei* was highly developed. If he did not want to scare her off he would have to rely on *kobudera*, the masking of true intent. Seduce her, charm her with beauty. And then, take from her the prize.

But first he would get to know all of her, even her secret places: the delicate dent behind her ear lobe, the hollow at the bottom of her spine, the slender arch of her foot . . .

And he would discover her dreams.

Was she dreaming?

He closed his eyes, letting time slip away from him. One part of his brain still registered the dripping of rainwater, the rushing gutters, the sound of a woman's laughter in the distance. But he was stilling his mind. At this moment the amplitude of his delta brain waves would be heightening as his energy flowed smoothly through his body. He could feel it drawing upwards from the soles of his feet, moving to the point behind his knees, pushing on through his legs and thighs and on and upwards, rushing from one chakra point to the other. He pushed his hands closer together and felt the energy of the magnetic field hot between his palms.

The texture of her dreams: their shape, vibration. He stood with eyes closed, swaying slightly, his mind filling with the shadow thoughts washing across the ceiling of her room. Dreams hanging in the darkness like unspoken wishes, floating like stars across a windswept sky.

CHAPTER TWELVE

Dragonfly had posted another comment on Kime's discussion board.

It looked as though the guy was going to become a regular, Nick thought. He noticed that Dragonfly had added a number of icons next to his name as part of his call sign and that the symbols looked like Japanese or Chinese ideograms. Which probably meant the man was a vogue: vogues loved that kind of thing. Grunts, on the other hand, tended to post pictures of themselves striking a heroic pose or celebrating victory in the ring.

Nick turned his eyes away from the screen for a moment and speared a salad leaf. God, he hated this part of his training. He could handle the five o'clock runs and JC's hammering but the food thing broke his spirit. He looked up just in time to see Flash bite into a thick, squelchy sandwich filled with gooey something or other. Probably a thousand calories in one bite. And the kid was as thin as a rake.

Nick sighed. He had only himself to blame, of course. It was perfectly within his power to end all of this agony right now: he could simply hang up his gloves. He had received his first pair when he was six years old and since then he had never stopped fighting – not even when he was living in New York. But thirty was in sight. Why the hell was he still putting himself through the pain? Certainly not for the money, which he didn't need and which was pitiful anyway. Why, then?

He sighed again and turned back to the computer.

The modern world, despite its superficially exciting technological advances, is not what we were built for. Our emotions and our wants evolved in a world without keyboards and screens. The modern world has little heroic content and it fills us with deep malaise. It drains us of our vital energy. It makes us behave in unnatural ways.

This is why fighters are blessed and cursed in a way outsiders can never understand.

Locked body to body with your adversary, you spring to life: vital energy fills your heart. You smell your opponent's body odour — it sticks to your skin, enters your nose, clings to your tongue; the tang of his breath is in your face. Like a coma victim prodded to consciousness by the voice of his beloved, you wake up. Desire runs through you like quicksilver.

Huh? Nick lowered his fork, bemused. Maybe

Dragonfly was a ring fighter, after all. And maybe he was a total nutcase.

```
But the fighter is cursed as well.
Vulnerability, pain, grace: for the fighter
they are inextricably bound together. You look
into your opponent's eyes to see who he is —
and to know who you are. In his eyes you find
the truth.
```

A nutcase, definitely. Nick wondered what Kime's grunts would make of this.

But as he looked across the room at Flash, who was still munching away happily, he couldn't help but wonder if Dragonfly didn't have a point. In Flash's world, social interaction was masked. Drago of the Deep, say hi to Cassandra, Queen of Shadows. Drago likes underwater basket-weaving; Cassandra is an urban witch. A beautiful friendship was sure to follow in make-believe land. Looking into someone's eyes was pretty much becoming a redundant activity these days. Not to mention finding out what someone smelt like.

His thoughts were interrupted by Flash, who was still chewing but now also trying to speak at the same time. 'I meant to tell you,' Flash swallowed deeply, 'that friend of yours called again — what's-'is-name? — the sports writer.'

'Lee?'

'That's the one.'

'Did he say what it was about?'

'Hmm. Mmm.' Flash opened a carton and took out a slice of chocolate cake.

This was too much. Nick picked up the phone and faced the window so that his back was turned on Flash.

Lee sounded rushed. 'Listen, I'm not sure if this means anything, but I thought you might want to check it out in light of your personal interest.'

'Check what out?'

'Four other fighters died in the UK over the past five years. All of them died outside the ring.'

'So?'

'Their hearts stopped. For no reason.'

'You mean . . . like with Valentine?'

'I don't know all the details, but I have the names here somewhere . . .' Lee paused and Nick could hear paper rustling. 'OK, I found it; have you got a pen?'

Nick grabbed a pen and started writing as Lee rattled off the names.

'Could be something, could be nothing,' Lee said, sounding distracted. 'Have to run. Keep me posted.'

Nick replaced the receiver and looked at the names. He didn't recognize any of them. But something reeked: five healthy blokes, fighters all, dropping as though someone had pulled their plug. What was it Lee had said? Might be something, might be nothing.

Something, Nick thought. Something.

CHAPTER THIRTEEN

In 1844, the French missionary Aimable Petithomme came upon the widow of the great Polynesian chieftain Latete. It was thirty days after the chieftain's death and the queen was busy removing her husband's skin with her fingers. If the goddess Oapu was to accept the chieftain into the afterlife, the queen knew she needed to purge certain tattoos from her consort's body.

Molly had told this story to Mia many years ago as a cautionary tale. A tattoo is not just for life, Molly warned, it follows you into death. A tattoo can be a blessing . . . but it can also be a curse.

Tim's skin was angry. The blood welled underneath Mia's fingers as she pressed Angelique to his shoulder. But the outline of the swastika was finally softening – a curve was replacing a hook.

'I was only eighteen,' Tim explained to Mia the first time he walked into her studio. 'I was a stupid kid, full of rage. I hung out with some vile people. This was my first tattoo and I wanted to show I belonged. But now it feels like I'm carrying around bad luck. Can you help?'

Covering up an unwanted tattoo with another design

was one of the most demanding things a tattooist could be asked to do. If the offending image was black and bold, like this one, it took some seriously creative thinking.

And it took time. Mia straightened. Her back was aching from sitting in one position for so long.

She reached out and gave the hand mirror to Tim.

'Oh.' He stared. 'It's great. It's really beautiful, Mia.'

She smiled. 'It works.'

She had submerged the swastika into a larger, more flowing image and had softened the unrelenting black with blue and green. The design now seemed whimsical.

She started applying A+D Ointment to the skin. 'And mind you take care when you take off the dressing,' she told him as he got ready to leave. 'Be gentle – use cold water – otherwise you'll yank the colour right out.'

'I'll remember. And thanks again, Mia. Rosemary's going to love this. You're invited to the wedding, OK?'

Mia removed her gloves and yawned. For the third night in a row she hadn't slept well. No nightmares this time, but she kept waking up, as though someone was constantly touching her shoulder. And at one stage the room had felt bizarrely cold and she had even left her bed to close the window.

The studio seemed very quiet now that Tim had left and Angelique was no longer humming. Lisa was still at the dentist.

Maybe she should use this time to call Amy. Mia looked at the phone, debating. She had left two messages already and Amy hadn't called back. Best to face facts: Amy still hadn't softened to her even though Valentine was dead.

An e-mail might have more success than a phone call. She didn't want to pester Amy, but she needed to know. Why had Valentine not told her he was returning to the ring?

After a moment's hesitation, Mia walked over to the keyboard.

Dear Amy,
I was so very sorry to hear of your loss. Please know . . .

A shadow fell across the threshold and she looked up.

It was a man. He stood in the doorway and with the sunlight behind him he was at first only a tall, dark shape. But then he stepped fully into the room.

For a moment they looked at each other, not speaking. And in his eyes came a look, if not of recognition, then, surely, of acknowledgement. But she had never seen this man before, had she? How disconcerting, then, when he smiled at her slowly as if they shared a secret.

'Can I help you?'

He smiled again. His face was exceptionally attractive with its light-grey eyes set under sweeping brows, long mobile mouth and strong, almost beak-like nose. His hair was dark blond; the exact shade of her own. He was wearing a crisp white shirt, blue blazer and understated silk tie, but he moved with a kind of whippy strength that seemed at odds with the formal clothes. Not that the clothes meant anything: body art had lost its street-cred, blue-collar exclusivity years ago. Everyone from models, to dentists, to Dame Helen Mirren had tattoos these days. But somehow she doubted this guy was interested in having his sweetheart's initials inked into his pecs.

But maybe she was wrong. He gestured at the thick albums filled with designs. 'Would you mind if I browse?'

'Please do. Anything you're looking for in particular?'

'I'll know it when I see it.'

That's when she noticed it: the calluses on his fingers. The kind of calluses you develop only from gripping the lapels of the stiff *dogi* worn by martial-arts practitioners in judo or aikido. The man might look like a banker, but he was a fighter.

He opened one of the albums and started leafing through. She looked back at the screen in front of her but found it difficult to concentrate. She was acutely aware of his presence. Some people's energy filled a room without their even trying: Valentine had possessed this quality as well. He would enter a room crowded with others more attractive, more articulate, more powerful, but still he was the one to whom you paid attention.

She glanced over her shoulder and found her visitor watching her. The album was open in front of him but he was looking in her direction, hands in his pockets, rocking almost imperceptibly on his feet. A tiny movement, but it managed to convey explosive power.

He nodded at the open book. 'This is lovely work. Are they all your own designs?'

'Some are my mother's. But I can replicate them.'

'There's one here that caught my eye.'

She slid off the stool and walked over. When she reached the bench he pushed the book across. He made no movement to touch her, but his gaze was so hot and intense, she hesitated. There was something here she didn't understand.

He tapped his finger on the page. 'This one.'

'Oh, yes.' Mia nodded. 'It's a one-off I did for a girl who brought me a drawing she made of a dream.' A very rough drawing, she remembered. It had not been easy translating those hesitant pencil outlines into ink on skin.

'Dream?' His eyes were keen.

'Yes. She kept having the same dream again and again. Every night she'd fall asleep and this image would appear in her mind like clockwork. And then she'd wake up. It always happened only a few minutes after she switched off the light.'

'Hypnagogic sleep.'

'Excuse me?'

'Hypnagogic or sleep-onset dreams. We all have them. They can be highly coherent, if completely surreal. They come to you in your pre-sleep phase before you slip fully into the sleep cycle and only last about ten to fifteen seconds. At that point your brain is closer to a meditative than a sleep state.'

'Oh . . . right.' A banker who did judo and watched the Discovery channel.

His lips curved. 'I'm a chronobiologist.'

She did not like the creeping amusement in his eyes. Did he think she would be intimidated by a big word?

'I'm sorry,' she said, keeping her voice cool, 'I don't know what that is.'

'Something not as boring as it sounds.' But he didn't elaborate.

She stared at him, still feeling slightly hostile. But he really was impossibly good-looking – beautiful, even. Not that there was anything remotely effete about the regularity of his features . . . and there was just something in the set of his mouth and the way he carried himself that warned he might be an ugly customer to take on in a fight.

He looked up and into her eyes and she felt herself blush. Damn it.

But his voice was casual. 'Maybe you can help me out with something else? I'm looking for a good gym in this area.'

'There's Horton's . . .'

He shook his head. 'I've already looked at that one.'

'And then there's Scorpio.' Why did she feel as though she shouldn't have mentioned it?

'That sounds more my thing.'

'It's not swish.'

'I'm not looking for swish.'

With a leisurely movement he reached out and touched the tattooed symbols encircling her wrist. A small shock ran through her.

'These are Usui Reiki symbols, aren't they?'

She didn't answer.

'You're a healer.'

Still she didn't respond. She was so aware of the warmth of his fingers.

He smiled and drew his hand away. She looked down at her wrist as though she expected him to have left a visible imprint.

There was a sound at the door and his eyes looked past her shoulder. Mia glanced behind her. It was Lisa, back from the dentist.

'I'm running late, I'm afraid.' He nodded at Lisa, who was looking at him with undisguised interest. 'I'll have to drop in again another time.'

At the doorway he paused. His eyes met Mia's and she felt her breath catch. There it was again – that flame of recognition. The next moment he had turned away and the doorway was empty.

Lisa stared at Mia, eyebrows raised. 'Who was *that*?'

'A potential client.'

'Well, I'm booking my seat when you do that one. Can you imagine him without a shirt?'

Mia pulled a face. 'Don't forget the popcorn.'

She walked to the computer and moved the cursor to her favourites list, then clicked the mouse on the entry for Wikipedia. When she entered the search term, she hesitated a little over the spelling, but she was spot-on.

```
Chronobiology: the field of science that
examines periodic (cyclic) phenomena in living
organisms. 'Chrono' pertains to time and
```

```
'biology' pertains to the study, or science,
of life. The related terms chronomics and
chronome have been used in some cases to
describe either the molecular mechanisms
involved in chronobiological phenomena or the
more quantitative aspects of chronobiology,
particularly where the comparison of cycles
between organisms is required.
```

There followed a paragraph about infradian, ultradian and tidal rhythms, which seemed to cover everything from sleep cycles to menstrual cycles to the behaviour of oceans. And who knew there was a four-hour nasal cycle or that growth hormone was produced every three hours?

All interesting, but hardly illuminating. She still didn't really understand what the guy did for a living.

She sighed, irritated with herself. He was just another scientist. Why was she so interested? Not that she met that many scientists in the course of her day, admittedly, and he certainly did not look like the stereotypical image of a stoop-shouldered beaker carrier. But it didn't matter: she would probably never see him again.

She thought back, recalling the look in his eyes. No . . . she would see him again.

As she turned away from the computer she realized he had not told her his name.

CHAPTER FOURTEEN

The Book of Light and Dust
For Rosalia
XXXI

Electric world. Its energy runs through the veins of us all. My energy signature — singular to me alone. Yours too — a unique marker. Billions of beings, each with our own energy signature as distinctive as a fingerprint.

We are all aware of one another's energy and react to it intuitively and without conscious thought. Is your energy strong, is it weak? Does it drain me, does it replenish me?

Vital energy flows sluggishly in most of us. We walk and our footprints leave uneven imprints in the dust. We list. We are out of balance.

But there are those in whom the flow of energy is a sword of light. They walk with power.

We are drawn to them. We seek them out. Dimly we realize that they hold within them the one answer to many questions.

I looked into her eyes today and I saw labyrinths and mysterious things. I told myself: pay attention. She is the most important person you will ever meet.

THE WAY: EYE GATE

BLACKLIGHT: DIR: GB13 GB19, FRC: 2, TIME: 9, SUs: GB14 GB18
Whitelight: no whitelight possible

CHAPTER FIFTEEN

When Nick entered Scorpio's changing room he wrinkled his nose. The air in here was ripe: damp socks, damp wraps, malodorous gloves. And no excuse, really. He bet it didn't smell like this in the female changing room.

He was tired. For most of the day he had been on the receiving end of a barrage of phone calls from an irate parent berating him for allowing the man's son to sign up to Kime. The son was fifteen and, according to the father, too young to become a member of a social networking site that 'celebrated violence'. Considering that the kid probably played Grand Theft Auto on the sly and had a merry old time decapitating and torturing virtual opponents, Nick found this a little rich. But the parent was a big shot in a sports goods company that paid a hefty sum to advertise on Kime, and Nick had had to choose his words carefully.

By the time he had managed to placate the man, his head was pounding. When stressed, he usually turned to fighting or writing, but his attempt to write the next instalment of *Rick Cobra's Adventures* hadn't turned out brilliantly either: his hero was acting disappointingly lazy and becoming scarily inarticulate to boot.

And there was something else that was nagging at Nick: those five fighters dying without any obvious cause. As he tapped in the code on the keyboard of his locker, Nick thought again how much it bothered him. As soon as he had managed to sort out Rick, he should take the time to look into their deaths a little more closely.

He took out his gear. Next to his locker was Okie's — wide open and empty. The sight made Nick realize how much he missed his friend and also that he still hadn't lined up a new training buddy to take Okie's place.

Changing into his workout clothes, Nick caught a glimpse of his figure in the mirror. He had lost almost four pounds this week — not bad going — but the weekends were always his undoing and he was meeting Mia for dinner tonight at Luciano's. Mia had suggested they have sushi to help him avoid temptation but he had always found it difficult to get enthusiastic about raw fish. He would just have to be strong and stay away from the cream sauces and the vino.

He turned to face the mirror full-on and looked at himself critically. Below his one eye was a slight bruise. He had walked straight into JC's cross the other day — a really stupid move for someone who was about to do a fight — and he could count himself damn lucky it wasn't his nose that had connected with JC's paw.

Nick touched his finger to the tip of his nose. Vanity was not his vice — some of the other guys in the gym peered and preened in front of the mirror as though they wanted to date themselves – but he had to admit: he was pretty damn proud of the fact that he had never broken his conk. Most fighters sported the 'squashed' look with their noses flattened or ridged, but he had been lucky so far. And if he had his way, he would stay lucky. He tapped his finger to his forehead. Touch wood.

Well, time to stop admiring himself. He turned away from the mirror and headed for the door.

The dojo was packed. The air was filled with the *whump* of gloved fists striking at leather bags and the *whap* of bodies hitting the mat. He passed by a group of tiny vogues – no more than ten years old – who were practising their drills in unison, every now and then emitting an ear-splitting spirit shout. Kids were the life-blood of the dojo: the next generation. And every kid who thought it was cooler to kick like Jackie Chan than join a gang was a kid with a chance.

Scorpio did not have a dedicated boxing ring and sparring sessions took place on the mat at the far end of the room. JC was already waiting, watching a fair-haired man throw a combination of punches at one of the heavy bags. Nick did not recognize the man – he must be a new member – but he was hitting the bag well. When you hit a bag hard, the idea was not to make the bag swing wildly – pushing was always the first sign of a beginner – but to hit it with such solid focus and elastic force that the bag would absorb the power and move only slightly. If you did it right, the sting of the glove against the leather made a very distinctive sound. This guy was doing it right.

'Nick.' JC nodded at him. 'Say hello. This is Adrian Ashton. He joined today.'

The fair-haired man dropped his fists and turned towards Nick.

'Hi.' He smiled. His teeth were white and even. 'Call me Ash. JC tells me you have a fight lined up.'

There was genuine interest in his eyes and Nick found himself returning the smile. 'Yes, for my sins.'

'You can motor, my man.' JC punched Ashton on the shoulder. 'Are you interested in a fight yourself? Can I set one up for you?'

'No, thanks. I don't fight.'

'Why the hell not?' JC stared at him in disillusionment.

Ashton smiled faintly. 'I took an oath. First do no harm.'

'You're a doctor?' Nick blinked. The man looked more like a pro athlete.

'I don't ring-fight' – Ashton glanced back at JC – 'but I'm always up for a spar.'

JC was cheered. 'Great. How about giving Nick here a rumble? You guys are pretty evenly matched in the size department.'

'Certainly. Say the word.'

Nick slipped his mouth guard on to his teeth and grinned. 'Let's rock.'

Death is the shadow man. Inside the ring, every punch you throw, every kick you receive, could be your last. The idea of death resides in a place in the fighter's brain that lies beyond words. A place where Ali said he could 'hear snakes screaming'. A blur of movement, a lethal whiplash, and the fighter's brain smashes against his skull with the impact of a high-speed car crash. Death is always at his shoulder.

A sparring session is altogether a different thing. It requires trust. Sparring partners are engaged in a relationship of give and take: a relationship that is generous and unforgiving at the same time. You trust your opponent not to hammer your head in but you don't expect him to pull his punches either. He is going to hit you but he is not going to try and win at all costs. A good spar is a spar in which partners do not allow their egos to interfere. You are not there to pulp your opponent, but to learn from him.

Ashton was a model sparring partner. He was light on his feet and moved with economy and speed. He made Nick work. Oh yes, he certainly made him work. Nick shook the sweat out of his eyes.

In some weird way, though, it felt as though the guy wouldn't fully engage. Yes, his punches were crisp and once he slipped Nick's right and countered with an uppercut that was certain to leave a bruise, but most of the time it felt as though Ashton was simply keeping him at bay with his jab and some fluid footwork. He had tried to work the angles on Ashton without much luck. Nick was an inside fighter: favouring lots of pivoting, side-to-side stepping and head and shoulder movement, which allowed him to utilize his powerful body punches. But Ashton was Mr Elusive. It wasn't that Ashton was running away, but it was certainly a hell of a job to get close to him.

After three rounds, they switched from hands only, to hands combined with feet. Ashton's kicks were hugely impressive and a few times the kicks zinged dangerously close to Nick's head, but there was that same sense of energy kept at bay. Usually, after sparring with a bloke, you had a fair reading of who you were dealing with. Not now, though. Nick simply had no idea how Ashton might shape up in an actual fight. A spar revealed your opponent's temperament. Okie, for example, had a tendency to lead with his chin, which had landed him in big trouble more than once, but that was Okie: all part of his 'watch out, here I come' machismo and temperament. Ashton? An enigma. Nick had no idea what pushed his buttons.

But JC was pleased. 'What Nick needs.' He slapped Ashton on the shoulder and helped him take off his gloves. 'Keeps him from going off half-cock.' He turned to Nick. 'How's your roadwork coming along? Six miles tomorrow, right?'

Nick nodded glumly. He wondered if it would be raining again tomorrow. Running in rain was the pits. Running was the pits anyway.

'Looking for company?'

Nick glanced over to where Ashton was standing, watching him. He hesitated. Normally, he would jump at the offer – running with someone at your side helped take your mind off the pain and the excruciating boredom. But this guy . . .

'I could show you some stuff that can help with your kicks. I travelled round Asia for a few years. Northern China mostly. Picked up a few moves.'

Nick studied him with interest. 'I bet.'

Ashton shrugged. 'I also studied internal martial arts: Qigong, Hsing-I, Ba Gua. They're excellent for developing chi sensitivity.'

'Really?' Internal martial artists were nothing but loopy philosophers and woo woo mystics, as far as Nick was concerned.

Ashton seemed to read his mind. 'Don't worry.' His voice was dry. 'I won't start chanting on you.'

'In that case, you're on.' Nick clamped his head guard under his arm. 'Let's meet at five thirty. Pagoda. North side of the park. Know where it is?'

'I'll find it.'

'Great.' Nick nodded. 'Sorry, but I have to run. I'm meeting someone for dinner.'

JC turned round from where he was talking to another member. 'I heard that.'

'Don't worry, JC. It's Mia.'

'Ah. OK. That girl will keep you away from the bread basket. Give her a kiss from me, will you.' JC had a soft spot for Mia, and Nick knew that the old man had been hopelessly in love with Molly. The fact that Molly had never reciprocated JC's feelings hadn't fazed his dogged devotion and the only time Nick had ever seen tears in

JC's eyes was at Molly's funeral. He hadn't been the only one smitten with Molly, of course: there had always been numerous admirers hanging round Mia's mum. It couldn't have been easy for Juan, come to think of it.

Ashton spoke again: 'Mia . . . Is she the body artist at the Mystic Ink studio?'

'Yes.' Nick looked at him in surprise. 'Do you know her?'

'I dropped in there earlier today. Her work looks very professional.'

'She's the best. I've know her since childhood.'

'Oh? Has she done work on you?'

Nick shook his head. 'I left this neighbourhood before she set up in business and I only returned fairly recently. But I promise you, she's good. Barry—' Nick stretched out and grabbed the arm of a burly man who was walking past. 'Show Ashton your tat.'

Without a word, Barry pulled up his shirt and looked impassively into the distance. On his chest was tattooed a snake. The fine-line details were exquisitely rendered – smooth coils, flat diamond head, cold eyes.

'Nice.' Ashton nodded.

'Thanks.' Nick slapped Barry on the shoulder. 'Barry here isn't the only one. Mia has done tats for most of the guys in the gym. Ask around.'

'Any protection tattoos?'

'Protection? Not sure what you mean. Billy over there has his mum's name on his shoulder.' Nick grinned. 'He swears it brings him luck.'

'Not quite what I had in mind.'

'Well, talk to Mia. I'm sure she'll be able to help you out.' Nick glanced up at the large clock above the door. 'Shit. I'm late. I have to make tracks. See you tomorrow, yeah?'

Ashton nodded. 'Tomorrow.'

As Nick was about to step through the door, he looked back. Ashton was watching him. There was something in the blankness of his expression that made Nick pause. But then Ashton smiled and sketched a salute with his hand.

Nick returned the smile. Interesting guy.

CHAPTER SIXTEEN

Mia had not arrived by the time Nick walked into Luciano's and he was surprised; it was unlike her to be late. He ordered a bottle of mineral water for himself and a glass of Mia's favourite red and started reading through the menu.

A soft hand touched his shoulder and he looked up, smiling. But it wasn't Mia. It was Claudine Normandy, looking rather fetching in a halter-neck dress.

'Nick.' She leant towards him and kissed him on the cheek, allowing him a dazzling glimpse of cleavage. Oh, boy.

'Why are you sitting here lonely and sad?' Claudine, Nick always thought, was very attractive but her conversation often sounded as though it came straight from one of Okie's romance novels.

'I'm waiting for Mia.'

She didn't respond but a small furrow appeared between her eyebrows. 'I'll keep you company until she arrives.' She sat down and brushed her hair away from her face with a sinuous motion. 'Now . . . tell me *everything*.'

The woman was over-the-top and Nick had heard

stories of her being a real ballbreaker, but the fact that she was willing to turn on the seduction routine for him was flattering all the same.

'Of course.' He smiled back at her. 'Tell me what you'd like to hear.' Good grief. He sounded like a Mills & Boon character himself.

But it was all quite pleasant. They were still flirting amiably and Claudine had started touching his arm every so often, when he spotted Mia entering the restaurant. And wasn't it just amazing how he lost all interest in Claudine at once?

Mia's hair was slightly dishevelled and her cheeks were flushed from the wind. She had on slim-fitting black trousers and a scarlet blouse. Her leather biker's jacket was hooked to her middle finger and slung over her shoulder but still she looked totally feminine. She was not the most glamorously dressed nor the prettiest woman in the room, but as she walked towards his table Nick noticed that every male head in the place turned to look at her.

'Hi, Claudine.'

'Mia.' Claudine's voice was cool. 'I took pity on poor Nick. He was sitting here all alone and bored with himself.'

'Sorry, Nick.' Mia made an annoyed gesture. 'Those idiot builders next door shorted the electricity supply to my house. The second time this week, would you believe. I've been on the phone trying to get it fixed – that's why I'm late.'

'Did you get it sorted?'

'No. I'll be without power until tomorrow. Lisa and I had to cancel our last appointments today. We couldn't use the machines.'

'Well, I'll leave you two to it.' Claudine got up from the chair, but before moving away she brushed a finger against Nick's cheek. 'Don't forget our date, handsome.'

Nick coloured under Mia's gaze. 'She promised to cook me a celebration dinner after the fight.'

'Sweet of her. Careful, Nicky. She'll feed your heart through her Magimix.'

'Well, you know me – I'm in favour of extreme sports.'

Mia grinned and raised her glass of wine in a mock salute. 'Here's to living on the edge. But when she turns your pretty blue eyes brown, don't say I didn't warn you. Anyway' – she dismissed Claudine from the conversation and reached for the menu – 'what looks good?'

They took their time over dinner and talked with the ease that comes from long friendship and from growing up together. Twelve years he had been away but those years seemed unsubstantial, of no consequence. This was what was important, Nick thought; this right here. Mia was telling him a story about Lisa's new boyfriend – a funny story – but he wasn't really concentrating. He was content merely to be with her and to watch her face: the wide-spaced eyes, the mouth that turned up at the corners, making it look as though she were always just about to smile, the charmingly skewwhiff nose he loved so much.

But the years he had been away had also left gaps in his understanding of who she was. She lifted her hand and pushed a strand of hair from her face. Her sleeve fell away from her wrist and on the pale skin the inked Usui symbols looked like the indecipherable footprints of birds in dust. He knew those symbols were associated with Reiki and healing and energy transference, but he had no real understanding of what they meant – she had acquired them after he had moved to Scotland. Things had happened to her during those twelve years of which he knew nothing. Secret things. Sometimes he even had the fanciful idea that she lived another life as well, like some mysterious, beautiful cat who explored the dark after everyone had gone to sleep.

He loved this woman. He should try to move things between them to the next level. Why couldn't he find the right words? But he knew why. If he crashed and burned, it might be the end of their friendship and he did not think he would be able to bear that. He used to have more courage when he was younger. 'Mia Lockhart, will you give me the key to unlock your heart?' he once wrote to her. Considering he was only thirteen years old at the time, it was not a bad effort. Mia had been kind but firm. She would probably still be kind today but once he said the words and she rejected them, the continental drift would start.

Towards the end of the evening, over coffee, they talked about Valentine.

'I have to admit I hardly ever thought of him while I was away,' Nick said. 'But now that I know I'll never see him again, I badly want to have a beer with the guy.'

'I keep thinking of that bomb the two of you made in your mum's garage when you were ten.'

'It's a wonder we didn't kill ourselves.' Nick shook his head, remembering. He and Valentine had jammed a marble down a lead tube and then tried to blow it out of the tube using household cleaning products and petrol. The subsequent explosion had ripped a crater in the floor of the garage and had cracked the windows of four houses. The marble stayed put.

He looked at her. 'You and Valentine kept in touch over the years.'

Her eyes were lowered now; he couldn't see her expression. 'Not so much after he left for Liverpool. But, yes, we kept in touch.'

'Did you know he was coming out of retirement?'

'No.' Her voice was almost inaudible. 'He didn't tell me.' She hesitated. 'Nick . . .'

'Yes?'

'Do you remember Jeff Carruthers? He used to train at Scorpio. He was transferred by the company he works for and now lives in Manchester. He left Scorpio about a fortnight after you came back.'

'I think I remember him.' Nick thought for a moment. 'Welterweight, red hair?'

'That's him.'

'What about him?'

'He's fighting next week.'

He waited for her to go on, but she was quiet, seemingly intent on stirring her tea.

'He's a friend of yours?'

'Yes.'

For a moment he had the feeling that she wanted to add something. Something important. 'Mia? What's wrong?'

'No. It's nothing. Forget it.' She glanced at her watch and her voice became brisk. 'If you're going to be pounding along the road at dawn, we should probably get you to bed.'

'Speaking of which,' he said as he signalled for the bill, 'it looks as though I have a new training buddy.'

'Good. I was hoping JC would find someone to take Okie's place. Who is it?'

'New guy by the name of Adrian Ashton. Actually, he told me he met you today.'

'Ashton . . .'

'Tall. Blond.'

'Oh . . .' For just a moment an odd expression flitted over her face. 'You sparred with him? How did he handle himself?'

'He's fast.' Nick shrugged. 'Good hand speed. Great kicks. But at heart he's a vogue. He studied internal martial arts in Asia.'

'Interesting that he likes to spar.'

'Yeah.' Nick took the bill from the waiter. 'Let me get this.'

'The answer to that would be No.' She smiled but her voice was decisive. 'We go Dutch. As always.'

Right. As always.

Outside in the street, he helped her with her jacket. 'I'm

parked right there.' He pointed at his car, a gun-metal Aston Martin DB7 Zagato. Even though he could now afford it, Nick did not treat himself to toys very often but the Aston Martin was the apple of his eye. The car, and the Krell Evolution Music System he had installed at great expense in his flat a while back, were his two major extravagances. 'Give me a minute, Mia, and I'll follow you home.'

'There's no need, Nicky. I'll be fine.'

'You're not getting your way on this one, Ms Lockhart. It's late. Besides, Lisa told me there was some creepy stalker lurking in the park the other day who freaked you out.'

'Lisa likes a good story. There was a man, but there was no real menace. I was just jumpy, I think. It was the day after you told me of Valentine's death. I was still ... shaken.'

'Nevertheless, I'm seeing you home.'

And as he followed the red tail light of Mia's bike as she weaved through the traffic, Nick felt a sense of contentment. He liked the feeling that he was watching over her.

It was a beautiful evening. The sky was a deep, dark blue and you could see stars. A helicopter, glittering bright as a jewel, hovered for a few moments overhead before clattering away like some beautiful alien insect. Mia suddenly took a turning fast, leaning low to the side – a manoeuvre graceful and thrilling – and then they were close to the river and there, in the distance, was the London Eye, blue and pink and purple, floating weightlessly in a sky that showed not a ribbon of cloud. Nick breathed in the night air rushing through the open car window. The river was in full tide and he could smell wet leaves and earth: strong as bitter tobacco.

In front of her house, Mia stopped her bike and kicked down its stand. Nick got out of his car but left the engine running. As he walked up to her she took off her helmet and shook loose her hair.

'Isn't it a magical evening?' She smiled at him with uncomplicated delight.

Ah, Mia. He placed a hand on her arm. He should tell her how he felt. This was the right time – now – when her eyes reflected a star-filled sky and she was happy.

Her eyes moved past his shoulder and she brought her finger to her lips. He turned round.

The headlights of the car threw beams of yellow that chased the shadows. Caught in their glare was an urban fox. It was one of the thousands of light-footed animals living nocturnal existences in the streets and gardens of London, prowling around dustbins, flitting through leafy squares. Ghosts. You never saw one during the day.

The animal's eyes shimmered with a phantom sheen. One paw was lifted hesitantly. Nick and Mia stared back at the poised animal, holding their breath. The air between them seemed to glisten and thicken. A magical evening . . .

Someone slammed a window shut at the end of the street; the sound echoing off the walls of the other houses. The fox turned its head and disappeared into the shadows.

CHAPTER SEVENTEEN

Mia watched the orange tail lights of Nick's car disappear round the corner and stepped into the house. Shutting the door behind her, she automatically reached for the light switch on the wall. Nothing. The power was still off.

Her good mood starting to ebb, she navigated her way slowly down the dark steps into the kitchen, one hand steadying herself against the wall, the other outstretched in the gloom. She had some candles in the larder, she remembered. Was there a box of matches as well?

The candles were on the top shelf, but she could not find the matches. She seemed to recall seeing some in the drawer next to her bed – one of those small matchbooks you find in restaurants. Candle in one hand, she made her way up the stairs once more.

A breath of cool air made her pause. The window on the first landing was open. In her rush to meet Nick, she must have forgotten to close it. Stupid of her to be so careless.

For a moment she stood quietly, her hand resting on the windowsill. She was looking out on to the dark expanse of garden that lay to the back of her house. Her own outdoor space was small, little more than a patio with overfull tubs of flowers, but backing on to her property were the long narrow Victorian gardens of her neighbours. She could smell the star jasmine drifting in from old Mrs Quinn's hedge and the sluggish scent of roses. Someone was playing a Byrds CD, the sound faint but the song so familiar, she could repeat the words in her head. 'A time to be born, a time to die . . . a time to kill, a time to heal . . .'

It used to be one of Molly's favourite songs.

She suddenly wished fiercely for her mother. She missed her father too, of course she did, but Molly had been the dominant force in her life. Maybe it was being with Nick tonight and revisiting old memories, but an overwhelming wave of longing swept over her. Since Valentine's death she had the strongest feeling that things were changing irrevocably and that soon everything that was safe and familiar would be gone and she would have to walk where she did not want to go. Molly would have been able to reassure her.

'We make our own stories, Mia.' Molly smiling at her where she sat in front of the dressing table, brushing her hair with long, firm strokes. 'Never be afraid. Never back off. Don't let anyone stop you from living your own story now.'

That had been Molly's talent – to live in the moment. Growing up with a mother for whom planning was anathema presented its own challenges, of course. Equal part exhilaration and apprehension was probably the best way to describe it; like taking a ride on the big dipper without strapping yourself in first. Molly was bright colours, creativity and laughter. She was temper tantrums and mood swings. Nothing about her mother had been muted. Not her loves, nor her hates, not the way in which she had lived her life.

But in other respects Molly had made sure she gave her daughter the opportunity of growing up conventionally. Juan's job as a diver had taken him all over the country but Molly had decided it was not in Mia's best interest for them to follow him around. Mia had lived her entire life in this one house: you couldn't get more stable than that. And if it was up to her, she would never leave this place until the day they carried her out, feet first. She felt rooted here to an extraordinary degree. Even now, as she stood looking out of the window, it was as though she could sense the secret lives behind the walls of the darkened houses around her – as though she were connected to every drawn breath. If she closed her eyes she could swear she felt the city itself breathing – in, out – a vast sentient presence pressing on her heart. This was where she belonged.

Something cold touched her hand; something soft. Mia gave a small scream. But it was only Sweetpea.

'Hey, girl. What are you doing here?' Sweetpea nudged her again. Chameleons were supposed to be deaf but Mia had never believed this. She hefted Sweetpea on to her shoulder. 'Let's go to bed, what do you say?'

She closed the window and continued walking up the stairs, but when she reached the second landing she thought she heard a sound down below. A door closing? She paused, listening.

Nothing. It was her imagination. She was still skittish from the scare Sweetpea had given her, that was all. She continued up the dark stairs, her hand trailing the balustrade to guide her.

Inside her bedroom she deposited Sweetpea on top of the headboard of her bed before groping inside the drawer of the bedside table. Her fingers brushed the matchbook and she gave a sigh of relief. The matches were thin and bendy but she finally managed to strike one into life and light the candle.

The tiny flame threw large shadows. Mia took a nightdress from the cupboard and started to undress. Her figure – all long, spindly arms and legs – moved across the wall next to her like an elongated shadow puppet. Taking the candle with her, she crossed the room and knelt down in front of a large trunk. As she opened it, a fugitive scent of verbena and bitter herbs escaped from its depths. Hidden underneath a stack of jumpers were two small wooden boxes embossed with silver filigree work.

She sat down cross-legged in front of the old-fashioned standing mirror in the corner of the room. Her reflection seemed to be floating and the mirror's surface shimmered with shadows and light.

Mia opened the first box. Inside was a nest of stainless-steel acupuncture filament needles – already sterilized by autoclave – and a small plastic bag filled with sticks of moxa: herb mixture.

She carefully touched the flame from needle to needle and ignited the moxa, causing it to smoulder. Breathing out slowly, slowly, she inserted the first needle into her skin approximately two finger widths away from the crease in her left wrist. Almost immediately she could feel the *deqi* sensation at the point of insertion. The second and third needles went into the *he* and *gu* points in the web between the thumb and the palm and the fourth at the base of her throat. She could feel her skin turning warm from the conducted heat.

Slowly she lifted the lid on the second box. Inside were three pictures. The top one was of Valentine. He was wrapping his hands in preparation for his gloves and his face was uncharacteristically pensive. A feeling of sorrow touched her mind but she pushed the picture to one side and reached for the one just underneath. Jeff Carruthers had been photographed in a typical fighter's pose: fists raised, chin lowered, his expression ferocious.

Over the past days it had been very difficult for her not to check on Jeff obsessively. Valentine's death had spooked her but she had to keep reminding herself that there was nothing to suggest that Valentine's death had been anything but a natural tragedy. There was another full week to go before Jeff's fight and there was nothing to suggest that anything was wrong. If she kept calling him, he would become alarmed.

But with Jeff getting ready to enter the ring, it was time for her to go to work: time to start doing what she did best. Tonight was only the first phase. On the night before

Jeff's fight, she would follow in the footsteps of Keepers over the centuries and step out fully. *Stepping out.* Even though she had done so many times before, the idea alone still filled her with excitement.

Against the wall above her bed, Sweetpea threw an oversized shadow: humpbacked silhouette; one big round eye. Mia blew out the candle and Sweetpea's shadow melted into darkness.

Some people can run fast. Some people can do maths. She was good at keeping fighters safe. That's what Keepers do. It was as simple as that. And as complicated.

The energy flowed cleanly through her body. Keeping Jeff's face in her mind, she closed her eyes. Her intent absolute, she reached out to him. *Hon Sha Ze Sho Nen.* No past, no present, no future. The Buddha in me reaching out to the Buddha in you.

Time floated like petals on water. When she opened her eyes again the hands on the alarm clock were twenty minutes further along. She removed the needles from her body and replaced them along with Jeff's photo inside the boxes. Tomorrow night she would repeat this long-distance healing ritual and she would continue to do so until Friday, when she would step out fully.

She was very sleepy now, as was always the case when she did this. Because of the heat of the night, she lay down on top of the sheets, not underneath.

She was starting to slip into sleep, her fingers twitching involuntarily, her eyeballs moving underneath their closed lids. Jeff's face was fading in and out, becoming jumbled up with the flotsam and debris of her subconscious mind . . .

. . . *Haragei* and a stranger watching her from across a garden square filled with rain and shadows. Nick pouring wine into her glass and a stray drop staining the tablecloth like a crimson tear. A fox staring at her with gleaming eyes. The sound of a song drifting through dark gardens: 'a time to kill, a time to heal . . .' Molly saying, 'We make our own stories, Mia.'

Stories. Old stories. Ancient memories . . .

CHAPTER EIGHTEEN

It was an old, old story: the battle-scarred warrior and the beautiful woman taking him into her keeping. And like all powerful myths, it was repeated in different incarnations in different cultures. Odin's fair-haired Valkyries carried slain warriors to an everlasting feast in Valhalla. Irish Morrighan demanded of the warrior of her choice that he make love to her before going into battle. If he accepted, he was victorious; if he refused, he died.

Sex, ritual, bravery, death. The stuff legends and dreams are made of. The thief believed in dreams: he lived his life by them. And he believed in legends. But could legend survive in an age of binary code? Could it survive in a time in which physical strength and courage were no longer celebrated as the ultimate male accomplishments? In a world in which ritualized, hand-to-hand combat was marginalized, was there still room for a Keeper?

Before he met Valentine, his answer would have been no. But when he met Valentine, he made a discovery. Somewhere out there among the rows of soot-blackened houses and dirty streets, the high-rises, the television aerials, CCTV cameras, beeping mobile phones, city grit and rattling Tube trains, there lived a Keeper. A warrior woman who possessed the gift of healing energy.

The moment he first became aware of her existence was still fresh in his mind. He and Valentine had just finished training and were getting dressed in the men's changing room.

Valentine stripped off his T-shirt, stretched and scratched himself. He was not tall but he was powerfully built. On one muscled shoulder was tattooed the head of a wolf – his fighter's emblem. But it was the other tattoo, the one on his heart, that was key.

Two eyes were inked into Valentine's skin. Contained in one eye was a symbol that looked like a circle with three lines entering it at an angle. As he stared at Valentine, he knew he had seen this tattoo before, if only he could remember where.

Valentine noticed his interest. 'I got it done when I first started fighting professionally.'

'Very cool. Who did it for you?'

'A very cool lady.'

'Why eyes?'

Valentine flashed a grin. 'She insisted.'

And he now remembered where he had seen these eyes with the mysterious symbol before: it was on the wall of a monastery in Thailand. It was a protection tattoo – the mark of a Keeper.

During the years he spent travelling in Asia he had heard stories of women who protected warriors who were preparing for hand-to-hand combat. These Keepers used the ancient art of *fa gung* – the transmission of chi through meditation – to protect their charges against harm and always left their mark of protection on the skin of the men in their keep. For the rest of his life, the warrior would carry with him an amulet, a talisman.

These stories were rarely written down. They were part of the secretive lore of *Okuden*, the '*deep-inside* hidden teachings' of martial arts. Knowledge of Keepers was passed on from mother to daughter and from Keeper to warrior. And just as many martial-arts techniques were lost in the mists of time through a tradition of oral instruction and obsessive secrecy, so the Keeper and her true purpose had become an enigmatic fragment in a half-forgotten tale of magic and valour.

Could it be that he had found one? The possibility blew his mind. And it added an additional challenge to his quest. Valentine had something he wanted. Usually, that would not be a problem – he would simply steal it. But this time, he would have to mislead a Keeper.

How?

It had taken him weeks to crack that riddle. In the end, he found the answer in an obscure volume of *Bugei*. '*For the Keeper has two tools: she must hold him in her dream and mark him with her sign.*' One sentence only, but it was enough. It had enabled him to slip in under the Keeper's radar. She couldn't hold Valentine in her dream if she didn't know he was about to fight. It was that simple. And once he had stolen from Valentine what he needed, he had turned his attention fully to tracking her down.

He had found her.

He was inside her house.

The open window had been an unexpected bonus – he should make the most of this opportunity. As he walked slowly up the stairs he could smell the mugwort she had burnt. For a moment he hesitated at the threshold of the room, but his eyes were already dark-adapted from waiting downstairs inside the pitch-black studio and he had no difficulty making out her quiet form on top of the bed.

Her head rested on her pillow at an angle, the hair curtaining her face. One leg was pulled up to form a relaxed, lopsided triangle. Her hands were resting on her breasts as though posed.

She had already slipped from meditation into proper sleep: her brain waves slowing from the 4–7Hz theta state of deep meditation into the 3Hz sleep state. She was oblivious to the world. She would not sense him.

He stood silently next to the bed, looking down at her and the desire to take from her what he wanted – *needed* – was so great he tasted it in his mouth. He could steal it from her right now. It was why he had tracked her down and moved to London.

Take it. It would be easy . . .

Her angled, pale neck looked vulnerable.

He balled his hands into fists and swallowed deeply. Not yet. He was curious. He wanted to be there when the time came for her to step out fully . . . The rush of blood in his ears slowly subsided and he knew he had managed to repress the hunger.

For now.

As he looked down at her he wondered who else was in her keep besides Valentine. He already knew it wasn't Nick. Nick did not have a tattoo and a Keeper's charge always carried her mark.

Somewhere on her body must be her own mark. Somewhere secret. Her nightdress was rucked up high on one thigh and he was tempted . . .

Another time.

I want to play with you, sweet Mia. Will you play with me?

And after playing with her, he would move in and satisfy his hunger. Steal from her the ultimate prize.

She was breathing so quietly. Her chest seemed hardly to move.

Take care, little stranger. Dreams can be like bondage. They leave bruises.

He sat down in the armchair next to the bed to watch.

CHI

... energy's seed sleeping interred in the marrow ...

Octavio Paz, as quoted in Robert O. Becker,
The Body Electric

CHAPTER NINETEEN

Sweat rolling off his brow, Rick Cobra turned to confront, once again, the man facing him. Cobra was close to exhaustion: his razor-sharp reflexes blunted and his movements sluggish. The man in front of him smiled and the ruby in his front tooth winked in the feeble light of the lamp-post that lit this seedy side of the docks with a stale yellow glow.

'Tired, little man?' he growled.

Cobra knew he had no strength left to beat the giant rushing at him with outstretched hands. Time to think outside the box. Time for Dragon's Breath. What a good thing he had chewed on burdock root over the past few days. An old Ninja trick, and one Gonzo would be unprepared for. As Gonzo's fingers stabbed at his throat, Cobra exhaled mightily into the face of his foe. Gonzo staggered back, gagging, his eyes rolling upwards in shock—

Nick stopped typing and glared at the screen. This wasn't working. Did he really want his hero to win the day because of bad breath?

Maybe he should try it himself, Nick thought sourly. The idea of chewing on stinky herbs was not attractive but he supposed he could simply stop brushing his teeth for two weeks before the fight.

The fight. Shit. He glanced at his watch. If he didn't leave for the park right this minute, Adrian Ashton would arrive there well before him. It was bad form to keep a training buddy waiting. He grabbed his keys.

He was lucky. Because of the earliness of the hour, there was little traffic and he arrived at the park in minutes. He also had no trouble finding a parking space for the Aston Martin right inside the north entrance.

As he jogged into the park, the horizon was pink with light. A faint mist was rising and there was dew on the grass. Usually he hated doing roadwork: running was boring, boring. And most of the time he wondered why the hell he was still doing this. The constant training. The dieting. The bruises and aching muscles. JC screaming abuse. His next fight would be his first title fight: Southern Regional. If he won the belt, that would probably be as much as could be expected of him as a shot at a British title was unlikely to be on the cards. On a morning like this, though, he could not imagine doing anything else.

The long lane of trees was coming to an end and ahead of him was the red and gilt pagoda. Standing on the bottom step was Ashton. He looked rested and bright-eyed and clearly had a good night's sleep behind him.

'Sorry, mate. Have you been waiting long?'

'Not at all.' Ashton shook his head. 'I just arrived. So, shall we set off?' Without waiting for an answer he started jogging in the direction of the bridge.

No small talk, then. Right. And the guy was keeping up a hell of a pace. Nick stretched his stride.

He had just found his rhythm, when Ashton kicked up the pace another notch. Shit. But like hell was he going to ask the man to slow down.

Ten minutes later and Ashton increased the speed again. And five minutes later, even more. They were practically sprinting by this time. Did Ashton want to kill him? Nick's breath burnt in his chest.

Ashton suddenly stopped in his tracks. In front of them was a small but steep hill. He turned and looked at Nick. 'I'm going to get on your back and then I want you to run up that slope.'

'What!'

'You do this every day and your endurance and strength will increase like you will not believe.'

Or give him back problems for the rest of his life. Nick looked uncertainly from Ashton to the hill.

'Come on, Nick. Trust me.'

Hesitantly he got down on one knee. Christ, this was going to look really strange. It was a good thing there were so few people around.

Ashton was bloody deadweight. How much did the

man clock on the scale, after all? It felt as if there was an elephant on his back. Nick started shuffling up the slope. 'Try increasing your speed.' Ashton's voice came from behind his ear. He sounded as calm as though he were having a cup of tea.

Nick gritted his teeth. Driving from his hips, shoulders bowed, he attacked the hill. By the time he reached the top, his thigh muscles were quivering.

'Now run down backwards.' Ashton pointed to the bottom of the hill. 'I'll meet you down there. And then we do it again.'

The hill was not the end of it. After Nick had staggered up the slope for the third time, Ashton made him do a series of plyometric exercises. Nothing was more energy-sapping than squat thrust jumps and explosive hand-clapping press-ups. After ten minutes, Nick was close to collapse. What was galling, though, was that with the exception of the hill, Ashton had matched him move-ment for movement and looked little the worse for wear.

'Time to stretch you out.' Ashton slapped him on the shoulder. 'By the way, I know this is a kickboxing fight and you won't be going down to the mat, but I'm a firm believer in groundwork.'

Nick nodded and winced as Ashton pulled back his arms and pushed his elbows close together. 'JC is too. Wrestling is part of my training.'

'Good. We can roll together. I did a stint at Gracie Barra in Rio.'

Nick looked at him with respect. Gracie jiu-jitsu was

the best in the world. 'I thought you said you were into internal martial arts.'

'I like to cherry-pick. A little bit of this, a little bit of that. I know there are martial-arts masters who frown on training in more than one system, but I don't believe in getting attached to any one style.' Ashton stepped back. 'Right, you're done.' Turning away, he opened his rucksack and took out two bottles of water. 'Catch.'

Nick managed to grab the bottle – a remarkable feat considering that his reflexes were shot to hell with fatigue – and twisted open the cap.

For a while it was quiet between them. Nick looked over at the other man, who was staring into the distance. His blond hair was dark with sweat but he looked completely at ease. The guy was super fit.

'So, you're a doctor?' Maybe Ashton was related to Dr Mengele.

'I started out as one.' Ashton took a swig of water. 'After a few years I switched to pure research and worked at the chronobiology institute at Exmare. In their sleep clinic.'

'Hanging out with sleeping people.' Nick grimaced. 'That must be exciting.'

Ashton smiled lazily. 'All kinds of interesting things happen to your body when you sleep. You'd be surprised. A dangerous time, nighttime. But I'm no longer at Exmare.'

'Why did you leave?'

'Let's just say I decided to walk down a road less travelled.'

'The road less travelled sounds like an interesting place to be.'

'I like to think so. Although some people might call it an exercise in futility. Or trying to catch a white crow.'

Nick blinked. 'Crow . . .'

'A term used by William James, an American behavioural scientist. He used it to describe those things in life that did not fit. Anomalies. That's where I like to potter around. I am trying to prove something that has never been clinically established inside a laboratory. Not everyone approves.'

'I thought that was what scientists are supposed to do. Find proof.'

'You'd think so, wouldn't you. But in this case, my colleagues did not agree with my . . . activities.' Ashton shrugged. 'I started off by doing some acupuncture experiments to see if it could help with sleep disorders. I used the conclusions of some of Robert Becker's experiments – he's an American orthopaedic surgeon who specializes in biomedical electronics – and found what he did: that there are electrical charges separate from the pulses of the body's nervous system, which correspond to the body's acupuncture meridians.'

With his left hand, Ashton suddenly lobbed his empty water bottle in the direction of a rubbish bin about fifty yards away. Nick watched as the bottle sailed unerringly into the bin. How long would it take him before he would be able to pull off a move like that, he wondered dispassionately. Probably never.

'Acupuncture points have been researched before, of course.' Ashton looked back at him. 'Other scientists have proved that there are differences in the levels of potassium and sodium in acupuncture points compared with the surrounding tissue. Acupoints also exhibit lower skin resistance – in other words, these points conduct electrical current more efficiently. What's interesting is that this lower skin resistance is even measurable after death. Isn't that cool?'

Cool? Yes, that was one way of looking at it, Nick supposed. Not that he was really all that interested in what happened once you copped it. When you're dead, you're dead, and it didn't much matter if your skin still crackled like a transistor radio.

'Despite all of this evidence, acupuncture doesn't get much respect in the West. It is still considered wild territory.' Ashton sighed. 'In China it is different. The codified Chinese acupuncture studies go back two thousand years. So I went looking for my white crow in Asia. I studied *The Emperor's Classic of Internal Medicine* – sort of the historical equivalent of the Western Corpus Hippocraticum.'

'Did you find your white crow?'

'I came closer. I did further research into sleep patterns and it confirmed my belief that they are correlated to cycles and fluctuations of vital energy.'

'Vital energy. You mean chi?'

'Exactly. You know about chi?'

'A bit.' You don't work out next to a group of vogues

every day without absorbing some of that stuff through osmosis, Nick thought. And Mia, of course, believed in it absolutely. 'It has to do with internal energy flowing through your body? Or something like that?'

'Something like that. Chi enters the body through acupuncture points and flows through twelve meridians and two midline collaterals and through paired yin and yang organs. The movement of chi builds up in wave-like movements, completing a cycle every twenty-four hours. In the early-morning hours, chi is at its lowest ebb. That's when many people have trouble sleeping. And when many people die in their sleep, incidentally.' He shrugged again. 'The Western medical mind has difficulty with the concept of chi. It cannot be dissected under a microscope and does not fit the empirical model. You can't exactly cut through an artery wall and look at it.'

Nick frowned. 'Seriously? I always thought chi was so much mystical mumbo-jumbo.'

Ashton lifted his eyebrows. 'I once saw an operation in Guangzhou province. A woman was having a goitre removed. She was completely conscious, with only a number of needles stuck into her neck. No anaesthesia, nothing. It was all about manipulating the hollows along the meridians and working on her chi. I watched the surgeon pick up a scalpel and cut her throat and she was just lying there, eyes wide open, smiling continuously. Don't know if you would call that mystical.'

'I'd call that creepy.'

'There's that, of course.' Ashton looked amused.

'You should talk to Chilli. He's into this kind of thing.'

'Chilli?'

'He is my friend Mia's instructor. He has been her sensei for ages. Actually, Mia will be interested in your ideas as well. She very much believes in chi: all part of the martial-arts philosophy taught to her by Chilli.'

'I could tell. It shows in her training.'

'You've seen her train?' Nick was surprised.

'I left my mobile at Scorpio last night. Before I came to the park this morning, I stopped to pick it up. Mia was there – training by herself. I didn't interrupt but I watched for a while. She's very, very good.'

Nick nodded. 'Her mother enrolled her with Chilli when she was only six.'

'Her mother is a martial artist as well?'

'Oh, yes. But she died a few years ago. She and Mia's father both.'

'What happened?'

Nick hesitated. But it was hardly a secret: everyone at Scorpio knew. And it had been in all the papers.

'They tombstoned.'

Ashton's eyebrows flew up his forehead.

'Tombstoning. It's an extreme sport. You jump off high cliffs. Really high cliffs. Mia's dad was a diver and he and Molly used to do this for fun.' Nick shook his head. 'On this day, Molly decided to sit it out because the current was so strong. Juan jumped alone but something went wrong. He couldn't get enough distance between himself and the cliff face and he hit a rock on the way down. When Molly saw what had happened, she jumped after him and tried to pull him ashore. The autopsy showed that Juan was alive when he hit the water but probably unconscious because of his injury and therefore unable to help Molly get him to safety. The current took both of them and they drowned.'

For a while it was quiet. Then Ashton said, 'It's a good way to die.'

'Excuse me?'

'Would you rather die hooked up to a tube, drooling all over your chin, or would you rather do something fearless and life-affirming before dying in the arms of the one you love?'

Point taken, Nick thought, surprised by the intensity in the man's voice.

Ashton glanced at his watch. 'I must go. I have an appointment with an estate agent. See you tomorrow, same time?'

'Will we be doing the hill again?'

'Of course.' A grin. 'Are you training with JC this evening?'

'No. JC and I will be at Mia's. Actually . . .' Nick paused. 'If you're free, why don't you come as well? Mia has pot luck at her place once a month – sort of an institution. All the fighters from Scorpio will be there. It'll give you an opportunity to meet some of the guys.'

'That would be great.'

'She lives in the same house as her studio. You know where it is, don't you?'

'I've been there.'

'Good. Any time after eight.'

'Thanks. I'd like to meet Mia again. I enjoyed watching her train this morning.' Ashton paused. 'She dances.'

CHAPTER TWENTY

The Book of Light and Dust
For Rosalia
XXXII

Last night I watched you sleep and saw you reflected in a million minds — as real as a hallucination; as seductive as a dream. This morning I watched you dance — part poetry, part lethal intent.

You burn with light, while I watch from the shadows with my mummified heart. You have what I steal.

Woman. Child. Angel. Temptress. The way I want to love you is the way I want to hurt you.

What does the Buddha teach us?

The Buddha teaches renunciation. The Buddha teaches repression of desire. Desire leads to dukkha. *Dukkha is suffering — an insatiable yearning that can never be satisfied.*

Is this truly the Buddha's message? Because without desire there is no energy. And the greatest desire of all leads us from dust to light.

No. The Buddha's message is misinterpreted. We fail not because we desire. We fail because we do not desire enough . . .

THE WAY: YANG RED

BLACKLIGHT: DIR: LU4 GB19, FRC: 8, TIME: 10, SUs: K9 PC2

Whitelight: mas. GB20

CHAPTER TWENTY-ONE

O ne of the fighters had rigged his iPod to Mia's music system and the Cheeky Girls were blaring from the speakers in the living room.

Mia sighed. She loved these guys but their taste in music was often execrable. Okie once did his ring walk to Chesney Hawke's 'The One and Only'.

As she headed to the kitchen to check on the pasta, Mia wondered if Nick had chosen a song yet. Choosing a song for your entrance was a big deal. Fighters spent hours trying to decide what song best embodied their personal credo or what might possibly intimidate an opponent into quivering jelly. Bon Jovi's 'Unbreakable' was a favourite on the fight circuit, as was Europe's 'The Final Countdown'. On the other hand, Billy over there was a fervent church-goer and liked to walk in to 'Amazing Grace'. But then Billy was an anomaly, Mia thought, looking at his freckled face and innocent eyes. Tall and spindly, he still lived with his mum. On fight nights he entered the arena looking mild as milk in a robe embroidered with the words 'Jesus is Lord' hanging from his bony shoulders. And then he'd step into the ring and kick his opponent's head in.

Caroline, Tom Williams's long-suffering wife, followed her into the kitchen.

'Is there anything I can help with, Mia?'

'No, thanks, Caroline.' Mia looked over her shoulder where she was standing in front of the stove. 'How are you holding up?' Tom had a fight coming up in two weeks' time, which meant poor Caroline was going to have to grit her teeth and think Zen to make it through the coming days.

'Tom's lucky trunks got mangled in the tumble-drier.'

'Oops.'

Tom was highly superstitious, Mia knew, especially when a fight was looming. The knowledge that he would not be able to wear his lucky trunks when entering the ring was sure to send him into a tailspin. He also kept to a regime that would put a monk to shame and, as one of the few vegetarian fighters around, was obsessive about his diet. But Tom was hardly alone, Mia thought, prodding the pasta with a wooden spoon. All these fighters were as vain as models and kept a watchful eye on their love handles. Which was why the pasta she was cooking was whole wheat and the sauce contained not a drop of cream. And most of the men tonight would not be drinking beer but sipping diet Coke from a can.

Caroline said, 'I've moved into the spare bedroom.'

Mia was shocked. 'Things between you and Tom are that bad?'

'No. It's so Tom won't get tempted.' Caroline snorted. 'It's all rubbish, of course. After all those hours of training, I could walk round the house dressed in only a G-string and he'd be too exhausted to lift . . . a finger. Banishing me from the bed is just so he can pat himself on the back for being so disciplined.'

Mia bit back a smile. 'Not long now.'

'No. And' – Caroline brightened up – 'the post-fight sex is great. All that testosterone and adrenalin and feel-good hormones sluicing round . . .'

'That's if he wins.'

Caroline shook her head. 'How I ended up with a fighter, I'll never know. You'd think a librarian would fall for a Woody Allen type. I sometimes think I'm like Françoise Sagan. You know – she said she liked her men to behave like men: strong and childish.'

Okie stuck his head round the door, dreadlocks swinging. 'Hi, ladies.' He smiled disarmingly. 'Some hungry blokes out there. When will the food be ready? Before Christmas?'

'Don't be cheeky.' Caroline tried to swat him with a dishcloth but Okie stepped back smartly. Okie prided himself on his reflexes.

'Almost ready.' Mia placed a colander over the sink. 'How's the rib? Better?'

'Yeah, the rib's on the mend.'

'Great. In that case you can make yourself useful.' She pointed at the colander. 'Empty the pasta in there for me, will you?'

Picking up a stack of bowls Mia headed back to the living room. The music system had been turned off but the noise level was still high as everyone had gathered in front of the TV to watch a video, which was drawing exaggerated cheers and groans. Mia glanced at the screen. It was an old rerun of a cage fight between Randy Couture and Pedro Rizzo.

'Now, that's heart.' JC jabbed a finger at the TV. Couture was lying on his back but still throwing a last desperate kick at an upright Rizzo. 'No retreat, no surrender.'

'That might be heart but Randy didn't deserve to win that one.'

Nick came up to her. 'Do you need help with those, Mia?'

'Thanks. Just pass them out to everyone, will you, and tell them to go and help themselves in the kitchen.' As he took the bowls from her she noticed he was stifling a yawn.

'You look tired.'

'I'm shattered. My new training buddy put me through my paces this morning.'

In her mind's eye came the image of grey eyes, sensuous mouth, elegant hands. And a sense of clamped-down power. Just thinking about the man made her feel short of breath. She frowned.

'Do you think it will work out?' she asked Nick. 'Having him as a training buddy, I mean.'

'If I survive it, it should work out fine. But I can't remember the last time I was this exhausted.' He yawned again. 'Let me get everyone rounded up for you.'

The noise level dropped as soon as they started eating. As Mia watched the men dig in, slurping their pasta, a wave of affection swept through her. She felt like a den mother. She had known many of the men for a long time. They were good guys. They did not live the glamorous lives of highly paid superstar sportsmen but worked as policemen, firemen, gym instructors, DJs, and there was even a hairdresser in the group. But whatever they had to do to pay the bills and whatever turmoil they had to deal with in their personal lives, the discipline of their training held them fast. Inside the dojo, friendship was of the true kind, not the virtual kind. In there you did not have the option to log off when you got bored. You had to engage for real.

Suddenly a cold hand rested on her heart. She looked at the group and it was as though she were looking at their laughing faces from a distance; as though the sound of their voices came to her from a long way off. There was something in the air – something lethal, menacing – and she had the strongest feeling all at once that the little gang gathered under the yellow electric light in her living room was under threat. She didn't know what that might be, but she was light-headed from the adrenalin pumping through her body. She stood there surrounded by friends and the sound of laughter, not understanding why her heart was suddenly beating like a triphammer.

'Mia!'

She looked up, shocked out of her stupor by Caroline's voice.

'Wasn't that the doorbell?' Caroline pointed to the ceiling.

She wondered who it could be. Mia walked up the stairs, still feeling slightly disorientated. The fighters knew to use the kitchen door at basement level. The front door was used mainly by clients, but the studio was closed on Monday nights.

The first thing she noticed as she opened the door was the orchid. He was holding a glazed pot from which grew a spray of moth-white orchids. The second thing she noticed was his eyes: those cool grey eyes with the intent gaze.

'Mia? Remember me? I'm Adrian Ashton. I was here at your studio the other day. I train with Nick.' When she still did not answer, he continued, 'Nick said to come. He said you wouldn't mind?'

'Oh, no, of course not.'

He looked at her arm, which was stretched across the doorway like a barrier.

'Sorry.' She dropped her arm, feeling embarrassed. 'Please come inside, Adrian.'

'Call me Ash.' As he stepped over the threshold, his body brushed against hers and for just a moment she felt closed in by his tall figure, the powerful shoulders.

'This is for you.'

She took the orchid from him and looked down at the creamy blooms that were shot through with veins as delicate as spider's thread. Lovely, but for some reason she felt slightly repulsed as she stared at the fleshy petals.

'Thank you.' He was too close. It made her feel breathless. And why did she have butterflies in her stomach all of a sudden, like some stupid teenager? She pulled herself up and tried to look dignified. 'This is very kind of you.'

'My pleasure.' His voice was solemn but there was laughter in his eyes.

She gestured to the staircase. 'Shall we go down?' She edged past him, acutely aware of his eyes on her as they walked down the stairs.

Nick's face creased into a smile as they entered the living room. 'Ash. Let me introduce you to everyone.'

Mia watched as Nick took Ash round. It was interesting to see how easily Ashton was absorbed into the group. This was a tight circle and although these men were good-humoured they did not readily allow outsiders in. She would have thought Ashton's extreme good looks, obvious wealth and subtle elegance would have made them look at him askance. But not so.

Nick had a similar ability to win people over, but then, Nick was very much part of the neighbourhood despite all his dosh and the success he enjoyed in his professional life. He and Ash could not be more different. Nick – easygoing, laid-back, non-judgemental – was the kind of guy other men liked to hang out with. Nick, Mia always thought, was like the favourite jersey you reached for when there was a chill in the air. He was the friend you called when the chips were down. With Ash it was different. You did not feel that immediate, easy familiarity with him but there was no doubt the others were responding to his presence. She felt the attraction as well – no use denying it – and she was intrigued by this man, but why, when she looked at him, did the back of her neck go cool?

Nick and Ash were now standing next to each other, slightly outside the circle. Nick was laughing at something the other man had said, his eyes crinkling with genuine amusement. Ash touched Nick on the shoulder and the gesture was brief, but strangely intimate. There was just something about that moment, the two men sharing a private joke, their heads close together, that seemed off-beat and flash-froze the image into her mind.

She was still staring at them when she heard the phone ring in the other room. By the time she reached the kitchen, Okie had already picked up and was speaking into the receiver. He obviously knew the caller.

'Oh, man, that's too bad.' Okie was shaking his head in what looked like commiseration. 'Is no one else able to replace him?' A pause while he listened. 'Man, what can I say? Go and eat a steak. Take your wife to the cinema. Something.' Another pause. 'Stop by Scorpio next time you're in town, yeah? Anyway, here's Mia. So long, mate, and sorry again. That's a bummer.'

Okie held out the receiver. 'Jeff Carruthers. His fight's been cancelled.'

She took the phone from him. 'Jeff? What happened?'

'Dammit, Mia. The bugger just pulled out. A day before the fight. Said he knew he wouldn't be able to make the weight at the weigh-in tomorrow so he wouldn't even be coming in. Bloody wanker.' Jeff's voice was filled with frustration. 'Twelve weeks. Twelve bloody weeks of training, wasted.'

'Jeff, I'm sorry.' And she was. For a fighter to pull out at this late stage was bad form. It left it too late to find his opponent a replacement, which meant that all the back-breaking training Jeff had put in, not to mention the effort of psyching himself up for the actual event, was for nothing. Jeff was at peak fitness right now but he wouldn't be able to keep to his excessive training schedule and stick to his combat weight during the weeks it would take his trainer to find him a new opponent. He'd have to go back to his cruising weight, get rested and then start again. Jeff worked as a computer engineer for a data-protection company and she knew he had agreed to work over the school holidays in exchange for taking time off to prepare for this fight. A big sacrifice considering his three children had all been looking forward to some fun time.

'I'm sorry,' she repeated, but this time she also knew she was lying. Much as she sympathized with Jeff, she couldn't help feeling relieved as well. Only at this moment did she realize how much Valentine's death had scared her. With Jeff not fighting and Okie still out of commission, she could relax.

'Well, I just called to let you know, Mia. No stepping out and no dreams on my behalf tonight. You can have a good night's sleep.'

'You too, Jeff. Try and chill, OK?'

'Yes.' His voice sounded tired now. 'I'll try.'

Back in the living room everyone had an opinion about Jeff's former opponent.

'No class. They should ring-ban him for months . . .'

'Hang him by the balls . . .'

Nick walked over to her. 'I think I should hit the sack, sweetheart. I'll be facing the torture meister tomorrow.' He nodded at Ash, who had come up to them.

'OK. Good luck,' She leant over and kissed him on the cheek.

'I'm heading out as well,' Ash said.

'Thanks for coming.' She looked up into his eyes and then quickly away again.

He lingered. 'Would it be possible to see you this week? I'd like to discuss that tattoo I've been thinking about.'

'Of course. Stop by or call me.'

'Will do.'

She watched the two men cross the courtyard. The yellow light within, streaming over her shoulder, cut into the darkness and created long shadows in their wake: two black shapes – clearly separate at first – gradually merging as they walked together up the steps.

CHAPTER TWENTY-TWO

He wondered if the man whose fight was cancelled was one of her charges. It seemed likely. Which meant that she would not be stepping out soon, which was a great pity. A Keeper stepping out – he could not imagine anything more exciting.

But there would be another fighter in her keep; he just needed to find out who it was. And when she stepped out on this man's behalf, he would make sure to follow close behind.

He looked over to where Nick was talking on his mobile. Interesting that Mia hadn't adopted Nick as one of her charges. He wondered why. They were obviously close.

He and Nick had just finished another round of training together and Nick's hair was slick with sweat. But his eyes were sharp with concentration and his voice crisp. From what he could tell by eavesdropping on the one-sided phone conversation, Nick was considering a buy-out offer for Kime. A very lucrative offer, by the sound of it.

He was surprised by Nick. This was a man who had

achieved substantial professional success in his life. Most local boys made good couldn't wait to move away from their roots and tended to layer their lives with all the trappings success had brought within their grasp. But not Nick. Nick travelled lightly.

Nick closed his mobile and slipped it into the pocket of his shorts. 'Sorry about that.'

'I couldn't help but overhear. Are you thinking of selling Kime?'

'It's a good offer.' Nick grimaced. 'And I'll need to discuss it with the shareholders. But I am still the majority shareholder and I think I'm going to recommend we pass.'

'Why?'

'I'm having too much fun.' Nick flashed a sudden grin. 'When it stops being fun, that's when I'll move on.'

'Is that when you'll stop fighting too? When it is no longer fun?'

Nick had been about to turn away, but at these words he stopped. 'Fighting isn't fun.'

'No?'

'No.'

'So why fight?'

Nick shrugged.

'What about death?'

'What about it?' Nick's face was suddenly guarded.

'Do you ever think about it? When you're in the ring?'

'Not when I'm in the ring.'

He watched as Nick turned away to pick up his

sweatshirt where it lay crumpled on the grass. Many years ago, as a trainee doctor, he had studied the brain scan of a boxer who had died in a fight. The brain, connected to the side of the head by blood vessels, had rotated bizarrely at the moment of the knock-out punch. The vessels had severed and the wildly careening brain had crashed from side to side inside the man's skull, a stream of blood pouring into the cranium. It hadn't helped that the fighter, struggling to make his weight allowance, had allowed himself to dehydrate, robbing his brain of the essential fluid that might have helped protect it.

He remembered staring at the scan – at the ethereal, almost spectral image floating within its depths: three pounds of tissue and blood and murky dreams and searing desire. The brain – easily bored, easily blue, relentless in its search for the white-hot thrill of feeling truly aware. And he had thought how it was that at the brink of death one feels most alive.

Nick's head emerged from the sweatshirt. 'Well, I'm off. See you tomorrow?'

'Tomorrow.'

His eyes followed Nick as he crossed the street towards his car and he thought how things had changed. In the beginning he had sought out this man solely because he knew he was friends with Mia. After all, if Nick accepted him as a friend, Mia would be inclined to do the same. But since then, his interest in Nick had deepened. When they had first been introduced he had thought Nick to be only another weekend fighter – not vastly ambitious, not extraordinarily talented – but he had come to realize very quickly that behind the good-humoured exterior was a steely core and a great heart. The man was a warrior.

Nick had something he wanted. He decided he would steal it.

CHAPTER TWENTY-THREE

Nick did a double take as he passed by Flash's desk. 'What the hell?'

Flash looked up. 'Wicked, eh? What do you think: crop-top or T-shirt?'

'What on earth are you doing?'

'I'm dressing Desiree.'

'You're playing with dolls?' Nick stared disbelievingly at the screen. Seated on a chair was an avatar: a long-legged girl with Bambi eyes and pigtails. She was also naked from the waist up and, judging by the pubescent breasts, Desiree was, as the Britney song said, not yet a woman, no longer a girl.

'Crop-top, I think.' Flash's fingers moved over the key-board. 'And maybe I'll give her a belly ring as well.' Another few taps on the keyboard and Desiree was suddenly presentable. Grateful, Desiree blew a kiss.

'Seriously, what is this?'

'It's a new social networking site developed by a friend of mine. A little bit like Cyworld. You should check it out: it's a fun site. See, I've built my own room. Desiree here is my roommate. And there's my profile.'

Nick squinted at the screen. 'I notice you do bungee jumping in your spare time.'

'If you read on, you'll see I also know who killed Tupac.' Flash took a swig from his Coke can. 'I'll build you a room too, if you want. You can tell me how you'd like it decorated. And if you ask nicely I'll let you play with Desiree. All my friends can play with her.'

'You're a pervert.'

Flash waved a nerveless hand. 'Why are you sweaty, by the way?'

'Because I just worked out, mouse potato.'

'I thought you usually took a shower first before coming in.'

'I did.' Nick touched his forehead. It was damp at the hairline. Even though he had stumbled into a cold shower after his torture session with Ashton, he was still sweating. Probably delayed shock. What surprised him – and amused him a little as well – was that he was getting quite desperate to impress the man. Looking for a pat on the back was not usually his style.

Wincing as a muscle in his thigh protested, Nick sat down at his desk and quickly scanned through the posts on the communal board. As he expected, there was another one by Dragonfly. The guy had become one of the most prolific of Kime's contributors and, although the entries sometimes still hovered on the dark side of weird, Nick was starting to look out for them. The man had an interesting take on things, to say the least.

What makes a great fighter? Is it the fighter who is un-defeated? Is it the intelligent fighter with the long-range style and graceful footwork that keeps him out of harm's way?

Or is it the fighter who takes the punches? The fighter who moves forward no matter what the punishment — who does not care that he may already have lost — who staggers out of his corner again and again until bloodily defeated or bloodily victorious.

A fighting great is a skilled fighter: a champion worthy of admiration. But a great fighter is a fighter with that most elusive of qualities: heart.

Well, he couldn't argue with Dragonfly on this one, Nick thought. Heart was where it's at.

He logged off and swivelled his chair round to open the bottom drawer of his desk. He wasn't going to spend any more time on Kime today. He had managed to post Rick Cobra's new adventure on time and there were no other looming crises. Which meant he could finally turn his attention to checking out the information Lee had given him.

After rummaging round in the drawer, he found the piece of paper with the four names of the dead fighters. He placed it next to the computer and entered the first name on the list into his favourite search engine.

For the next hour Nick surfed the Net, moving from link to link. As he expected, all these fighters had been low-profile weekend fighters — just like Valentine. At the time of their death none of them had suffered from any injuries or stealth medical problems.

But he could find little else they had in common. The fighters all lived in different parts of the UK and they all fought out of different gyms. The first fighter had died five years earlier, the last one – not counting Valentine – a year ago. One was a boxer. Two were kickboxers. Valentine was a Thai fighter. The fifth fighter, Bill Muso, fought in the cage. One fighter died a day after his fight. Three of the men died two days later and Valentine's death came three days after he had stepped into the ring. One of the fighters had lost his fight, one drew and three, including Valentine, had been victorious.

There was only one common denominator: the fight itself. These men had all died within days of their fight. Despite all the signs to the contrary, the answer to their deaths must lie in the ring.

Nick picked up the phone and dialled directory enquiries. He wanted to talk to Valentine's wife but he didn't want to ask Mia for the number. No use upsetting her with far-fetched theories at this point.

He had never met Valentine's wife. They had no personal connection and he wasn't quite sure what he was going to ask her. Do you think someone might have killed your husband? Not a great opening line.

But introducing himself to her was easier than he had expected. She accepted without problem his explanation that he and Valentine had been childhood friends and sounded grateful when he offered his condolences. And without much prompting she started talking about

Valentine. In fact, she hardly drew breath. The headlong rush of words made him realize: she was lonely.

'There's no one here in Liverpool who knew him when he was a kid,' she said at one point. 'It's good to talk to someone who really knew him from way back.'

'Did he like Liverpool?'

'Yeah. But he missed London. He missed Scorpio and the fights. You know he had retired — before this last fight?'

'Yes, I know. A mutual friend told me. You probably know her: Mia Lockhart.'

'Mia? You're a friend of Mia's?'

OK. Something was wrong. The tone of her voice had changed from one of gentle reminiscence to open animosity.

'Well,' he hedged, 'we all grew up together in the same neighbourhood, you know. Mia, Valentine and me — we all lived within spitting distance of each other when we were children. And I know she's always been interested in his fighting career.'

'Interested? That's one way of putting it. Valentine was far too dependent on that woman.'

That woman? Oh, no. Did Mia and Valentine . . .

But Amy probably realized what impression her words had created, because she immediately continued, 'Let me make it clear: my husband did not have an affair with her. Valentine would never do that. But she had a way of worming herself into his life, you know?'

No, Nick thought. He did not know. This was getting stranger by the minute.

'Fortunately,' Amy continued, 'I wasn't the only one round here who thought it was time he cut the umbilical cord. He couldn't simply accuse me of playing the jealous wife.' In the background a child started crying. 'I'm sorry,' she said, suddenly sounding rushed, 'I have to go.'

'I understand. Thank you for speaking to me.'

'It was a pleasure.' Her voice was small and forlorn. Just before she hung up she said, 'I have no one to talk to about him, you know?'

CHAPTER TWENTY-FOUR

Art was bleeding profusely. Mia was annoyed with herself. She should have realized right away that the man was drunk. When he entered her studio his attitude had been borderline belligerent and he reeked of Listerine. Normally that would have alerted her and she wouldn't have brought Angelique to within a foot of him. Alcohol in the bloodstream can cause one to bleed excessively and this made life very difficult for the tattooist. But for some reason she had missed the signs that the guy was sloshed and now it was too late: she'd have to push on. Wiping the bubbles of blood away with a paper towel, she pressed down on the foot switch once again.

'Mia . . .'

She looked up. Lisa was standing in the doorway, her handbag under her arm. Lisa jerked her head to one side, indicating she wanted a word in private.

Mia pushed back her chair. 'I'll be right back,' she said as she pulled off her gloves and left Art to stare at the ceiling on his own.

'Are you off home?' she asked as she joined Lisa outside the door.

'I'm meeting Rufus at the cinema. We have tickets for the late show. But I don't want to leave you alone with that character.'

'It'll be OK. I've almost finished.'

'I don't know, Mia, I'm getting a bad vibe off this one. He's a Biro boy.' Lisa was referring to the fact that Art had tattoos on his arms and knuckles that had been done with a ballpoint pen. This was usually a sure sign he had received them in prison. But if she and Lisa turned away every bloke who had done time, they would lose a fair number of clients.

'I'll be fine.' Mia nodded her head encouragingly. 'You go and have fun. Go on,' she repeated, waving Lisa out of the gate.

When Mia stepped back into the room, she found Art sitting bolt upright and peering down at his chest.

'What the fuck have you done to me?' He jabbed at his chest with a stubby forefinger. The ink and the blood had mixed and instead of a clean-lined tattoo the image looked like a child's finger painting.

Mia sat down on her heels and fished in the bottom drawer of the trolley for a fresh pair of gloves. 'Don't panic,' she said over her shoulder. 'It's all superficial. All I need to do is blot off the excess ink and blood. Why don't you lie down again.' She gave him what she hoped was a soothing smile before turning her attention to the drawer once more.

It was stupid of her to have turned her back on him. With surprising speed he launched himself from the chair to right behind her and slammed her head into the trolley. 'Don't lie to me, bitch!'

The pain as her forehead hit the sharp edge of the trolley was instant and intense. She was sitting on her heels when it happened and the force of the impact made her lose her balance. As she toppled to the side, he pushed her – hard – and sent her sprawling on to her stomach. The next moment he had placed one knee on to her back and grabbed her by the hair.

The unexpectedness of it all stunned her. She struggled and pushed down on her hands to try and move out from underneath him, but he was too heavy. She threw one hand backwards and grabbed him by the arm, boring her nails into the soft skin of his wrist. In response, he jerked her by the hair so sharply that her neck snapped back and her eyes watered. Then he placed his other hand round her throat and squeezed.

He did not have a comfortable grip but he was strong and flashes of light and dark spots started to blur her vision. And she was unable to scream. She hoped he would turn her round – on her back she would have far better mobility and might be able to use her knee or elbow or crash her palm into his nose or gouge his eyes – but he was obviously going to wait until she had passed out.

Which seemed to be imminent. There was a roaring in her ears and she could feel herself slipping . . .

The next moment the pressure on her throat disappeared and the weight on her back lifted. Art made a strange bleat-like sound.

As fast as she could, Mia rowed forward with her arms, snaking away from him. When she reached the wall, she turned over, breathless. Propped up on her elbows, she stared disbelievingly at the scene in front of her.

Art was standing upright but his legs were buckling. His head drooped, chin to chest, and he was gasping – deep, horrible gasps – as though desperately searching for air. Standing behind and to the side of him was Adrian Ashton. He was gripping Art's forearm, pulling it sideways.

He looked at her. 'Do you want to call the police?'

She hesitated. Then she shook her head. 'No.'

'Sure?'

She nodded.

Ashton switched his grip to Art's upper arm and pulled him backwards. Opening the front door, he jabbed his palm into the man's back, then pushed him outside. By the time Mia had scrambled to her feet, Ashton had closed the door.

'Is he gone?'

'He's gone.'

'Is he OK?'

'He will be. He might have an attack of diarrhoea within the next twelve hours but that's about it.'

She looked at him doubtfully. Not that she didn't like the idea of Art under bathroom arrest but he had looked truly deathly. And that sound he made . . .

'What was that you did to him?'

'I combined a wrist lock with pressure to a *Dim Ching*

point in his forearm. Very painful and it causes shortness of breath and weak legs.' He smiled. 'And stomach problems.'

'But you're certain he's going to be OK?'

'Don't worry, Mia. It's a pressure-point technique taught to riot police in Tokyo. It works well but it's harmless.'

She suddenly realized that her throat ached fiercely. She coughed, painfully.

He moved towards her at once, his face concerned. 'The important thing is: are you OK?'

'I'm fine.' If fine meant nauseated and shivery. She touched her hands to her scalp, feeling for bald spots. It felt as though he had ripped out chunks of hair.

'Why didn't you want me to call the police?'

'I don't want the publicity. Can you imagine how many clients I'll attract if he starts talking to the newspapers, saying he lost it because I messed up his tattoo?'

'Did you?'

She gave him a look.

He grinned. 'OK. You can't blame me for asking, though. I came here tonight to give you a job, Ms Lockhart. But we'll talk about it later. This is not the time.'

'No.' She started walking in the direction of the workbench. Strange how her legs felt like straw. 'You're here. Let's talk. What did you have in mind?'

He looked at her for a few moments. 'A couple of years ago, I visited Wat Phraw monastery near Bangkok. There was a group of monks there, doing tattoos for visitors. These tattoos were supposed to grant protection to the wearer – help him in his journey through life. I was hoping we could do something similar: something unique and customized.'

'Why didn't you ask one of the monks to do it for you while you had the chance? They're masters at manual body art.'

'The idea of some muscular monk attacking me with a three-foot-long chopstick did not appeal. And I'm still enough of a squeamish Western quack to want to know that the instruments are properly sterilized.'

'What do you think you'll gain from this tattoo?'

'Protection, what else?' His voice was light.

'Protection hinges on the person giving the tattoo. It has nothing to do with the actual markings. See that?' She gestured at a design that was pasted up on one of the studio walls. It was in the shape of a mandala and filled with delicate glyphs. 'That's a protection tattoo. It looks attractive and all those symbols appear heavy with meaning. But, really, it could just as well be Donald Duck instead of a mandala filled with charms. It is all about the intent of the person giving the tattoo: that person's energy. Not the tattoo itself. The symbols are meaningless without the intent behind it.'

'So?'

'I'm not a monk, Adrian.'

He touched the Usui symbols round her wrist. 'No, but you practise Reiki. You heal through energy.'

She moved her hand away, feeling suddenly irritable. 'Tattoos can lie ... just like people can. Tattoo lore is filled with stories of tattoos bringing curses and bad luck.'

'I suppose I'll just have to trust you.' He smiled faintly.

She stared at him, perplexed. 'You're a scientist; a doctor. And yet you're talking to me about healing – not through drugs, but through energy. I find that ...'

'What?'

'Surprising,' she added lamely.

'Good. I would hate to be predictable.'

All of a sudden she felt tremendously tired and she realized just how much her forehead ached. 'Maybe we should talk about this another time, after all.'

'Absolutely. And now I'm going to make you some tea. With lots of sugar. You're in shock.'

'No, really, I'm OK.'

'As you said, I'm a doctor. You should do as I tell you. Come on.' He placed his hand gently under her elbow and steered her towards the door. 'Let's go. The kitchen's down there, right?'

Once inside the kitchen, he insisted that she sit down. Without asking her permission, he opened the fridge door. 'Have you any ice?'

'Ice? No.'

He pulled open the freezer drawer and looked inside. 'Never mind. This will do.' He removed a bag of frozen Brussels sprouts and wrapped it up with a dishcloth. 'Here. Hold this to your forehead while I make the tea.'

She kept the sprouts in place and watched as he filled

the kettle with water and removed two mugs from the cupboard. His movements were neat and graceful. It was oddly relaxing to relinquish control as it were: to simply leave everything to him.

'Tea?' He looked over his shoulder.

'In that canister there.'

He poured her tea, and not only spooned sugar into the mug but even stirred it the way one would do for a small child or an invalid. Under normal circumstances, this might have seemed over-the-top, but right now it felt enormously comforting.

'Thanks.' She dropped the bag of sprouts on the table and picked up the mug. The warmth between her hands was comforting too.

'Who's that?'

She looked up quickly. He was pointing in the direction of the window.

'That's Sweetpea.'

He walked over to the curtain and placed his finger against Sweetpea's side. 'She doesn't want to come to me.'

'She's not that kind of girl. You'll have to win her trust first.'

'To be continued, then.' He gently touched Sweetpea's dorsal crest. 'Where did you find her?'

'I've always had chameleons in my life. My mum gave me my first Sweetpea when I was only ten years old.'

'Cool mum. Mine gave me a goldfish.'

'She's my third chameleon. They don't live that long, you know.'

He walked back to the table and sat down next to her. 'There's an African legend that the gods had planned to give the chameleon the gift of eternal life.'

'But?'

'The chameleon blew it. He was too slow and turned up late. The gods were insulted and left.'

'That's a sad legend.'

'Most legends are.'

He stirred his own tea, looking down at his cup and frowning slightly. The long lashes masked the expression in his eyes.

He really was beautiful. She had always believed that small imperfections were necessary to save beauty from blandness, and this man's features were so perfect they should have given him a kind of vacant attractiveness. But Adrian Ashton was anything but bland. The curve of his mouth was too sensuous; the intelligence in his eyes too obvious. He had amazing skin for a man. It was stretched taut over prominent cheekbones; smooth, poreless and glowing with a high sheen of good health.

The two times she had met him before, there had been something about him that had made her look at him warily. She had no way of articulating to herself what it was. Maybe it was the sense of almost brutal energy that he projected: as though he had to purposefully clamp down on some inner wellspring of explosive power. The fact that his movements were always measured and relaxed merely accentuated this quality. Tonight, though, she found it rather attractive. But then she supposed it was only right to feel kindly disposed towards a man who had just come to your rescue like some knight in a story-book.

She pushed the mug away from her. 'OK. I'll do it. I'll do your tattoo.'

He looked up quickly. 'You mean it?'

'Yes.'

'Great.' He sounded truly elated. 'It will be an adventure: my first tattoo.'

'Do you have anything specific in mind?'

'Yes. But let me get back to you on that. Right now, I think you should go to bed. You look all in.'

'I'll let you out.'

The night air was warm and soft. The light from the kitchen fell into the courtyard and the darkness glowed orange.

She held out her hand formally. 'Thanks for stepping in.'

'Right time, right place.' He ignored her outstretched hand and touched her forehead briefly, his touch gentle. 'You're going to have a bump.'

She sighed. 'Some martial artist, I am.'

'There's fighting and there's fighting, Mia. What you do in the dojo is something very pure, very clean. In the street, it's different.'

'This didn't happen in the street, it happened inside my home.'

'Your own home is the most dangerous place because that's where you feel safe. You don't feel the need to stay alert.'

'I suppose.'

'Were you afraid?'

She thought for a moment. 'No. It happened too fast. Fear is anticipation of what's coming, not the actual event.'

'Yes, it works like that, doesn't it.'

She watched him cross the courtyard. As he placed his foot on the first of the steps that led up to street level, he looked back at her where she stood, framed inside the door.

'Sleep well, Mia. Sweet dreams. You deserve them.'

THE THIEF

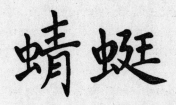

We only live once, but if you work it right,
once is enough.

Joe E. Lewis

CHAPTER TWENTY-FIVE

The Book of Light and Dust
For Rosalia
XXXIV

The Dragonfly is associated with illusion, magic, visions and dreams. It is the totem of the god Hiro, the god of thieves.

Hiro, with his avaricious heart and sleight of hand, carried with him a swarm of dragonflies hidden inside his cloak. Upon entering the house of his victims, he would release the dragonflies and the beautiful, glimmering wings would so delight and dazzle the occupants, they would not notice they were being robbed.

Beauty can be treacherous. Beauty and truth are not one and the same. Beauty can be used to catch the light . . .

THE WAY: YELLOW DRAGON
BLACKLIGHT: DIR: S13, FRC: 1, TIME: 6, SUs: K5 PC
Whitelight: LU2

CHAPTER TWENTY-SIX

It had turned into a lovely summer. The days were luminous and the nights languid and warm with a shiny crescent rising in a ginger-ale sky. Night after night it grew, a tiny sliver of light, until one evening Mia and Nick and Ash stepped outside to find the darkness filled with a big, yellow story-book moon.

How had it happened? How had someone who was a total stranger become absorbed in the rhythm of her days so quickly? That moment when he had come to her rescue was the turning point. Almost overnight, Mia could no longer imagine Adrian Ashton not being part of her life. Why had she ever thought he would be difficult to know? Why was she ever wary of him?

The two men. It was as though she could no longer think of the one without the other. She would close her eyes and see the two of them side by side: the one dark, the one fair. Nick with his blue eyes and curly hair: heavy-boned, shorter than Ash. Ash with graceful hands and tall, elegant body. In her mind's eye, they were running towards her where she waited for them at the pagoda in the park. Sweat glistened on their arms and foreheads.

Their teeth were white in their tanned faces. And then they were suddenly upon her; exuberant, overwhelmingly male, cracking a joke among themselves, cuffing her playfully against the head, picking her up and swinging her by the waist. And she would squeeze her eyes shut to fight the dizziness as the red of the sun pressed against her lids.

At first she accompanied the men when they went running, but there came a day when she had to stop and watch them go on by themselves. She could no longer keep up with their long strides. Squinting, she brought her hand up to her eyes and watched their figures move away into the distance, and she couldn't help but feel a little sad.

Nick was changing. His body was becoming toned and muscled. When she watched him train in the dojo, she was struck by his focus. Chilli once told her that, according to Buddhist philosophy, when a student is ready for the right teacher, he will be there. Ash had certainly come at the right time. Even at this halfway mark in Nick's training, Mia could see he was already far better prepared than for his previous fights.

It was a summer of beauty and friendship. She wondered if she would remember these days, one day when she was old. Would she look back to when they were all young and confident and energy was flowing strongly through their bodies? And would those memories be vital and glowing or drained by old age? If only one could stop time. Sometimes she'd be training in the dojo surrounded by voices, laughter and movement and the desire to halt time in its tracks would be so strong it took her breath away.

Weeks later, when the nights had become cold and the daylight weak, she would look back at those months and realize she had become lost in beauty and tricked by it. Beauty can slip under your guard and leave you vulnerable. A bright sun made for deep shadows.

'They're males.'

Mia followed Ash's gaze. Skimming low across the water and perched on reeds and rushes were dozens of dragonflies. The sun made their wings glimmer with light.

'How do you know?'

'Females don't have those bright colours.' He gestured at a pool of shade. 'Let's sit down under that tree and watch Nick do his thing.'

Mia glanced over to where Nick was slowly walking into the stream. He was dressed in waders. The sight of bag-punching Nick with a fly-fishing rod in his hand still seemed unreal to her. Fly-fishing had a veneer of affluence to it: it belonged to a world of expensive whisky and heavy tweeds. It was at times like these that she realized Nick had picked up habits in Scotland that were alien to her.

She sat down next to Ash, who had propped his back up against the tree and was once again watching the swarm of dragonflies.

'Why are there so many males?'

'They're on the prowl.'

'For food?'

'For women. Any female that shows up now will get

pounced on.' He lifted an eyebrow. 'It's quite brutal, actually: at the tip of a male dragonfly's abdomen are hooks, which he slams into the female's head before dragging her off.'

'Charming. How do you know so much about it?'

'I admire dragonflies.' He nodded. 'They're the ultimate predators. Fast, deadly, beautiful. And they're the ultimate survivors too: there are dragonfly fossils that are more than 350 million years old.'

She looked back at the darting wings glistening like silk. She had always thought of dragonflies as pretty things belonging in fairy-tales. More fool her.

Ash gestured at the insects. 'Dragonflies have globular heads with enormous eyes that give them 360-degree vision. They're incredibly acrobatic and can change direction so rapidly, their prey has little chance of escape. And their legs are lethal – studded with sharp spines that allow them to scoop their prey out of the sky and consume it while still in flight. Actually, that's how some of them have sex as well.'

'They eat the females?' Mia was horrified.

His lips twitched. 'No, they mate while flying. But only chaser dragonflies, I hasten to add. Some of the other species do it right and cuddle up for hours . . . if that makes you feel happier.'

'Not at all. First the poor female has horns stuck into her head and then she's forced into tantric sex.'

'Ah, well.' He smiled lazily. 'Life's not just.'

For a while it was quiet between them. Nick had

reached midstream. He cast a line and it unfurled deep into the river, the tip trailing sweetly in the shandy-coloured water.

'He's good,' Ash said. 'That's not easy.'

'Hmn.'

'Nick is a good guy.'

'Yes, he is.' Mia nodded. 'I don't think he has even one enemy. People always like him.'

'Nick has an unambiguous way of looking at life, that's why. If you read his Rick Cobra adventures, you see that clearly. It attracts people: that kind of confidence. Most of us do not feel within us such certainty.'

'Rick Cobra is just a fictional character, Ash.'

'Yes, but Nick writes from the heart. Nick really does believe good will triumph.'

'You're saying it's an unsophisticated way of looking at life.' She suddenly felt as though he was criticizing Nick and she had to defend him.

'Not at all. Uncomplicated is not the same as un-sophisticated. Nick is lucky. I envy him.'

She did not answer. Nick was fiddling with something on the line, his profile a study in concentration.

'Why are you and Nick not together, Mia? You must know he's crazy about you.'

For a moment she hesitated, not certain that she wanted to answer something so personal. Or try to articulate emotions she herself felt so confused about.

'I can't really say.' She sighed. 'What Nick and I have is . . . pure.'

She stopped, embarrassed – unsure how to explain to him her fear of all the treacherous things people in relationships did to their partners. Hurting each other, manipulating each other, becoming needy or indifferent. In a relationship there was usually the one who kissed and the one who was being kissed and even her parents had found this equation troublesome. She had always fought against the attraction she felt for Nick – and there were good reasons for that. Nick was her safe harbour. If their relationship changed, it would be exciting, but the waters might be turbulent. Why risk that?

She got to her feet, feeling suddenly restless. 'I'm going to join him. That stream looks cool.'

When she reached the river bank opposite Nick, she kicked off her sandals. Lifting her dress above her knees, she slowly lowered one foot into the water.

Nick waded over and, after laying the fishing rod on the bank, reached out a hand to help her enter the water fully. He smiled at her. As she placed her hand in his, she looked into those blue, blue eyes. He *was* a great guy. In her heart she had always known they were meant for each other, so why was she hesitant? She should have more faith in him and in herself. She wasn't her mother. Molly had loved Juan but she could be moody and dismissive too. Molly was the great passion in Juan's life, but her father had never made peace with the idea of Molly being a Keeper, even though her relationship with the men in her keep had been as chaste as sister to brother. Still, it needn't be like that for her and Nick. Mia took another step forward.

'Oh!'

'What?' Nick frowned. 'What's the matter, Mia?'

She looked down. The honey-coloured water was clear enough to see the red blood spiralling from her foot and the chunk of glass embedded in the soft part of her sole.

Nick swore. The next moment he had scooped her up and was stepping out of the water and on to the river bank.

She clung her arms round his neck, feeling suddenly light-headed and, despite the sun on her skin, cold. She could feel Nick's heart beating fast and agitated against hers but everything else seemed slow and dreamlike. Small things were magnified and stood out with preternatural clearness. The veins on Nick's strong forearms and the bruises on his knuckles. The creases round Ash's eyes as he cradled her foot in his hands.

'We need to get this out.' Ash looked at her. She noticed a small nerve jumping at the corner of his mouth. 'Are you ready, Mia?'

She nodded, still feeling as though things were happening in slow motion. Dimly she was aware that Nick was holding one of her hands in both of his own.

'Deep breath in' – Ash gripped the chunk of glass – 'and out.' The next moment his fingers twisted and the glass slid out of her foot and, bloodily, into his hand.

'Christ, that must have hurt.' Nick's face was white.

She shook her head. For one moment intense pain had flared inside her body, but now that the glass was out it was bearable.

'This needs stitches.' Ash peered at the gash. 'But until then, let's get some dressing on.' He took from his pocket a white handkerchief and wrapped it skilfully round the arch of her foot. 'How does that feel?'

'Fine. I'm fine.'

'Are you sure?'

'Yes.'

And suddenly, as she looked at the concerned faces of the two men, a wave of affection for both of them swept over her – so strong, she felt it prickle her throat.

'Mia? Are you all right?' Nick's eyes were deeply worried.

She blinked. 'Yes, I am. Really. Thank you for rescuing me. And you' – she turned to Ash – 'for patching me up.'

'The warrior and the healer.' Ash was smiling.

'My heroes,' she answered in return, and stretched her arms out to both.

CHAPTER TWENTY-SEVEN

The hunger was overwhelming. The hunger had driven him from the confines of his flat and out into the night. More than anything, the thief wanted to go to her house. But he could not trust himself.

And so he continued to crisscross the West End, walking for hours through streets alive with sound and streaming with light. Light everywhere. Radiant cinema names, flashing lights at crossroads, glowing signs at restaurant doors and white light illuminating the immaculate windows of shops. And around him bodies – surging, jostling – and these bodies, too, filled with light. He stared at the faces with their shiny eyes and glistening teeth and he imagined he could see furtive light speeding through the veins of their bodies like quicksilver, mingling with caustic enzymes inside iridescent cells, charging up the pale, spiky column of the spine and sparking the electric brain.

The hunger. He had to ball his hands into fists inside his jacket and he could feel the sweat blooming in his armpits. The hunger was so strong, he had difficulty keeping it in check. But he knew exactly what had triggered it.

Her small, strong foot inside his palm. The blood streaming red and potent over his fingers.

A streak of pollen lay like a yellow exclamation mark on the shoulder of her dress. Her face was stippled with the shadows of the leaves above her head and her skin seemed translucent. Her mouth was slightly open with pain.

For a moment, it felt as though his own heart was entraining with hers — the agitated beat of her organ speeding up his own. He looked back at the wet blood on his hand. It came from inside her body and would be charged with light.

His heart trembled. He couldn't remember ever desiring anything as much.

CHAPTER TWENTY-EIGHT

'You are looking good, Nicky.'

Nick smiled at his mother. 'You too, Mum.' It was true. With her flashing dark eyes and thick mink eyelashes, his mother was still an attractive woman. She was plump but curvy and had neat ankles, which she liked to show off with very high heels. Her voice was attractively husky. The Greek accent and wobbly syntax, which still marked her English even after years of living in the United Kingdom, was appealing.

'Help yourself.' His mother pushed a plate of biscuits towards him.

'No, I mustn't. I'll be fighting soon, Mum.'

His mother frowned. 'Why you always want to fight . . .'

Nick looked at her with affection but he wasn't going to get sucked into this conversation again. They had had it too many times before.

He took a sip of his tea. 'Mia sends her love.'

His mother's face cleared. 'Ah, Mia. How is she?'

'She's doing fine. She had an accident with her foot the other day but she's already back in training again.'

'You two are meant for each other, Nicky. Destiny. That's what I say to Molly when you and Mia are born.'

'So you keep telling me.'

'If you don't take her, someone else will. You must be more strong, Nicky. You must grab her and kiss her and tell her she is beautiful. What am I saying this for you? You should know that.'

'That the way to a woman's heart is through her vanity?'

His mother gave him an exasperated glance. 'You are flying back to London tonight?'

'In three hours. But I have one more stop to make before heading for the airport. Which means' – he got to his feet – 'I should probably go.'

Outside in the driveway, they hugged and Nick kissed his mother on top of her head. 'Are you happy, Mum?'

'I am, Nicky. Donald is a good man.'

'I know.' He meant it. It couldn't have been easy all those years ago for his stepfather suddenly to accept a truculent, teenage boy into his life, but he had done so with equanimity and Nick was grateful. And Donald was good to his mother, which, in the end, was all that mattered. His own father had walked out on them before he was born.

Nick opened the door of the rental car and got behind the steering wheel. As he pulled away, he opened the window. 'Grab her and kiss her and tell her she's beautiful?'

'Yes.' His mother nodded vigorously. 'Like that.'

He was still smiling as he steered the car on to the road, but as he glanced at his watch the smile disappeared. He had spent too long at his mother's place. He was going to have to hurry if he wanted to fit in his next appointment and make it to the airport on time.

One of the names on the list of fighters who had died mysteriously was Bill Muso, a cage fighter. Nick had flown to Scotland to visit his mother but also to meet Barry Driver, Muso's trainer at his gym in Edinburgh. Muso had no wife or girlfriend, which meant that the trainer would be the best person to talk to about what went on in the fighter's life.

Driver's Gym was pretty down-at-heel. It was located in a basement behind a steel door and there was no natural light inside the rectangular room. The heavy bags were punched out and scarred with duct tape. But it was still a dojo where men came to work hard. As Nick stepped inside, he felt immediately comfortable.

Driver was wrestling with a lanky youth who was breathing past his mouth guard like Darth Vader. Nick watched as the coach put a head crank on his student, causing the kid, after a few futile movements, to tap out.

From his position on the floor, Driver looked up at Nick. 'Can I help you?'

'Nick Duffy. I phoned.'

'Oh, right.' Driver jumped to his feet with springy grace. Nick noticed that he had absurdly small feet and rosy toes. 'Let's go to my office.' He turned back to the youth. 'Nice work, Jimmy. Go for a steam now, yeah?'

Based on the spartan appearance of the rest of the gym, Nick had expected the office to have the appeal of a prison cell, but Driver's office was surprisingly comfortable. Thick carpets. A decent flower arrangement on the desk. On one wall was a pinboard with snapshots of fighters and gym members.

'So you want to know about Bill?' Driver sank into a swivel chair behind his desk and gestured at Nick to sit down.

'What can you tell me about him?'

'He was one determined fighter.'

'Any bad habits? Clubbing? Drinking? Women?'

'Not Bill. Dedicated, he was. And he never trained as hard as he did for that last fight. He was at his peak.' Driver got to his feet. 'I have a picture of him here. Let me show you.'

Driver walked to the pinboard and unerringly removed a snapshot from among the dozens of photographs.

Nick stared at the picture. Muso had obviously just worked out; his body was glistening with sweat. Like most cage fighters he had massive shoulders and his upper body was strongly muscled. In the photo he was laughing open-mouthed. Someone was standing next to Muso, but the picture was cut off and all Nick could see was the other man's arm around Muso's shoulders.

'This photo was taken during the last sparring session Bill had. Two days later he stepped into the cage for his fight. This man here' – Driver pointed at the arm – 'was Muso's training buddy.'

'Is he around by any chance? Can I talk to him?'

Driver shook his head. 'After Bill's death, I never saw him again. He told me he couldn't cope with coming to the gym any more. Too many painful memories. Understandable, I suppose: they were pretty tight, those two.'

'What were Muso's most outstanding characteristics?'

'He was always jumping. Strong energy. Never still for a moment. Lots of self-confidence.'

'If you had to use one word to describe him?'

Driver stood for a moment, thinking. 'Heart. He had a lot of heart, that man. He did not always win, but he never gave up. That's heart. You either have it or you don't. Can't beg it; can't borrow it; can't steal it.'

CHAPTER TWENTY-NINE

There was the matter of Ash's tattoo. Mia kept stalling.

'It's going to be painful. Especially if you persist in wanting it . . . where you want it.'

He sighed. 'I'll try not to scream too loudly.'

'This is your first tattoo. You do understand that once it is on, it's on. No chance for a do-over.'

'I'll take my chances.'

'Are you sure this is what you want?'

'Come on, Mia; let's get on with it. It's going to look great. What's your problem?'

What indeed? She couldn't understand herself why she was so nervous about the whole thing.

Ash seemed restless today. He was tapping his fingers on the surface of the table. The expression on his face was tense and there were shadows under his eyes.

'Are you all right?'

'Of course. So when are we doing this?' He gestured at the sheet of paper on to which she had drawn the tattoo.

She looked down at the drawing. Even though she said

so herself, the design was attractive. He had wanted it unique, and unique was what he got.

The tattoo would be largely made up of glyphs, symbols, oriental ideograms and icons. He had provided these himself and it had been her task to fuse them into an attractive visual image. She had decided to arrange them into a long, flowing snake-like design, which would sit low on his hips, stretching from one side of his body to the other. He had told her he wanted the tattoo in the *hara* zone – and she could understand why. The *hara* was the storeroom of energy and the centre of life. In the West a shot to kill would be targeted at the head or the heart. In the East it would be the *hara*. Chilli once told her that *hara-kiri* literally meant 'to cleave the stomach' – to obliterate chi – which was why samurai who committed seppuku had disembowelled themselves by plunging their swords into this zone.

She had no idea what the meaning was of many of the symbols she would be transferring to Ash's skin, which made things difficult. Even though she would be using a stencil, it was easy to make a mistake and it was important that every one of the glyphs and ideograms she transferred to his skin be absolutely identical to the original. A lapse in concentration could be disastrous: just one wrong stroke, and the entire meaning of a symbol could change. She would never forget how a friend of hers once tattooed a giant Chinese ideogram on to a client's back. The sign was supposed to symbolize something profound and life-changing but, because of one incorrect line, ended up signifying 'chicken feet'.

Mixed in with all the oriental ideograms and idio-syncratic signs Ash had given her were a few numerals: 8, 15, 33, 81, 271.

'These' – he tapped his finger to the paper – 'I want tattooed exactly on the *kikai tanden*.'

The *kikai tanden* was situated about two inches below the navel. It was the inner compass of the body and the centre for balance and breathing: probably the most crucial area in martial arts. The numbers must be important to him. Mia looked at Ash searchingly.

'What are they?'

'Numbers.'

'I can see that. What do they mean?'

He only shrugged in response.

She was irritated by his evasiveness. 'Your lottery numbers?'

'Great idea.' He suddenly grinned, the tenseness round his eyes slackening. 'Maybe I should; they could work out well for me. No, dear heart, those numbers are my energy numbers: the days when the light emissions from my body are perfectly correlated.'

'There is actual light shining from your body?'

'Not just mine, yours too.'

'Oh . . .' She stared at him, enchanted. 'Is that true?'

'Oh, yes, light inside the body has definitely been proven. A German scientist by the name of Fritz-Albert Popp – a Nobel Prize nominee, by the way, not some weirdo boffin – discovered definite biophoton emissions coming from humans.'

'Light in the body . . . That sounds like chi.'

He shrugged again. 'Who's to say this light is chi? I believe it is; many scientists do not. Some are still struggling with the whole idea of light-inside-the-body to begin with. But it's not just humans, of course: all living things emit a permanent current of photons, from only a few to a few hundred. Plants, animals . . . people.'

'Shiny happy people. I like that. It's very REM.'

'Well, don't get too carried away. A piece of broccoli emits more light than a person.' He smiled wryly. 'The higher you are up the evolutionary tree, the more difficult it is to find the light. But it is there – and it has huge implications.'

'I can't say I understand all this stuff about biophotons. But I do know I can feel chi.'

'Of course you can, Mia.' This time his smile was almost tender. 'And you don't need to be shown photon emissions in a lab, you simply know. I've watched you train: you're the real thing. The rest of us are still quibbling about semantics, but you simply tap into your energy intuitively.'

She looked away, confused by the look in his eyes.

'Anyway,' he continued, his voice light, 'it's important not to disturb the system: to keep your biophoton emissions coherent and the periodic rhythms stable. That's what keeps you healthy. And I've been lucky: my energy numbers have been constant for a long time now, the emissions on these days identical year after year. A good reason to have them tattooed on my body, don't you think? An affirmation as well as a wish.'

'Wish?'

'That they will continue. And never change.'

'All things change, Ash. You can't stop it.'

'Yes, you can. You need only to know how.'

Something dark flickered behind his eyes. For a moment she had the overwhelming sense that he wanted to reach out and touch her, but then he pushed his hands into his pockets and she could see him tightening his fingers into fists. Suddenly, she felt unnerved.

But his voice was casual. 'So when is D-Day? The design is finished. When are we going to walk the walk?'

Mia touched her hand to the long black flow of magic writing. 'It looks like a snake.'

'No, it looks like a wave.'

'OK.' She took a deep breath. 'Let's do it. But I need to make a stencilled copy of the images first. So shall we say . . . Thursday?'

He nodded in satisfaction. 'Thursday.'

He arrived at ten in the evening after the studio had closed. From her bedroom upstairs, Mia heard Lisa letting Ash in and, shortly after, shouting up the stairs that she was leaving. Lisa sounded petulant. Earlier she had asked Mia if she could watch, but Mia had been firm. She was still nervous about this job and the last thing she needed was an audience. Besides, she had a strong suspicion Lisa's only motivation was to ogle.

As Mia walked into the studio, she found Sweetpea

resting comfortably on Ash's arm. Sweetpea's initial truculence was long gone. Like everyone else, it seemed, she had been charmed by Ash.

He looked over at Mia. 'Aren't you worried she'll run away?'

'Run?'

'OK, maybe not run, but you know what I mean. I found her at the open window.'

Mia turned on the tap at the basin and started scrubbing her hands. Over the sound of the running water she said, 'She never does. I have never once found her on the outside windowsill. Inside, yes, but never outside. It's as though she doesn't want to leave.'

'Well, I can understand that. I wouldn't want to leave either.'

Mia glanced at him over her shoulder.

'I'm sure you spoil her to death is what I mean.'

'Yes, she's a pampered pet. But I'm pretty dependent on her too. I can't imagine life without Sweetpea.'

Mia dried her hands and pulled on her gloves.

'Right.' She took a deep breath. 'Why don't you take off your shirt.'

He had broad shoulders and narrow hips – like a swimmer – and he was muscular. But his chest was the flat chest of the boxer and martial artist, not the pumped-up breasts you find among weight-lifters. He lay back, loosened the belt on his jeans and tugged at them until they sat below his hips.

Mia felt suddenly shy. At the same time, she was

exasperated with herself. Ash was hardly the first guy she had worked on. Many of her other male clients had required her to do tattoos on far more private places.

'I'm going to have to shave you.' She spoke briskly to hide her embarrassment.

'Please do.'

Mia glanced at him sharply but his face was perfectly serious.

She picked up a disposable razor from the tray. As she placed the blade on to his skin, she was surprised to see her hand shaking. Stop it, she told herself savagely. Taking another deep breath, she gently dragged the blade across the silky hairs pointing downwards in a dark spiral.

She tossed the razor into the bin, smoothed a paper towel soaked with antiseptic across the area to be inked and blotted it dry. Then she took another piece of paper towelling and ran a stick of clear deodorant across it and pressed down. 'To make the stencilled images stick to your skin,' she explained to him, 'I need you to stand up again and face the mirror. I want to see how the tattoo will lie.'

Skin is not flat canvas. Muscles wrap and twist and will determine the appearance of the tattoo. A good body artist always takes the sitter's musculature into consideration, which was why she wanted to see the wave stencilled on to his skin before she started to work.

When he stood in front of the mirror, she sat down on her heels in front of him and pressed the stencilled image against his skin. She could feel his heat through her latex gloves and she sensed her face growing red. Keeping her eyes resolutely on the stencil in front of her, she peeled it off – slowly, slowly – leaving behind ethereal purple images.

The tattoo would sit well. The wave flowed gracefully. She touched her fingers to the purple shadows. 'Is this how you want it?'

'That's how I want it.'

She looked up at him. He was staring down at her with hooded eyes.

'Once I start working, there's no going back. You have to be sure.'

'I am sure.'

'Let's do it.'

Skin.

Nothing was more seductive or sensual. Or a more poignant reminder of your own mortality.

Marry ink to skin and you make a commitment for life. From now on you are marked, forever displaying a visual clue to what it is that stirs your soul. It can tell of desire, love, hope, It can tell of hate.

His skin was flawless. In the white glare of the lamp it glowed with a supreme gloss of vitality.

The lamp threw a tight pool of light but the far reaches of the room were dim and outside the window it was dark. There were few sounds drifting in from the street.

While she worked, they didn't speak. The air between them felt charged and she was conscious that his eyes never left her face. The relationship between tattoo artist and client is always an intimate one, of course. The intimacy is physical – skin, blood, nerves – but, more than that, it is emotional. The artist is entrusted with making visible a dream or desire so potent, the bearer wishes to carry it to the grave.

She sat back, closing her eyes for a moment. It was a challenging job. Not only do the ideograms have to be perfect, but they also had to look beautiful. Instead of merely filling in the outlines of the symbols, she was using the magnum shader almost like a brush to convey a feel of calligraphy. It was painstaking work with no room for error.

She shrugged her shoulders. 'Would you mind if we called it a night? I'm worried I'm losing my focus.'

'How many more sessions do you think we'll need?'

'If we shoot for an hour at a time . . . three, possibly four.'

Ash's skin was raised and irritated and dotted with scarlet flecks. How much bleeding there is differs greatly from one individual to another. Ash bled a lot – she actually had the fanciful thought that he had too much blood inside his body – and the gleaming drops pushed relentlessly through the skin, ringing the freshly tattooed charms with bright red. It was another reason she did not want to continue for too long.

Gently she dabbed the skin with a cold water and alcohol solution.

'Did you always know you wanted to be a body artist?'

She turned her head to look at him. He was lying flat on

his back, his head propped up on one strong arm. It was strange to find herself looking down at him for a change. He was inches taller than she was.

'I suppose so. It never occurred to me to do anything else. My mum probably had a lot to do with it.'

'Tell me about her.'

'My mother was a special person.' She hesitated. 'But she sometimes made people feel . . . uncomfortable.'

He didn't say anything, waited for her to continue.

'People called her a witch. She was accused of being weird and full of superstition.'

Which was not deserved, Mia thought. Yes, Molly had found luminosity lurking in the shadow of the mundane. She could sense forces hiding behind the dusty curtain of everyday living and the world she bequeathed to her daughter was an extraordinary one. But Molly had not been a superstitious woman. A black cat was only a black cat. Walking underneath a ladder was to be avoided not because it might bring you bad luck but because something might fall on your head. Werewolves, vampires, shapeshifters: these were creatures that inhabited the pages of a book.

'And your grandmother?'

'I never knew her: she died before I was born. My mother said she was a free spirit.' In actual fact, Molly had used the word 'adventurous'. Coming from Molly, this probably meant her grandmother had lived out on a limb.

She glanced back at him. 'What about you? How did you decide what you wanted to do with your life?'

'I come from a medical background. My father was a doctor. I once sneaked into his office when I was fourteen years old. He didn't hear me come in; he was watching a video that was taken in the room of a hospital where transplant donors are kept. These people are brain dead, you understand, but they are still hooked up to a machine and they look alive. They're breathing; their blood is warm. Anyway, the video my father was watching monitored the organ donation of one particular patient – my grandmother.'

Mia stared at him in horror. 'You mean you watched as her organs were removed? When you were only a child?'

'Well, I had already said goodbye to her in the hospital a few days earlier. And the removal of the organs was quite peaceful. The transplant surgeons came one at a time – not all of them together. One took her liver. Another her kidneys. Another her eyes. And her heart, of course. Did you know the heart can beat on its own, even when outside the body? I remember standing behind my father's chair – hoping he wouldn't turn round and find me there because then I'd have to leave, and I didn't want to, I was too fascinated.'

She was starting to feel queasy. '*Did* he discover you?'

'Yes. And gave me hell for snooping.'

'You must have had nightmares afterwards.'

'I had dreams, but that's not the same thing. And those organs are beautiful, you know. They glisten. But what I do remember is that this was the first time I believed my father to be mistaken – totally wrong. Up till then he was omniscient in my eyes: the repository of all knowledge. But that day, before he kicked me out of the room, he made very sure to explain to me that what I had been looking at was a dead person. That just because she breathed and her heart was beating did not make her alive, because her brain was gone. "The home of the soul" was how my father described it. My father was a religious man.'

'And you did not believe him?'

'No. I don't think the soul is caged inside the brain, or the heart for that matter. Even at that age I sensed that the soul or the life force – or whatever you feel like calling it – was much more pervasive and encompassing: that body, mind and spirit are indivisible.'

'So in a roundabout way your path was set by your father just as mine was by my mother.'

'I suppose so. But the real catalyst came later, when I was a young man. The person who is responsible for who I am today is a girl. Her name is Rosalia.'

She looked at him enquiringly but he merely smiled. 'Maybe I'll tell you about her one day.'

He lifted his arm above his head and glanced at his watch. 'It's late.'

Lying on his back meant he hadn't been able to monitor what she was doing to his skin. Mia took a deep breath, feeling nervous. 'Do you want to get up and take a look?'

He got to his feet and walked to the mirror.

'Do you like it?' She was concerned by his silence.

'Yes.' He reached out and touched his fingers to the

mirror's face. 'Yes,' he repeated. He turned round. 'It's more than I hoped for.'

She was relieved. 'I'm going to put a dressing on it and I don't want you to take it off until tomorrow, OK?'

He nodded. As he walked away from the mirror, he stumbled slightly.

'Are you all right?'

'It's my weak knee. An old injury. It doesn't give me too much trouble but it sometimes acts up.' He smiled. 'Keep it to yourself, OK? Don't tell Nick or he'll take advantage of me next time we spar.'

She nodded solemnly. 'Your secret's safe with me.'

After he had pulled on his T-shirt, she opened the door for him. As he stepped out, the muted chimes of a church bell floated towards them on the night air. Witching hour.

He touched her cheek with his fingers, a gossamer touch. 'I love what you've done so far. Thank you.'

'I'm glad you're pleased.' She was very aware of his hand on her face.

'Same time next week?'

'Same time next week.'

CHAPTER THIRTY

Flash had hooked up his iPod to his external speakers and was playing Skunk Anansie's 'Weak' at top volume. Nick could hear the music even as he entered the building. For some bizarre reason Flash had become impassioned with nineties protest rock and Skin was his new icon. At about the same time Flash had also suddenly become interested in Barbie dolls, bidding inordinate amounts of money on eBay and other sites to feed this new obsession. An army of plastic, blue-eyed blondes had taken up residence in the office: reclining gracefully on Flash's desk and peeping out roguishly from behind stacks of books and computer disks. They spooked the hell out of Nick.

'*Weak as I a-a-am, no tears for you . . .*'

Shit. The neighbours were going to kill them. As he stepped into the office Nick motioned urgently to Flash to turn down the volume.

'What on earth are you thinking? Do you want us evicted?'

Flash shrugged. He looked out of sorts. Flash rarely showed any strong emotion and Nick looked at him sharply.

'What's wrong?'

'Nothing. But Mr I'm-so-cool-can-you-stand-it dropped in while you were out.'

Flash was referring to Ash. Flash was the one person who had proven immune to Ash's charm. 'He's creepy,' he had told Nick after meeting Ash for the first time.

'Creepy how?'

'I don't know, but I feel it here.' Flash had slammed a bony fist somewhere in the region of his heart.

Coming from someone who counted among his friends people with names such as Lillith, Mistress of Darkness, and who hung out in chat rooms with other grown men who spent their savings on politically incorrect dolls, this was a bit much, Nick thought. He watched as Flash disconnected the speakers, his movements jerky.

'So what did Ash want?'

'Said he was in the neighbourhood and wanted to see if you could have lunch with him. I don't trust that guy, man. I tell you.'

Nick shook his head in warning. 'He's a friend, OK?'

In fact, Ash was fast becoming his best friend. Nick was slightly bemused by exactly how quickly the relationship had grown. Ash had become the kind of friend with whom you shared secrets. Nick had never talked to anyone about Mia – not even Okie knew his true feelings – but one night, after a particularly demanding spar, something had opened up inside Nick.

'I plan on taking things with Mia to the next level.'

Ash's face was calm. 'I'm surprised you haven't done so already.'

'It's fear, I suppose. My whole life I've been lucky.' Nick smiled. 'My mum will tell you the planets have always aligned right for me. But with Mia . . . I've always had the feeling that this might be where the planets will fall from the sky.'

'When will you talk to her?'

'Soon.'

'Before the fight?'

'No. Don't worry.' Nick shook his head. 'I'll wait until after.'

'That's good. You shouldn't lose your focus now.'

'Yes, you're right. But after the fight: watch me. I'm going to take my mum's advice and sweep her off her feet.'

Flash was gesturing sullenly at a large manila envelope. 'That came for you.'

Nick sat down in his swivel chair and opened the envelope. Inside was an old back-issue of *Fighter's Own*. Nick had sent away for it because it contained a feature article on Ben Dobb, one of the fighters who had died as mysteriously as Valentine.

Despite his growing frustration, Nick had not given up on his dead fighters. He was thinking of them as 'his' fighters now – they had become part of his life. Even when he was doing something else, they were ghosting through his subconscious: these men with their honed bodies, their bright eyes – full of piss and vinegar –

exhorting him to pay attention, to find out what had happened.

Once or twice Nick had been tempted to take Mia and Ash into his confidence, but every time he decided against it. He especially did not want to upset Mia – it would be better to wait until he had more evidence.

Evidence, however, was proving pretty tough to find. He had spoken to a host of people: trainers, girlfriends, wives, friends, even employers. Every one he had talked to had said the same thing: these men had no enemies and they were healthy and at peak fitness. 'Jumping out of his skin' was how Ben Dobb's trainer had described the physical condition of his fighter. 'He had never been this primed in his life,' said the trainer of Travis Dean, one of the kickboxers. And still, their hearts had stopped working.

Nick had also spoken to Dean's and Dobb's GPs. One had snubbed him, but the other had been more forthcoming. 'During the post-mortem they tested for everything, Mr Duffy. Allergies. Poisons. Drugs. They did very thorough bloodwork. They had to, because the man had a big insurance policy and the insurers wanted to make quite sure everything was above board.'

Insurance policy. Maybe filthy lucre was involved. Nick even toyed with the idea that all the wives and girlfriends had formed an evil conspiracy in order to collect fat pickings. A red herring, of course, and more suited to a plot twist in one of Rick Cobra's adventures. Dean had turned out to be the only fighter with an insurance policy on his life. 'We always meant to do it,' Lisa Engel, the girl-friend of Steve Grindle, the boxer, told him. 'Especially with Steve standing a good chance of getting hurt inside the ring, but we simply could not spare the money.'

The article in *Fighter's Own* was bland and did not provide any new information. Discouraged, Nick tossed the magazine into the waste-paper basket.

But there had to be something. Some small overlooked detail that was key. If he kept looking, he would find it.

CHAPTER THIRTY-ONE

It was many years since he had walked the hospital corridors as a doctor but the smells were instantly familiar, as was the green dusk in the darkened rooms where damaged bodies reposed on their high metal beds.

It was very late. Visiting hour was long over and in this long, empty passage the light was dim. He had used the stairwell in order to bypass the nurses' station and so far he had gone undetected.

He touched his hip and felt the dressing underneath the shirt. He had just finished another session at the studio and his skin was still tender from the needles.

These hours that he and Mia spent alone, wrapped up in their own space – the outside world kept at bay – were the most intimate he had ever spent with another person. He was even deliberately willing himself to dream about their time together: an obsessive attempt to relive those moments again and again. Behind his closed eyes would flit images of her face: the soft mouth, the angled cheek-bones, the skin blotted of colour – dramatized – by the bright light from the lamp at her shoulder. Her fingers touching his body with such skill, even as the needles sparked his jangling nerves. Pleasure, pain. She lifted her eyes, and they were ringed with lashes dark as pitch. As her gaze met his, he thought of summer nights and light enclosed in darkness and mirrored water.

Confusion.

The corridor stretched out in front of him, the linoleum floor gleaming with that peculiar hospital sheen. What was he doing here? He would have found it hard to express in words his reasons for this furtive, late-night visit. All he knew was that he was becoming confused and that he needed to remind himself what his journey was all about.

What was the greatest desire?

He lingered at an open door. This room was lit and he could see easily. The patient inside was a woman. The bed was raised and she was half-sitting, half-lying against the hail-white pillows. Her eyes were closed and her thin arms stretched out on both sides of her body. One foot peeped from the bedclothes.

He stepped inside and stopped next to the bed, staring intently at her face. She must have been quite lovely when she was young: the bone structure was elegant. But the skin round her chin hung loosely. The flesh underneath her arms was slack and wrinkled. Her scalp was very pink. He looked at her foot and saw that the toes were delicate. The toe-nails were yellow and thickened like horn.

He knew nothing about this woman but he did not need to see her charts to know that she was dying. It was as though he could sense the organs labouring; could sense the armies of restless bacteria lying in wait. He imagined he could see through the skin to where rampaging enzymes strained against the walls of fragile cells, getting ready to break through those glistening membranes like an acid deluge – eating, digesting, liquefying, cannibalizing the body until it collapsed, spent of light, on to itself.

The woman stirred and her head moved against the pillow. She opened her eyes. As her gaze rested on him, she gave him a smile of such sweetness, his heart ached.

Gratefully, he took her hand in his own. 'Thank you,' he said. 'You have helped me.' Her fingers twitched tiredly. 'Go back to sleep,' he whispered. 'Go back to dreaming.'

Obediently, she closed her eyes. He gently placed her thin hand on to the bed.

He walked along the empty corridor, his tall figure gliding past open doors and darkened rooms, now heedless of the patients resting inside, decay on their breath. He knew his resolve was steadied. He was back on track.

The greatest desire: to live for ever. What confusion could there be?

CHAPTER THIRTY-TWO

'Hi, there.' Lanice, Scorpio's night receptionist, lifted her eyebrows at Mia. 'What are you doing here? It's pretty late.'

'How are you, Lanice? How's George?'

'You just missed him.' Lanice smiled. 'But you won't recognize him, Mia. He's a different boy.'

George was Lanice's fifteen-year-old nephew and, until a year ago, a hell-raising kid. But when a video appeared on YouTube showing George fighting another boy and almost tearing off his ear, Lanice decided enough was enough. Mia remembered the video well. The images were grainy – the fight had been filmed on a mobile phone by another pupil looking on – but the ferocity and ugliness were in sharp focus. Kicking, biting, clawing at each other's faces: there was nothing remotely graceful or disciplined about the encounter. Even worse was the baying glee of the students – many of them girls – who were egging the two boys on. The very next day Lanice had marched George down to the dojo and given him into JC's care for an hour. JC stuck a headguard on the boy, pushed gloves on to his fists and told him to keep his chin down. George never looked back.

'Anyone else in the dojo?' Mia asked as she pushed through the turnstile.

'One guy, I think. And a few others upstairs in the weight room and in the swimming pool. But I'm getting ready to chase them out and close up.'

'I won't be long,' Mia promised.

The dojo was empty except for a lumbering, over-weight man she did not recognize who was desultorily punching one of the heavy bags. After ten minutes of throwing a series of awkward combinations, he left.

It felt strange to be alone in that giant room and made her realize anew how big the place was and how high the ceiling with its exposed rafters. As she moved from one position to the other, her reflection in the mirror seemed ghost-like. Turn, push, sweep, throw. Turn, push, sweep, throw.

She must have done these movements thousands of times before. Form, visualization, intent: Chilli's mantra. Get the technique right, visualize how you would use the technique against an opponent and then perform with intent. But as she slipped from one movement into another, she remembered Ash's words the night he had rescued her from Art's attack. There is fighting and there is fighting. The one is pure and idealized; the other, any-thing but.

How would she shape up if she found herself in a real combat situation? If her experience with Art was anything to go by, not very well. But combat was not her mission.

Her gift was to protect – not through violence – but through healing. Martial arts was a way of increasing her chi sensitivity and her healing powers, not a way to pound someone into the ground.

Lanice stuck her head round the door. 'Fifteen minutes, Mia.'

Mia lifted her hand in acknowledgement. She had time for one more set.

After she finished the set she walked from light switch to light switch, plunging the dojo into darkness one section at a time until finally she stood at the door.

She looked back at the empty room stretching eerily ahead of her and for one moment she thought she could sense the shades of long-retired fighters; hear the rasp of their calloused feet on the mats, the faint echo of their fists on leather. They lingered like ghosts who refused to accept their time had passed and there were no more fights to train for.

Turning off the last light, she closed the door softly behind her.

The ladies' changing room was locked. Mia turned the knob of the door a few times but it would not budge. Lanice must already have closed up, not realizing Mia still had to retrieve her gym bag.

Mia walked back to the entrance but the front desk was empty. The revolving glass doors were silent, the lobby deserted. Against the ceiling, a fluorescent light sputtered and hummed.

She simply had to get inside the ladies' room — her purse was in there. She could have tried picking the lock — it was a skill she had acquired a couple of years ago from a client who had done time for burglary — but she wasn't exactly in the habit of carrying picks with her. And even though the door was old-fashioned and might submit to a credit card, she didn't have one on her. It was inside her purse. Behind the locked door.

For a moment she stood, thinking. There was another way into the ladies', which, bizarrely, led through the men's changing room. Maybe she should take a chance and slip through. The overweight man who had punched the bags was probably gone by this time. Of course, it would be just her luck if the men's changing room was locked as well.

The door opened beneath her hand. The long, narrow room with its rows of lockers and stark wooden benches seemed empty. But she could see damp footprints on the cement floor and a pair of sodden swimming trunks lay in a wet puddle. There was the sound of water running. Someone was taking a shower.

She peered cautiously round the corner. Unlike the women's showers, the stalls in here did not have glass partitions and were completely open.

He was standing with his back to her and he was washing his hair. The shampoo ran in foamy bubbles down his neck and his muscled back. It was Ash.

She stared at his figure: the broad shoulders, the narrow hips. There was a clear tan line between his waist and his buttocks. On one cheek sat a tattoo: the bold black ideograms were large and beautifully executed – they could have been drawn by a master calligrapher. Chinese characters? Japanese? She did not know, but it hardly mattered. What mattered was that Ash had told her he did not have any tattoos.

There are moments in life when you recognize that something significant is happening but you do not understand what it is. Understanding only comes later, with hindsight. As she stood there, Mia knew this was such a moment.

He suddenly stilled his movements and she realized he had sensed her. He started to turn round, his hand groping for the towel. She gave a big step backwards. Turning on her heel, she rushed through the open door behind her and headed back to the entrance.

Lanice was once more at her desk. 'Whoah! What's up? You seen a ghost?'

'Open up so I can get my bag, Lanice. Where were you?'

'Oh, sorry. I went upstairs to hurry up the guys using the weight room. Here you go.' She tossed the keys to Mia.

Mia grabbed her bag but wasted no more time in the locker room – she would shower at home. She didn't want to take the risk of bumping into Ash.

Why had he lied to her?

The question stayed with her as she returned home and prepared for bed. She slid in among the smooth sheets and stared at the shadowed ceiling.

What did she know about this man?

She thought back on that moment she first saw him standing in the door: a black shape against the light. Darkness and luminosity – a glimmer man. Adrian Ashton was a man of contrasts. A healer who identified with combat. A man of great charm whose eyes hinted at a turbulent inner life. He was an enigma, and trying to fathom who he was, was like trying to see a rainbow in the dark. Was this why she found him fascinating? Maybe it was precisely the precarious balancing of forces, which she sensed lurking inside him, that so attracted her. And there was no use pretending any more. She was drawn to him.

Turning on her side, she pressed her warm cheek into the cool pillow. She remembered his powerful shoulders, the graceful legs and the water flowing down his strong back. The black tattooed marks vivid against the pale skin.

Why had he lied to her?

The question hovered on the tip of her tongue the next day when he came in for his appointment. But now she was presented with an interesting challenge: how to explain that she knew he had a tat without revealing herself as a Peeping Thomasina?

'So why have you never had a tattoo done before?' She pressed down on the switch and Angelique started to hum.

'I've never been tempted. Or maybe I just wanted to wait for the right body artist to come along.'

He smiled at her and she smiled back. She shouldn't be so judgemental, she chided herself. He probably had his reasons for not telling her. It was a small lie, after all.

She placed Angelique close to his skin.

A small lie, really. Of no importance.

Summer was edging into autumn. Dusk came a little earlier, and sometimes when Mia woke in the mornings she would give a small startled shiver at the chill that nipped the air. But it still seemed as though the golden days would never end.

And then came the phone call from Okie and everything changed.

STEPPING OUT

Human perception occur[s] because of interactions
between the subatomic particles of our brains and the
quantum energy sea.

Lynne McTaggart,
*The Field: The Quest for the Secret Force
of the Universe*

CHAPTER THIRTY-THREE

Nick touched his fingers to his reflection in the mirror. He turned his head first to one side and then to the other. He had the strangest feeling that he was looking at another man, not himself. His face seemed inscrutable, even to his own eyes. His body had changed as well. His abs were hard and he had not an ounce of fat on him. In fact, he knew he would probably never achieve this level of fitness ever again in his life.

Ash was adding new dimensions to his training every day. Lately they had focused on breathing. The first time Ash made him take the Wu Chi position, Nick felt idiotic. But things had changed. Yesterday, he had experienced a sensation unlike anything before.

He and Ash were in the dojo. It was very early – only a few minutes past five in the morning – and they were alone. He had just completed a full cycle of Gates of Life movements and had moved on to the closing minutes, sealing in the energy he had allowed to pass through the portal. He was resting in the position Ash had taught him: eyelids lowered, knees unlocked and his feet taking the full weight of his body. His right palm was on his lower abdomen and the left hand rested on top of the right.

Next to him was a window and he sensed, rather than saw, the clouds racing behind the glass pane with its over-lay of dust. Suddenly, a shaft of sunlight slashed through the grime like a knife. At the same moment he had the extraordinary sensation that he could reach inside his body and touch every organ. For one single moment the static inside his mind was wiped clean and he felt connected to the world around him as through a massive web of spider's silk.

The sensation was so unexpected and strong, he gasped. Looking up, he saw Ash watching him intently and then nodding as though understanding exactly what had happened. But they hadn't spoken about it afterwards and Nick was glad. Describing the experience would be like pulling the petals off a flower in an attempt to under-stand its beauty. And truth to tell, he felt rather spooked as well. This kind of thing was not where the grunts lived. This was vogue territory.

'Nick.'

He turned round. Okie was standing in the doorway of the changing room, grinning at him.

'Hey, you.' Nick walked over and hugged him hard. 'Are you back?'

'Yup. Rib's mended and JC's lifted the ban.'

'That's great news.'

Okie opened his locker and pushed his satchel inside with a satisfied smile. From one corner of the bag protruded a paperback. *Desperate Hearts*. Okie's reading tastes had not changed during his absence.

'I wanted to check with you, Nick. You still want me in your corner on the night of the fight, right?'

'Of course. Can't do it without you, mate.'

'Great.' Okie looked pleased. 'So, how about us hitting the road again together? Can I pick you up tomorrow morning?'

Nick hesitated.

'What?' Okie frowned. 'You think I won't be able to keep up?'

'I've been training hard, Okie.'

'I'm fit, man. I may not have been working the bag, but I cycled my arse off during the past few weeks. My fitness level is high, I promise.'

Nick was surprised at how reluctant he was to let Okie in on his training sessions with Ash. He had a strong feeling Ash would not welcome company either.

Okie slammed the locker door shut. 'OK, I get it. You have a new training buddy now.'

'It's not that, Okie.'

'I think it is.' Okie shook his head vehemently, making the dreadlocks dance. 'But forget it.'

Nick felt bad. 'It's just until the fight, Okie, OK? No hard feelings?'

'Yeah, yeah.' But Okie wasn't looking him in the eye.

'Okie . . .'

'JC's waiting.' Okie turned his back and walked to the door.

Nick lifted his hand as if to reach out, but then let it fall by his side. It was only until the fight, after all.

CHAPTER THIRTY-FOUR

Mia gently patted Ash's skin with a paper towel. 'Next week will be your last appointment and you'll be all done. Now, remember . . .'

'I know. Keep the dressing on until tomorrow.'

The phone rang. Not wishing to render her gloves unsterile, Mia left it to the machine to pick up.

'Mia!' The tinny quality of the answering machine couldn't disguise the enthusiasm in Okie's voice. 'You there? No? OK, great news: I have a fight! Yeah! Sunday at Lancaster Tavern. So remember to dream of me, little one. OK?'

Mia hastily grabbed at the phone, glancing at Ash and wondering what on earth he must be thinking.

'Okie? How can you have a fight? You've only been back in the dojo a week.'

'Yeah, I know. But this one guy who was supposed to fight has tonsillitis and they're looking for someone to take his place.'

'What does JC say? Surely you can't be fit enough?'

'JC's OK with it. It's only a three-rounder, Mia. A

lung-opener: it will help me shake off the ring rust. So it's dreamtime for you, yes?'

'Yes.' She glanced uneasily at Ash again, who was still lying flat on his back and who didn't seem to be listening to the one-sided conversation with much interest. 'I will do.'

As she replaced the receiver, Ash asked mildly, 'So when is Okie fighting?'

'This weekend.'

'Why are you frowning?'

'I'm worried. It's a small fight and I know he's been trying to keep up his fitness, but a fight is still a fight, you know. Three rounds or ten rounds, it's still dangerous.'

'I'll ask him to come and train with me and Nick over the next couple of days. It can't hurt.'

'That would be great. Thanks.' She hugged herself as though cold. For the first time in weeks she thought of Valentine.

'What are you thinking?'

She shook her head. 'Nothing. I still have to fix that dressing on you. Let me get a new pair of gloves.'

After she had taped the dressing in place, she pushed her chair back. 'There you go.'

'Thanks.'

She turned her back on him and started clearing the trolley. Her movements were automatic, her thoughts racing. If Okie was fighting on Saturday, that meant she would have to step out on Friday. Three days to go.

Stepping out. Her stomach twisted with that familiar feeling of anxious excitement.

She had forgotten about Ash and was surprised, when she turned round, to find him immediately behind her.

Suddenly she was so aware of his closeness. He still had to put on his shirt and she could feel his heat.

'You really are worried about Okie, aren't you?'

'He's a friend. I worry about all my friends.'

He leant a hand against the wall behind her, his arm forming an enclosed space. She could smell the musk of his bare skin.

'Your pulse is going like mad.' He lifted his other hand and brushed his finger against the hollow of her neck and she felt her skin prickle as though an insect had alighted there. Her breathing became shallow. She swallowed, and her mouth tasted of salt.

Slowly, slowly, his fingers traced the nape of her neck and lingered just inside the open-necked collar of her blouse. In the deep secret core of her, she felt a lick of flame.

'Mia.' His lips touched her forehead, her cheeks. 'Mia.'

She closed her eyes and his lips were on her eyelids too. He was murmuring things against her hair but his words were indistinct. Placing his hands on her waist, his fingers gripped her flesh through the thin cotton blouse. He suddenly slammed her against him while simultaneously pushing her up against the wall. The next moment he was kissing her and she felt her lips open and his tongue touching hers. A liquid sensation ran along her veins. Slow fire spread up her legs and she could feel a dampness under her arms.

And hadn't she known all along that this would happen? Wasn't this what she had secretly hoped for? Slowly, slowly, his tongue moved against the inside of her lower lip. His hands were hot through the gauzy fabric of her blouse and she felt his thigh straining against hers.

He was now kissing her hard and her mouth opened even wider under his. All of a sudden it was as though her mind became cold as ice and she was floating outside her body and looking down at them: at the man pushing forward urgently and the woman enfolded by him, her head tilted back.

She snapped into alertness.

'No.' Turning her head to one side, her mouth slid away from his.

'Don't be scared.' He leant in closer. His mouth was seeking hers again and his breath was warm on her cheek.

'No!' She pressed her palm hard against his chest.

For just the briefest of instances, she felt him resist. His muscles tautened underneath her hand and she was suddenly, overwhelmingly, aware of how powerful he was. But then he immediately stepped back.

'I'm sorry.' His face had emptied of emotion.

'No, I'm sorry, it's just . . .'

He made a gesture with his hand. 'Don't look so dismayed, Mia. It's not the end of the world.'

He walked to the chair where he had left his shirt and pulled it on, while she watched, trembling fingers against her mouth. She tasted blood, coppery-sweet from a cut lip.

At the door he paused. 'Be warned, sweetheart, I don't give up easily.' His expression was blank but behind that shuttered gaze she sensed a relentless, single-track concentration. 'You can deny it all you want, but you and I are a pair. Diamond cuts diamond.'

CHAPTER THIRTY-FIVE

The Book of Light and Dust
For Rosalia
XXXX

What is the essence of sexual attraction?

Fantasy.

Not safe. Not civilized.

Not shared.

Fantasy is, at heart, solitary. It needs no reciprocation. Reciprocation leads to familiarity and the death of fantasy.

But what if you meet someone who has fantasy in her bones, her blood, the electric current of her mind, the energy of her cells?

I looked into her eyes today and I had to remind myself: watch out. That which is fragile can still be deadly.

The Keeper

Kiss me, light, kiss me, dust . . .

THE WAY: YIN DREAM

BLACKLIGHT: DIR: LU9 GB2, FRC: 1, TIME: 8, SUs: GB1

Whitelight: no whitelight possible

235

CHAPTER THIRTY-SIX

It was the day before Okie's fight and time to step out. Time to push away from her all the issues and worries that nagged at her and sapped her energy. Ash, Nick and her own confused, messy emotions about them both: everything would have to wait. Tonight she was the Keeper and Okie her only concern.

Mia always told her charges that she dreamt of them, which was not strictly accurate. But dreams were something they understood and Molly had warned her to keep it simple. *Wai chi* and Reiki were not concepts with which grunts were comfortable. They may just, with difficulty, accept the idea of someone channelling healing energy through their hands, but usually the idea of a Reiki practitioner engaging in long-distance healing through meditation made no sense to them.

The practice of 'stepping out' required an even greater leap of faith. Concepts such as *samyama* and *siddhis* – spiritual powers used in Hinduism and Buddhism – lay far outside the frame of reference of most grunts. As for an OBE – an out-of-body experience – this was completely foreign to their thinking and made the men feel uneasy. So

Mia talked of dreams only and followed Molly's advice to keep it uncomplicated. Besides, the notion that she was dreaming of them fed the vanity of the dear souls no end. What guy wouldn't like the idea of a woman dreaming of him?

Stepping out . . . a maze within a maze . . .

The actual practice of stepping out had never been a problem for Mia. Mastering the practice itself had been intuitive. Usually Siddhi powers were gained through years of *sadhana* – rigorous meditation and control of the senses – but Keepers were born with the ability to have an out-of-body experience at will.

Molly had not been curious about this unique talent that was hardwired into her DNA; she had simply accepted it and revelled in its use. 'If you try to label a mystery, it becomes impenetrable,' she would say in response to Mia's questions. But Mia wanted to understand. And so she read: everything from whimsical New Age tracts to daunting neurological theses posted on academic websites. She read voraciously, joyously and with wonder.

She learnt that unlike her own, most out-of-body experiences were not the result of rigorous meditation but happened spontaneously. They were usually sleep-related and occurred just as the subject was on the verge of losing consciousness. Close cousin to lucid dreaming, an out-of-body experience was far more vivid and the person was fully conscious even as he or she lost contact with the sensory input from their corporeal body. Many OBEs were reported by people when they were close to death.

Conditions of either excessive or diminished arousal seemed to be essential: subjects were either half-asleep when it happened or experiencing great stress – child-birth, a car crash, a rock-climbing fall. The adventures experienced in an OBE were sometimes so strong that the brain became addicted and people would allow themselves to be subjected to extreme bondage – virtual mummifi-cation – in order to reach the desired state of sensory deprivation that might lead to an OBE.

Of course, the sensation of leaving your body behind, travelling through a modified reality and then returning is an old one: reports of OBEs go back thousands of years. But Mia learnt that science only became interested in the phenomenon after Celia Green's first extensive scientific studies on the subject in 1968. Since then, neurologists, using binaural beats to elicit theta brain-wave frequencies or stimulating the right temporal-parietal junction of the brain have tried to induce OBE-like experiences on command. But it wasn't until 2007 that H. Henrik Ehrsson performed the first experimental method that fitted a three-point definition of an OBE, inducing an out-of-body experience in healthy participants at the Institute of Neurology at the University College of London.

But if scientists were now able to induce an OBE at will, they still did not understand the journeys their subjects took, or why.

If you try to label a mystery, it becomes impenetrable . . .

Mia sat down cross-legged in front of the standing mirror. Usually, before stepping out, she would prepare herself for the event with a full week of prolonged meditation. But Okie's fight had come upon them so suddenly, she hadn't had the luxury on this occasion. No matter.

The lights in the room were switched off, but the moon outside was so bright she was able to see her reflection perfectly. Her feet were resting on her thighs. One hand lay on her knee; the other was holding a picture of Okie. How young he looked, the posed ferocity of his stance making him appear oddly defenceless. Keeping the picture in her sight, she gazed beyond it and inhaled, breathing energy from beyond her hand, through her hand, to her nose, down her throat and the central channel, making sure to reverse the passage of the breath in similar steps as she breathed out with intent.

Her mind emptied. But she was starting to sense the current. There it was, stirring in her abdomen – an urgent flow of energy rushing from abdomen, to throat, to the top of her head, the tips of her fingers and down to her feet: a vital tide surging through her body, lapping behind her eyes, chasing through the hemispheres of her brain, urging her to step out . . .

Stepping out. The moon washed the wall white, but as she passed by it she threw no shadow. This was the part of stepping out she disliked. She was a clumsy rag doll. At this early stage of her journey she was still unbalanced and her knees were apt to buckle. Her sense of direction was impaired and she was liable to walk into corners. Mia looked into the standing mirror to her left, expecting to see her head flop on her neck like a poppy on its stalk, but she was unable to see her face. The only reflection in the mirror was of the motionless woman sitting cross-legged behind her, clasping a photograph with slack fingers.

Her legs were feeling stronger now. She was regaining her equilibrium. By the time she reached the window, her mind was as clear as a bell. For a moment she waited, sensing the vast city outside with its millions of windows – brightly lit and hanging like glowing squares of yellow against the darkness. A city of light despite its cold, black river, its dark alleys and passageways and deserted offices closed for the night. A city of luminous streets, of humming power lines and trains charging down sub-terranean tunnels. A city of souls. She could sense tidy lives and haphazard existences; flowers blooming in garden squares, weeds breaking through boarded-up windows. Everything *connected*. And if she listened closely she could hear the city breathing . . .

It was time to go. The Retreat waited. Without giving the quiet seated body behind her a second glance, she walked forward.

Outside in the dark street, the Thief watched the Keeper's house, his eyes fixed on the open window on the top floor. He could feel her energy and the quality of the air around him was altered. He sensed her pale form, the soft push of her thoughts. She was stepping up to the open window. Her arms were held wide and her head tipped back, show-ing her white throat. The next moment she tipped her body forward, showing no hesitation, no fear. *Zenpo ukemi.* It was a perfect forward breakfall with no flinching or flailing of arms.

The Thief closed his eyes and watched the Keeper take flight.

CHAPTER THIRTY-SEVEN

Stepping out was a conscious act. Finding the Retreat was a serendipitous one. There had been times when her search was futile and she had to break the meditation and try again. But tonight she found it almost immediately; one moment she was still falling into nothingness and the next her feet touched solid ground.

The first time she had visited the Retreat was on behalf of Benny, her first charge. She had only just turned eighteen and Molly had still been alive. Benny had quick feet, a tough, wiry body, and enormous ears, which seemed to glow when the light was behind him. He had been in her keeping for only seven months before he retired. That was when she took on Valentine. Bill and Okie had followed in short succession. 'Three charges,' Molly had warned. 'Don't stretch yourself too thin, Mia. Three only.'

Every time, just as one of her charges was about to enter the ring, she'd step out and head for the Retreat to draw healing energy from within its walls. This was where she came to recharge her own chi to pass on to her charges. *Fa gung*. It was a centuries-old ritual and it was essential that her charges kept her informed of their schedule. Valentine had always, always alerted her to his upcoming fights. Why hadn't he done so the last time?

No. With deliberation she shut her mind to Valentine. If she thought of him now, she would become hesitant, her internal energy blocked, and she would be of no use to Okie.

The Retreat was still out of sight, hidden by a turn in the path. For a moment Mia stood still, her senses alert. The moon was up high, but the large trees surrounding her threw deep shadows. The track ahead looked as deserted as though no one ever came this way and, underfoot, the moss was smooth and untrampled. When she pushed to one side the gate barring her way, the catch felt stiff.

But as she let the gate swing shut behind her, her heart lifted. Home, she thought as her bare feet followed the mossy path. Home. And as she walked down the moon-ribbed track, she knew there were ghostly footprints underneath her bare feet, unseen markers leading her on, left by Keepers who had entered before her, many years in the past. Sometimes she would dream of them: of women with long necks and silver eyes, holding hands through the ages, drawing their dreams together even though the dream they shared and the burden they carried were no longer celebrated or understood.

Keepers were shaman, healers and protectors. Found in every part of the world, the Orient was still considered their spiritual home. In Ancient China and feudal Japan the Keeper's presence was accepted and her role welcomed. The relationship between the warrior and the woman who guarded him was one that drew respect. The Keeper was an integral player in a world part poetry, part violent death.

Keepers were usually yoginis, Reiki masters and martial artists. Martial arts might seem a strange pursuit for one who healed, but healing and martial arts had always gone hand in hand. Even today, Mia knew, if you visited China or Taiwan and made yourself known as a traditional martial artist, people would start telling you about their ailments.

But the world of traditional martial arts had also been a world of obsessive secrecy. The significance behind many of the movements was taught to only a few trusted students or family members. Over time a vast body of martial-arts knowledge was lost as vital information was buried, hidden or outlawed. The Keeper became part of the world of 'hidden teachings'. It was a claustrophobic world and the lack of oxygen caused the Keeper to sicken. In the mind of the masses, her role became distorted. She was considered no more than a prostitute for men who engaged in ritualized combat: a hanger-on, a groupie – her protective fire ignored.

The track underneath Mia's feet was narrowing. She was almost there and her heart started beating fast. She turned the bend in the road and there it was.

The building was long and low and you approached it

from the side. The walls were stone and the roof made of bamboo reeds. The thick wooden door, leading to the rooms inside, always stood ajar.

There was a smell of jasmine here in the clearing and wilder scents too. As she walked up the shallow timber steps, her presence made a group of fragile wind chimes shiver and their silvery sound filled the air. Painted on the half-open door in front of her was the Keeper's mark: two long-lidded eyes; and inside one of the eyes a circle and three lines entering it at an angle. The circle symbolized energy; the three lines represented the bridge that can be crossed to access it.

Placing her hand lightly on the half-open door in front of her, Mia paused. In this place resided the spirits of wise women. One did not rush into such a place. One entered it with awe: grateful for the inspiration and healing energy that was kept safe within its walls.

She pushed the door fully open.

The Thief watched as the Keeper placed her hand against the door and it opened wide.

He had not entered the clearing himself and was still standing just inside the edge of the woods. The Retreat was bathed in moonlight; he was in shadow. The boughs of the trees around him creaked in the night.

He had never been here before but the place was as he would have imagined it to be and he felt a vast contentment. There was a satisfying sense of solidity to the thick walls and the low, sweeping eaves of the roof. The slab of stone surrounding the door was etched with symbols and even from this distance he recognized them: earth, fire, water, metal and wood – the five *gogyo* symbols, which the Keeper shared with practitioners of ninjitsu. They were transformation symbols, all of them, and told of energy and its use in combat and escape. On the right side of the door the *gogyo* symbols were depicted in their productive cycle: every energy manifestation giving birth to another. On the left side were the symbols in their destructive phase: every energy manifestation being destroyed by another.

She had disappeared from view. He stared at the house with longing.

The lamps inside the Retreat were always turned low. Mia stepped into the Great Hall and found the vast space filled with buttery light and soft shadows.

The highly polished floor, pleasant against the soles of her feet, gleamed. The embroidery thread in the wall hangings shimmered, as did the rich crimsons and golds of the ink drawings on *washi* and silk that lined the walls.

Captured by threading needle and paintbrush were enigmatic symbols and ghost-like figures: brave samurai; warring monks; sloe-eyed women with cloud-like hair and pale fingers. There were men with heavy shoulders and muscled thighs; women with saffron streaks on their foreheads and obsidian mirrors hanging from their waists.

Here was a portrait of the tragic red-haired Brigante Keeper who had lived under the female ruler Cartimandua and whose charge had poisoned her, the reason lost in the mists of time. There, looking pensive, a Keeper who had lived after the Second World War as an Okinawan priestess on the island of Henza. In her hand she held a three-foot-long tattoo stick; at her feet was her charge, his entire body covered in ink.

There was even a painting of the treacherous Keeper Tembandumba, Queen of the Jaga, who had hoped to revive the Amazonian cult with its man-killing ethos. As Mia looked into the queen's heavy eyes, she remembered the cold December night Molly had told her the story of the Keeper who had declared war on all men, turning her intent from healing to maiming. 'Keepers can destroy as well as heal, Mia. They are creatures not only of light, but – if they allow themselves – also of darkness. Energy can be reversed. *Fa chi* can be dangerous. Never forget that.' She remembered how Molly's words had transported her from their house, with its snow-rimmed windows, to the steaming forests of the Congo, where a mad queen ordered mothers to kill their sons and make an ointment of the fat of their skins. '*Magige samba,*' the queen would whisper: 'smear on you the magic paste and you will increase your life force and live for ever.'

The Great Hall held many treasures but Mia passed them by without a glance. She had explored these talismans and energy objects before and tonight her only thought was to reach the dojo.

Finally. She entered the cool, austere space. There was no colour here, no scrolls or symbols, only sixteen mats and a room framed by mirrors.

Mia bowed deeply to the empty room, to the spirits of the teachers who had breathed here. She took her position. As she started her formalized *Ba Gua* Circle movements, she thought she heard far behind her the tinkle of wind chimes. The wind must be blowing.

The energy of this place was palpable. The Thief walked through the open door on silent feet.

He ached to explore but satisfied himself with merely glancing at the treasures on display as he passed through. Books, tortoise shells, bleached bones and bundles of dry herbs beautifully arranged in a simple wooden box. Cups of sand and an array of polished half-staffs displayed in another. A niche entirely devoted to Chiyome Mochizuki, the sixteenth-century *miko* head who had trained a group of runaway girls to become keepers for the Takeda family. And everywhere the Keeper's mark: pairs of eyes looking down at him from the walls, the ledges, even painted on the timber floor underneath his feet. It felt unnerving to be under the gaze of so many eyes.

He and the Keeper were not the only living creatures here tonight. As he stepped out of the vast hall and into a narrow passage where the planes of light shifted and deepened, the walls on either side of him seemed to move. It took him a while to realize that he was looking at thousands of black crickets. Their wings glistened darkly.

Vaguely he recalled that in Asia the cricket was considered the symbol of intelligence and luck and fighting spirit. The crickets covered the stone walls like a living wall hanging and he made his way through the passage carefully, trying not to brush against them. They were eerily quiet: no chirping, only the antennae moving ghost-like. He looked at them, fascinated, and, at the same time, just slightly repulsed.

The dojo was right ahead. He could see the Keeper's reflection in the mirror. Her face was completely relaxed, her limbs moving fluidly.

He stepped fully inside.

Let's see what you've got.

When the figure appeared behind her, Mia was so surprised, she lowered her guard. The next moment she went flying through the air. Even though the surface was padded, the shock when her shoulder connected with the ground took her breath away.

He had thrown her clear across the room. She scrambled to her feet in a low crouch and looked up at the figure watching her from the other side of the dojo. He was dressed all in black and he wore a hood, allowing only his eyes to show. Like some villain in a B-grade film, she thought angrily. Despite the ache in her shoulder, her confused brain refused to accept his presence. He had no right to be here. This was a Retreat: a place of contemplation and ritual, not of violence.

How long had he been lurking? Why hadn't she sensed

his presence earlier? She was certainly sensing his chi now; it pushed against her, confusing her, and she felt it viscerally against her skin. And it was interfering with the energy of the room, making it seesaw chaotically.

He moved forward with a smooth, deadly glide, a kind of skipping step in which his back foot kicked the front into movement. It allowed him to travel the distance between them with stupefying speed and her anger suddenly turned to fear. The next moment he was striking at her with a snapping wrist movement – a mantis attacking – his fingers pointed. She just managed to evade this inside body strike by stepping away at an angle.

He was so fast. And he seemed to sense her moves even before she had executed them. As she tried to defend herself against his attack, she knew she was signalling, allowing him to read her intentions. Her movements were predictable. Her thoughts were interfering and anxiety was blunting her defence. Desperately she struck at him with a hammer blow, tensing her shoulders violently. He brought up his arm and blocked.

Never use force against force if your opponent is bigger than you: the greater force will win. If there was one thing Chilli had taught her in all the many years she had studied with him, it was exactly this most simple and logical principle. And it was the one that she now threw out of the window first. By pitting her own physical strength against her attacker's, she had put herself toe to toe with a man far stronger and more powerful. Her best chance would have been to continue moving around and into his attack, using circular and slipping motions, going with his flow, listening to his rhythm, waiting for an opening to use the right angle or lever against him. *Aiki*: turning his body against his mind, borrowing his force instead of spending her own. But, of course, she had not. And now she was about to pay for her stupidity.

Their arms connected and it felt as though he had struck her with a lead pipe. Vaguely she realized he had targeted the radial nerve. Moving forward smoothly, he pushed against her shoulder and at the same time swept her ankle with his right foot. *Shao twei* – ankle cut. His precision was terrifying. The blade of his sole cut into the nerve-sensitive spot at the back of her foot and the scything power of his sweep was devastating. Her leg collapsed.

He was on top of her now, as she lay dazed and in pain. The face looking down at her, draped in black cloth, was unnerving. He was smiling, she could tell by the way the skin puckered round his eyes. She sensed his thoughts, as clear as though he had spoken them.

You die in here. You die out there.

She lunged at him, trying to rip the hood off his face, but he grabbed her hand and bent her ring finger violently away from her palm and she screamed and fell back.

Gently he smoothed the hair away from her forehead and then touched her face deliberately – the eyebrows, the cheekbones, the jaw. She tried to move her head away but he still had hold of her hand and the finger twist this time was so violent she screamed again and felt the tears come to her eyes. Slowly, slowly, his other hand travelled down the side of her neck.

His thumb came to rest on her collarbone, his middle finger on the hollow in her throat.

CHAPTER THIRTY-EIGHT

The Book of Light and Dust
For Rosalia
XXXXI

I came to you today with many questions, my curiosity burning.

How strong are you? How will you hold up? Are you air or are you water? Do you contain fire or let it loose? So many questions and, after our single battle, not enough answers.

I looked into your eyes and I thought of how we search for love as though it were a jewel lost in a sea of sand. If only we can find it, we think. If only we can close our grasping fingers round it, press it to our heart, make it our own — irrevocably our own — then our lives will be transformed.

Love and life: looked together throughout evolution like binary stars. Is the desire for love as strong as the desire for life? Which is the prime directive; which the secondary, weaker force? Love conquers all, we say, as though it truly has the power to defeat that older, darker imperative.

Does it?

The one is flint, the other gossamer. The one is oxygen, the other is song.

I wonder . . .

There can be only one answer.

THE WAY: FLOATING VALLEY

BLACKLIGHT: DIR: GB10 GB20, FRC: 1, TIME: 2, SUs: GB2

Whitelight: mas. B1 10

CHAPTER THIRTY-NINE

The Lancaster Tavern was smoke-filled, pulsing with heavy-metal rock and filled to capacity. Colourful and vibey, the Tavern was not a venue for the faint of heart. The action in the ring was often bloody and the spectators loud and critical.

A pot-bellied man wearing a T-shirt with an image of Ken Shamrock and the words 'I can see dead people' blocked Mia's path. He burped loudly and a stale whiff of beer wafted over her. As she squeezed by him, she felt her mobile phone vibrating briefly against her hip. Someone had sent her a text message. But she was carrying two water bottles and the big man was tough to get round, so she ignored it and continued to weave her way past tables crowded with spectators to where she could see the rest of the Scorpio gang huddled together on the other side of the ring. After depositing the water bottles on to their table, which was already chock-full of beer cans, peanuts, Krispy Kremes and other silly food, she pulled out a chair next to Lanice.

Lanice looked at her critically. 'What's up with you, Mia?'

'What do you mean?'

'You don't look so good, girl.'

'Had a bad night last night.'

Which must be the understatement of the century. She was still frightened out of her skull and had no idea why she was attacked in the Retreat or who her attacker was. The last thing she remembered was lying on the mat, a figure in black staring down at her, his hands on her. Her next memory was of waking up inside her house.

You die in here. You die out there. An unambiguous threat. Who was this man?

'Have a Krispy Kreme.' Lanice pushed the box over to her. 'Come on, it has the glaze on it and everything. Good for you.'

Mia felt a hand on her shoulder and looked round. It was Nick. He looked different. He had shaved his head in a buzz cut – the style many fighters affected when they were preparing to go into the ring – and it made him look stern. With a little shock, Mia realized that Nick's own fight was only two weeks away.

'How's Okie?' she asked him.

'He's fine. But he's still looking for his lucky penny.'

Mia sighed. It had become a ritual: Okie searching for a lucky penny on the night of the fight. It was to be a serendipitous thing – the penny was to 'come' to him. If it did, he was sure to win – according to Okie, that was. If the penny failed to materialize, he would drive everyone in the changing room crazy with his pre-fight jitters.

'Why don't you lot just leave one for him to find?'

'Don't think we haven't tried. JC's planted two pennies already but he keeps missing them.'

'Nick, is he fit enough?'

'He's not in top shape, but he's OK. He went training with me and Ash yesterday and I was surprised. He didn't do too badly. He even did a few rounds of grappling with Ash and his rib held up fine.'

She felt her face grow warm at the mention of Ash's name. 'Is he here?'

'Ash? No. Something last-minute came up.'

So one less thing to worry about at least. Since their little scene in the studio three days ago, she had avoided Ash. But at some point she would have no choice but to face him – for one thing, she still had to finish his tattoo. She didn't even want to think about that.

'Anyway,' Nick squeezed her shoulder, 'I need to get back. Okie asked me to be in his corner. And don't worry: Okie will be fine. This is not a big fight, OK?'

'OK. Give him my love.'

'Will do.'

The lights dimmed and the urgent strains of Kasabian's 'Club Foot' blasted from the overhead speakers. The first fight was on.

As the first two fighters started circling each other, Mia suddenly remembered the text message that had come through on her mobile. She eased the phone from her pocket and pressed the message button.

MIA. YOU ARE OKIE'S KEEPER. WHY DID YOU
FAIL HIM?

Her eyes flew to the sender's ID but the phone number
was unknown to her and obviously did not correspond
with any of the numbers in her contact list.

Her thumb moved stiffly across the keys. *Who are you?*

She waited, her breath tight inside her chest. Beside her
Lanice was shouting at one of the fighters, 'Punches in
bunches, James! Punches in bunches!'

WE MET LAST NIGHT AT THE RETREAT, REMEMBER?

This was ridiculous. She couldn't keep texting this
maniac. She was going to call him. But she couldn't do it
here: the din was too loud. Gesturing to Lanice that she
was heading for the Ladies, Mia eased out of her seat.
Making herself as small as possible, she made her way
through the tables in the direction of the exit.

The ladies' room had an avocado-and-orange-coloured
carpet and smelt of spilt beer and cigarette smoke.
Standing in front of the mirror was a girl dressed in a
leather skirt and a very low-cut top. She squinted at Mia.
'Mia, yeah? Remember me?'

As a matter of fact, Mia did not and if ever there was a
time when she did not want to engage in a conversation, it
was right this minute.

'Yeah.' The girl nodded enthusiastically. 'You're the
tattooist. We met at the McWhinney fight.'

'Oh, right. Excuse me—'

But the girl grabbed Mia's arm in a startlingly strong grip. 'See. I wanted to ask you. I want to have Apollo's head tattooed on my breast.'

'Apollo?'

'My boyfriend.' The girl tugged at the neck of her top. 'I have a few other tats already but I think you can maybe still find a spot.'

Or maybe not. The breast that popped into view was ample but it was crowded space. Apollo was going to have to fight it out with the initials GS, a cross dripping tears and an angel. The angel's one eye drooped in a surprisingly lascivious wink.

Mia felt hysterical laughter bubbling up inside her. 'Look, I'm sorry. I have to go.'

'No, but I want to ask you—'

The mobile on Mia's hip pinged and vibrated at the same time. Shaking herself loose, Mia walked into one of the stalls and slammed the door shut. On the other side, she heard the girl mutter something that sounded like 'stuck-up bitch'. Then the swing door leading to the outside swished twice and the room was suddenly dead quiet.

YOU FAILED OKIE.

Mia keyed in the phone number and brought the mobile up to her ear. But no one picked up. After ringing for a full minute, the phone made a long beep sound and went dead.

So it was back to texting again. She felt a slow lick of anger.

WHAT DO YOU MEAN I FAILED OKIE?

YOU LOST THE FIGHT AGAINST ME. OKIE WILL STEP INTO THE RING TONIGHT FOR THE LAST TIME.

She felt herself go cold. Before she could text back, the phone pinged and another message flashed on to the screen.

NEXT TIME WE PLAY YOU WILL HAVE TO DO BETTER. IF YOU WIN, YOUR CHARGE IS SAFE. IF NOT, HIS LIFE IS FORFEIT. WE WILL GO ANOTHER ROUND YET: YOU AND ME. KEEPER AND THIEF. BUT FOR OKIE IT'S TOO LATE.

CHAPTER FORTY

'Spread your fingers, Okie.' JC tapped the top of Okie's right hand. 'Yes, that's good.' JC finished twisting the thin gauze wrap round Okie's knuckles and taped it in place. Okie flexed his hand and nodded.

Nick watched as JC started wrapping Okie's left hand. No matter how often he watched this ceremony, he was always struck by a feeling of awe. The moment a fighter gets his hands wrapped is the moment a sudden alchemy takes place. An ordinary hand is turned into a lethal weapon. A man is transformed into a warrior.

But this was also the moment when Nick was reminded of exactly how fragile a fighter's body is. Because the truth of it is, a man's hand cannot hold up to the impact of a blow delivered with the full power of the body behind it. The metacarpal bones crack like sticks. The wrist tears and buckles. Skin splits. Wraps are essential to pad the knuckles, keep the thumb straight and strengthen the wrist. And even then, a fighter could still end up with crippled fists.

Okie jumped off his seat and started pacing, rolling his shoulders and punching the air. JC took Okie's silk robe from the peg and waited for him to insert his arms into the wide sleeves.

'Nick . . .'

Nick turned round enquiringly. Roach Harper, the cut man, was sticking his head round the corner of the door.

'What's up?'

'Someone out front wants to talk to you.'

Nick frowned. 'Tell him I can't come now.'

'She says it's urgent. Said to tell you her name's Mia and she has to see you.'

Nick hesitated. But it was Mia, after all. She wouldn't call him out for something frivolous.

As he walked down the corridor towards the door giving access to the arena, it opened and the fighters who had just finished their match walked in with their corner men. One fighter was bleeding profusely from a cut on the eyebrow. The referee had probably stopped the fight, Nick thought, which meant Okie was up next. He'd have to tell Mia that whatever she wanted to talk to him about would have to wait until later.

She was standing right outside and she did not give him time to say anything. As soon as he stepped out, she grabbed him by the arm.

'Nick. You have to stop Okie. He can't fight tonight.'

He could hear her struggling to keep her voice level.

'What? Why?'

'He is going to get hurt tonight. You have to stop him.'

'Mia, he's going to be fine. This is not a big fight. Okie can handle himself.'

'Listen to me.' She was actually shaking him. 'Stop him now! He is in danger!'

She had two high spots of colour burning on her cheeks. Her eyes were desperate.

'Mia. Calm down.' He was trying to calm down himself but it was fair to say she was doing a good job of freaking him out. 'What the hell's going on?'

'There isn't time to explain it to you, Nick. Just trust me. He shouldn't go out there.'

He stared at her, feeling at a complete loss. But before he could say anything else, the lights dimmed and a roar of sound erupted from an overhead speaker: the Backstreet Boys launching into 'Larger than Life'. It was Okie's fight song, which meant he had started his walkout to the ring.

'I have to go.' He removed Mia's hand from his sleeve, giving her fingers what he hoped was a reassuring squeeze. 'Don't worry, OK? I'm going to be right there in his corner. Everything will be fine.'

Without giving her another chance to speak, he turned on his heel and hurried back.

CHAPTER FORTY-ONE

He typed in the URL for the Lancaster Tavern score-board and waited for the screen to load. Then he moved the cursor to the menu and clicked on the flashing LIVE UPDATE link.

The first fight, Brown vs. Dorking, was over and the judges' scorecards were up on the screen. Five rounds and from the scorecards it was clear that Brown had dominated. The second fight had been stopped early on by the referee because the cut man had been unable to seal the gouge above one of the fighter's eyes. The third fight, Rodriguez vs. Little, was into the final round with two minutes left. Okie was facing the last stretch.

He leant back in his chair and closed his eyes.

Right at this moment Okie's body would be awash in adrenalin and catecholamine, his cerebral cortex alight with electricity. If he had an injury, he would be insensible to the pain. If a spectator shouted abuse at him, he would not hear it. The baying crowd with their open mouths, the white upturned faces of the judges: none of this would register with him. His ears would be filled with the drumbeat of his own heart and JC's commands coming at him as if from a long way away. Maybe his mouth was dry. Maybe he was shaking the sweat from his eyes. Three rounds only. But no one who didn't fight himself could possibly understand how incredibly tiring nine minutes of full contact fighting was. By now, Okie's legs would start moving just a little bit sluggishly and he would have to concentrate just that little bit more on keeping his hands from slipping as fatigue started taking its toll. And on the other side of the punches and kicks slamming into his face and into his body would be the eyes of his opponent. Who could dig the deepest? Who had the greater heart?

He opened his eyes. The screen in front of him had changed. The judge's scorecards were up, 9–10, 9–10, 9–10, in favour of Rodriguez. Okie had lost.

As he logged off, he wondered how long Okie still had to live. Two days, probably. Maybe three.

CHAPTER FORTY-TWO

The dream was back.

She could hear her mother's voice calling her name, leading her hesitant footsteps towards the weak pool of light bleeding into the darkness.

Books all round her but only one book that mattered. *The Book of Light and Dust*. A precious book, this; you knew it from its weight, from the carefully tooled leather. A book of secrets.

Her pulse racing, she opened the first page. And went blind.

Such despair! Her heart slumped and tears ran down her cheeks as she stared into the mirror and found her withered eyes staring back at her, dead and useless. No energy, no life . . .

No! Mia came to with a gasp like a swimmer breaking water. Her eyelids flew open. Her heart was thudding. For a moment she did not recognize her bedroom: rain was pearling against the window and the light inside the room was opalescent.

She touched her fingers to her cheek and realized she had been crying. For a few more moments she continued to lie with her body coiled. Then she swung her feet over the side of the bed, placed her elbows on her knees and propped her head on her hands. She couldn't remember the last time she had felt this miserable.

It was four days after Okie's fight. He was alive and, as far as she could tell, well. But she remained scared. And she still had no idea what was going on.

What would her mother have done? The answer to that was easy: Molly would have stepped out. If a Keeper was in doubt or encountered difficulties, the Retreat was where she headed. But her mother had never encountered a shadowy figure who wanted to kill her.

You die in here. You die out there. Having an OBE was a liberating experience for a Keeper but it had its dangers. Mia was fully aware that it was important not to drift too far away from the body and to return in good time. And many researchers believed there was a reason so many people who experienced OBEs were near to death. If you die inside the alternative realm created by your brain, it might be the signal that your physical body was shutting down as well.

Mia was too frightened to go to the Retreat. It used to be her sanctuary, but her sanctuary had been breached. Who knew who was lurking there, waiting? And how had this man managed to step out with her? How had he managed to access her meditation space? The only person who had ever managed to accompany her to the Retreat was Molly.

Mia reached for her mobile phone and flipped open the

lid. For the hundredth time, she read the final text message:

WE WILL GO ANOTHER ROUND YET: YOU AND ME. KEEPER AND THIEF. BUT FOR OKIE IT'S TOO LATE.

Okie. He was her big worry. But he seemed all right. His pride had been bruised and he was sulking after his loss but he was in fairly good shape. There was a nasty bruise on his cheekbone and despite the protection of the mouth guard he had split his lip, but these injuries could hardly be considered life-threatening.

After the fight, she had apologized to Nick for her strange behaviour. She had experienced a panic attack, she told him. She could see he found her explanation hugely unsatisfactory but what could she say? 'I forgot to mention I'm a Keeper and I lost a fight against an intruder who is threatening Okie'? She could imagine how well that would go down with feet-on-the-ground Nick.

Still, she had made up her mind to tell him everything after his own fight was over. He would probably think her a basket case, but so be it. She was tempted to take him into her confidence right now, but that would not be fair: this was not the time to mess with Nick's focus. His fight was ten days away and he was concentrating on it to the exclusion of anything else – as he should. Their conversation would have to wait. She also knew Nick was still training with Ash and because of that she avoided them both.

Ash. Just thinking about him made her feel lost and confused. But she also longed for him. What was it she really wanted from this man? Unquestionably, she felt sexual desire. When he had kissed her, she had been tempted to give herself over to him completely: for him to do with her as he wanted. She remembered the scent of his skin, the feel of his hands sliding down her back, the taste of his mouth. But then came that moment – black and cold – like a viper's darting tongue, and she had drawn back. Something was wrong.

Ash or Nick . . . The choice should be easy. She loved Nick and when she thought of him her spirits lifted and she felt warmed and nourished in a way that felt right. And Ash? Her heart sagged. With some dreadful inner knowledge that rang completely true, she recognized Ash as her true mate, not Nick.

But her feelings for the two men were of no importance right now. Okie was the only one who mattered: everything else could wait. And so far, so good. Four days had passed since his fight: surely that must mean he was safe?

She might even be overreacting. Maybe the intruder wasn't really dangerous. Maybe he was simply taunting her. It was time for her to stop obsessing and get on with things. And tonight she would make sure to swallow the strongest sleeping pill she could lay her hands on. No creepy dreams allowed: no books with weird titles, no voices calling her.

She was starting to feel better. And as she walked into the kitchen, the rain stopped. She opened the window and a fresh, light breeze blew inside.

She was drinking her second cup of tea when the call from Nick came to tell her Okie had died on the bus on his way to work.

CHAPTER FORTY-THREE

Okie's memorial service felt deeply unreal to Nick. The low-ceilinged, impersonal room where the service was held seemed utterly bland and completely wrong. As he sat there listening to JC reading laboriously from his overworked eulogy, Nick realized that he had always vaguely believed that one day, when his own time came, he would be buried outside where the air was clean and there was a scent of flowers. An old village church-yard maybe, filled with headstones leaning sideways like drunken men.

It was a wistful fantasy. With the shortage of burial space, cremation was becoming the most common form of disposing of the dead. Scenes of mourners congregating round open graves set in bright green grass were rare. These days you were asked to say goodbye in places like this.

The room was packed. Scorpio's members had turned out in full force and the men were trying to do it right: most of them were wearing jackets and ties. The women were dressed in muted colours, except for Claudine Normandy, who was dressed in a scarlet waist-nipping outfit. As he glanced over his shoulder, Nick noticed Ash standing at the door. When he saw Nick looking at him, he inclined his head in a slight nod.

Sitting next to Nick was Mia. Her hand was inside his and it was so cold. Her eyes were fixed on the lectern where Okie's favourite pair of boxing gloves were arranged next to each other. The gloves were an eye-popping yellow – 'dazzling', to use Okie's word. None of your boring run-of-the-mill black or red leather gloves for Okie.

Okie was dead. The thought kept repeating itself in Nick's head like a needle sticking on a scratch in a vinyl record. Okie was dead. The words meant little.

At the front of the room was a big photograph of Okie in his fighting stance, with rounded shoulders and raised fists. Sweat pearled on his dreadlocks. But it was the uncomplicated expression of joy in his eyes that grabbed you: *I am young. I am strong. I am alive*.

And suddenly it hit home for Nick. He would never again walk into the locker room at Scorpio and find Okie, propped up on the bench, eating liquorice and reading *Passion's Harbour*. Never again would he witness the fluid grace of that devastating left hook or smell the nutmeg scent of Okie's skin as they clinched. Okie was dead. The macho swagger, the ready smile, the immense capacity for friendship: all of Okie was gone. For a second the feeling of loss was so complete, Nick found it hard to breathe.

JC stumbled through the last few sentences and then

the service was over and mourners started filing out one by one. Mia excused herself and disappeared into the ladies' room. Nick looked around in search of Ash but he was nowhere to be seen. Nick made a mental note to call his friend later. He needed to fill Ash in on his meeting with JC.

The meeting had been to decide whether Nick's fight should go ahead.

'I'll be straight with you, Nick.' JC's voice was heavy. 'You're not injured. You can make the weight. This is a fight for the Southern Regional belt. If you pull out now, the promoters won't be able to find a suitable opponent for Burton with little more than a week to go. Also, a large number of tickets have already been sold. Frankly, it is doubtful you will ever be allowed another shot at the title.'

Nick nodded. 'I know.'

'But none of this matters. You need to go in there focused. If Okie's death is going to screw you up don't do it, mate. This is a ten-round fight. Lose concentration for one second and Burton will kick your brains in. He's an aggressive bastard.'

Nick nodded again.

'So what's it going to be?'

'I can't quit now.' Nick took a deep breath. 'The fight's on.'

'There's another question.' JC sighed. 'Who do you want in your corner now that Okie . . .'

Nick spoke quickly. 'Ashton.'

'No.' JC shook his head. 'Ash is a great training buddy

but he has no ring experience. I'll ask Dennis. OK with you?'

'Dennis is a good man.'

'Great.' JC slapped him on the shoulder. 'And remember: stay focused, Nick. I mean it.'

Mia was coming towards him. She looked frail, Nick thought. The grey jersey dress she was wearing drained her skin of colour. Only her hair was still a cloud of gold. When she reached him, he noticed her lips were dry and flaky.

He placed a hand on her elbow. 'When was the last time you ate?'

'Oh . . . it doesn't matter.' She drew a tired hand across her eyes. 'I'm not hungry.'

'Before I take you home I'm going to feed you.'

Ignoring her protests, he took her by the hand and started walking. There was a café only a few blocks away, which he had visited once or twice before.

After they had placed their orders, he looked her straight in the face. 'Mia, what's wrong? And I'm not just talking about Okie. This started long before. What's going on?'

Her eyes welled with tears. 'I think . . .' Her voice shook. 'I think I'm responsible for Okie's death.'

'What!'

'Nick,' she touched her lips with trembling fingers, 'I need to tell you something. But I want you to give me time to finish before you start asking questions or telling me how crazy I am. Just hear me out first. All right?'

'OK.' He nodded obediently. But as soon as she started talking, he found it difficult to keep his promise. Once or twice he tried to interrupt but she waved his words away. Even when their food was being served and she had to pause, she would not allow him to jump in. 'Wait. Just wait, Nick. Listen.'

When she had finished it was quiet between them. And now, suddenly, he could think of nothing to say.

'So?' She took a deep breath. 'You're going to tell me I've lost it, right?'

'Let me see if I have this straight. You are a . . . guardian angel . . . to a group of fighters.' She was right. This *was* insane.

'Three fighters. But only one left now. Okie and Valentine are gone. And if Jeff's fight hadn't been cancelled, who knows? He might be dead too.'

'So you believe that because you lost a fight against some Ninja character in your dreams, Okie died.'

'Well, they're not exactly dreams . . . but close enough, yes.'

Nick tried to focus his scattered thoughts. 'Did you fight against this guy before Valentine's death?'

'No.'

'So Valentine's death is not connected to Okie's.'

'I don't know . . .'

'All right. Let's take a step back.' He spoke slowly, picking his words carefully. 'I need to tell you something as well. I've been investigating the deaths of four fighters: they all died a few days after their fights for no apparent

275

reason. I think there's a connection but I don't know what it is. And I think Okie and Valentine's deaths may form part of the pattern. I spoke to Okie's GP, who spoke to the coroner on my behalf. What happened to the others also happened to Okie. His heart stopped. Why? They don't know, but apparently it does happen often enough among athletes – not just boxers – that it doesn't raise eyebrows too much. And because these deaths are scattered and took place over such a long period of time – five years – no one has picked up on any connection. Personally, I think there's monkey business involved. Maybe some kind of secret poison or something. But what's important is that you were not the . . . Keeper . . . to any of these other guys, so I really don't think this has anything to do with you. And I don't know where Ninja man fits in. If he does.'

'You don't believe I actually fought him, do you?'

'You weren't exactly wide awake when it happened, Mia . . .'

She rummaged angrily in her bag. 'Before you make up your mind that I'm insane, I want you to look at this.' She flipped open the mobile phone. 'Read that. These are the text messages I received at the fight.'

WE MET LAST NIGHT AT THE RETREAT, REMEMBER?

'So you see, he knows about the Retreat. How could he know about the Retreat if he wasn't there himself?'

Nick stared at the phone, feeling as though he had woken up inside the *Twilight Zone*.

'Did you try calling this number?'

'Only a few hundred times. No one picks up. And I tried texting as well and no response either.'

'And you have no idea who it is?'

'None.'

'He says he's a thief. Not a killer.'

'But a thief of what? Lives?'

The kitchen door beside them opened with a bang and a waiter narrowly averted bumping into their table. Nick lifted his hand and gestured for the bill. 'We can't talk here. Let's go to my place. I'll show you the stuff I've collected on the other fighters and you can tell me if any of it looks familiar to you.'

They were quiet driving to his flat. It was only five in the afternoon, but already the sun was lowering in the sky. Dry leaves skittered across the tarmac.

When he pushed open the door of his flat, Nick remembered belatedly that the place was not exactly neat.

'Sorry.' He gestured awkwardly at the scattered newspapers on the sofa, the piles of paper on his desk. 'I've been a bit lax with the housekeeping.'

She wasn't paying attention. She was facing the wall, looking at the heavenly map Molly had drawn on the day of his birth: gold-rimmed planets and luminous celestial bodies spinning through a predictable future.

Mia touched her fingers to the frame. 'Do you believe our paths are set?'

He stood behind her and placed his arms round her shoulders. 'No. I believe we shape our own journeys.'

She leant back against him and her hair was fragrant. She felt so soft in his arms. He couldn't help himself, he placed his mouth against her temple and kissed the tendrils of gold that grew there.

She twisted round and looked up at him with dark eyes. Her eyebrows were slightly raised, her lips parted. She looked poised for flight.

Carefully he placed his hands on her shoulders and turned her round so that she faced him fully. He wanted her so badly, but he moved slowly, afraid of startling her. She hadn't drawn away. She was still staring at him with those wide eyes.

He lowered his head and softly, but quite deliberately, placed his mouth on hers.

For a moment her lips lay passively against his, but then she reached out and placed her hand behind his head and leant into his embrace.

Something broke inside him. He made a sound and kissed her hard, forcing her mouth to open up underneath his. It was too desperate; he knew it was. Into that kiss went years of pent-up desire and frustration. He was scaring her with this kiss – it was hungry, far too urgent – but he couldn't help it.

'Wait.' She placed her hand against his chest.

He stopped, breathing hard.

'Your fight.'

'To hell with that.' He leant forward and scooped her

up and she wrapped her arms and legs round him. He carried her into his bedroom, where a late-afternoon sun flashed blood red through the half-closed shutters.

She smelt of flowers and the contours of her collarbone jutted out startlingly prominent below the soft shadow in the hollow of her throat. He pinned her wrists above her head and the skin on the inside of her arms gleamed like silk. Her breasts were small but beautifully formed. Spread across the pillow, her hair was a tangle of dark gold.

Her legs were sprawling open, and the ache in his groin was urging him on. *No. Slow. Slow*. He had waited too long for this moment to rush it now.

He placed his fingers on the inside of her leg. A trailing garland of roses was inked into the pale flesh, starting mid-thigh and reaching all the way up to the crease: soft green tendrils, dusky pink blooms. He brought his head down and his tongue traced their outline. She gasped and her fingers tightened painfully on his shoulders.

When he covered her body with his, she threw her head back so that her throat formed a white arc. Her mouth was half-open and she looked up at him with heavy eyes. He had known this woman for most of his life, but suddenly she seemed almost like a stranger. The touch of girlishness he associated with her was no longer there. She seemed powerful. Elementally female.

Such a strange, wonderful combination of strength and fragility, of innocence and knowledge. Slender, muscled arms and strong, shapely legs. A ribcage that felt as brittle as a bird's. Her skin pale and fair, but on the one side of her body a tattoo: an intriguing shadow. Her eyes were filled with secrets, but her mouth was open and trusting. He entered her, slipping deep, deep inside her, and it felt as warm as the blood pulsing inside his veins; dark as the dusk pressing against the window. She moaned and moved her head on the pillow from side to side.

He turned her over. The bones of her spine were like pebbles and her delicate shoulderblades pressed like fossilized wings against his chest. He lifted the thick hair to expose the defenceless nape of her neck and placed his lips to her burning skin.

She moved slowly, deliberately, underneath him, matching his rhythm, holding him in a melting grip, leading him on until she pushed her face deep into the pillow and arched her back. He cried out, shuddering, and his eyes filled with tears. It felt like birth. It felt like death.

Outside the window, the day finally ended and the sky turned black.

CHAPTER FORTY-FOUR

'She's beautiful.' Nick ran his finger along the delicate figure in blue ink. The lamp on the bedside table threw a pool of light on to Mia's skin.

Mia, propped up on one elbow, looked down at her hip underneath his hand. 'I'm glad you like her. She'll grow old with me.'

'What is this symbol in her eye?'

'The eye is the inner eye, which the Keeper uses to visualize the Retreat. The circle represents chi. The three lines symbolize the bridge by which the Keeper gains access to chi.'

'This whole "stepping out" thing – it's . . .' He paused.

'Weird?'

'Strange,' he amended.

'Did you know that Thomas Edison deliberately induced out-of-body experiences? He'd hold a stone above a bucket while sitting in a chair and letting himself fall asleep. Just before the stone fell and woke him up, he'd have an OBE. He said it helped him solve problems when working on his inventions. For all we know, the idea of electricity came to him while he was floating outside his body, looking down at himself.'

'That's creepy.' Nick shivered.

'Lionheart.'

Nick grinned. 'I still can't believe Okie never told me about you being his Keeper.'

'I asked him not to. He made me a promise.'

'Can I ask you something?'

'Anything.'

'Why did you never offer to be my Keeper?'

'I wanted to.' She paused. 'But I knew, if I did, I would close a door.'

He frowned. 'I don't understand.'

'Keepers are not supposed to have intimate relationships with their charges. Once a Keeper takes a fighter into her keep, the dynamics of the relationship between them changes for ever. It becomes this formalized thing. When Keepers have broken this rule, it has always led to heartache.'

'We did not have an intimate relationship.'

'I know. But I thought one day we might.'

'You did?' He smiled, delighted.

'Yes. But I didn't know if you were up for it.'

'Of course I was up for it.'

She pushed down on her palm and sat up straight. 'No, Nick. You don't understand. Molly and my father had problems because he could never really make peace with the idea that she was a Keeper to these other fighters. He was jealous. Possessive. It created all kinds of trouble between them. I didn't want that for us.'

'And now?'

'Now I will never be your Keeper. Especially not with this maniac running around. If I placed my mark on you it would be like painting a bull's-eye on your heart and turning you into a target.'

'I take it that means I'll be going into the ring unadorned.'

'Nick. Please don't do this fight.'

'JC and I talked about this yesterday. I have to, Mia.'

'Don't do it, Nicky. Please, please, don't do it. We don't know what we're up against. Please!'

'Listen to me . . . No, Mia, don't look away.' He gently turned her face back to him. 'Nothing is going to happen to me. I am probably not even on this guy's radar screen. As you said. I'm not your charge and you're not my Keeper.'

'Apart from Valentine and Okie, those other fighters weren't my charges either.'

'Sweetheart, don't worry. It's going to work out. I'll be on my guard against any strangers from now on. All right? And tomorrow I'm flying to Liverpool to meet Amy face to face. I'm still hoping Valentine had told her something of importance and that she can provide the information we need to crack the puzzle. I promise you, I won't stop looking until I find out what's going on.'

'Nick . . .' Her eyes were wide and held a sheen of tears.

'Shh. It's going to be fine. Come here, let me hold you.' He tried to joke. 'I'm like Rick Cobra. He always beats the bad guy and he always gets the girl.' Pulling Mia down next to him, he drew her into the curve of his body. He placed his arm round her shoulders and held her close.

For a long time they stayed like that, with his body enfolding hers. Her breathing was slowing, he could sense she was falling asleep. He continued to lie with eyes open.

Should he give in to Mia's entreaties and bow out? Everything inside him screamed at this idea. It was his first and possibly only shot at a title. He had worked hard for it. He was due. And he wasn't getting any younger.

For a moment he thought back to when he was a six-year-old boy, receiving his first pair of gloves: a birthday gift from his uncle. That's when it had started for him. Over the years, he had had a lot of flak from others who could not understand his compulsion to fight. While living in New York, he had even given in to the wishes of a girlfriend who had insisted he needed therapy. The therapist had been surprisingly sympathetic. A Freudian, the man had murmured the words *homo homini lupus* — man is a wolf to man — and expounded learnedly on how the 'restrictions of instinct' were at the heart of modern man's depression and feelings of malaise. 'The imperative of violence and domination is hardwired into our genes, Mr Duffy. You see it in the businessman demolishing his rival; in the teenager playing a violent computer game. But we are told to repress the urge. And so we live vicariously through the fighter's experience. It is tactile combat. It gratifies the social machinery in our minds definitively.'

Whether this was true, Nick had no idea. He himself had never felt conflicted about his passion for fighting. If it was a throwback, primitive impulse, so be it. All he knew was that whenever he had tried to ignore it, he had become unhappy. Better, then, to give expression to it within the confines of the ring, where he faced someone of equal stature and skill in a controlled environment.

Mia mumbled something and moved restlessly in his arms. For a moment he thought she was waking up, but then her breath became even again.

He closed his own eyes and tried to relax. Things would turn out all right. After all, he and Mia could take on anything that came their way. Together, who could stop them?

CHAPTER FORTY-FIVE

H e pointed to the pagoda at the end of the avenue of trees. 'Run and touch the first step and then jog back. One last sprint, Nick, and then we're finished. OK? Ready? Go.'

He waited at the gate and watched as Nick drove forward smoothly and powerfully. Even though he had to say so himself, he had done a good job with him.

Nick had reached the pagoda and was now jogging back. He saw Nick's eyes go past him and his face breaking into a smile.

He looked over his shoulder. Mia was standing a few paces behind. How long had she been there? And how surprising that he hadn't sensed her.

Nick ran past him and swept Mia into his arms. He lifted her off the ground and swung her round in a full circle. She gave a small shriek and laughed.

When Nick placed her back on her feet, she glanced up self-consciously. 'Ash, hi.' She was smiling but there was just the hint of uncertainty in her voice.

For a moment he flashed back on the kiss he had given her in the studio. The feel of her tongue moving against his. The warmth of her skin where his hand had lingered at the crease of her blouse. He remembered the rush he felt at the knowledge of her beating heart against his palm, of the meridians of energy flowing cleanly beneath the tips of his fingers.

She cleared her throat. 'How's Nick looking for Saturday?'

'He's going to be unstoppable.'

There was something different about her, he thought. She had bruises under her eyes but they were not shadows left by worry. Her lips, he noticed, were just slightly swollen. Nick was looking down at Mia and the expression in his eyes was veiled, but there was no mistaking the tenderness with which he brushed a tendril of hair from her forehead.

They were lovers. The realization struck him with the force of a blow.

'Ash?'

He looked Nick in the face and for a moment he had difficulty focusing. 'Yes?'

'I've got to dash. I have a plane to catch.'

'Oh?'

'Work. But I'll be back later tonight. And we'll meet up at the dojo tomorrow morning. Final spar before the fight, right?'

'Yes.' He looked away from Nick to Mia. 'You still need to finish my tattoo.'

'I know.' Her eyes slid away from his. 'Let's plan on doing that after the fight.'

'OK.'

He watched them walk away down the lane with its russet-coloured trees. Mia was wearing a long dress in some kind of pale, floaty material, her waist cinched by a big leather belt. She was talking to Nick and her face was tilted up to his. Nick had one arm round her shoulders, his head bent down to listen. The effect was as determinedly romantic as a Kodak moment.

He closed his eyes. He had a blinding headache.

CHAPTER FORTY-SIX

After Nick had left for Liverpool, Mia felt restless. Even though it was a typical autumn day with muted sunlight, the air felt suffocating and oppressive. The day passed slowly. In fact, it was so quiet in the studio that she and Lisa decided to close shop early. Hoping to escape the sense of foreboding, Mia headed for Scorpio.

On the front desk was a photograph of Okie and a black ribbon trailing across it. The atmosphere inside the dojo was subdued. Someone laughed and then checked himself abruptly.

She trained hard for an hour but the feeling of serenity that usually followed after a demanding workout was proving elusive. As she stood at the water cooler, drinking from a plastic cup, someone touched her elbow. It was Chilli.

Chilli was half Portuguese, half Japanese, and had been her sensei since she was a little girl. But as she looked at his narrow, clever face, she realized again how little she knew about him. He was divorced and had a daughter and a son who lived with their mother in Portugal; that much she knew. But whether he was close to his children she had no idea. She had never even met them. Still, Chilli had been a part of her life for as long as she could remember. He was her martial-arts mentor in the most important sense of the word, helping her in her search for the way – *do*. She and Chilli might not ever have spent much time exchanging personal information, but he was her sensei and she was his student and this was a profound relationship.

For a few minutes they stood silently side by side, watching the fighters and trainers at work – this small, tight-knit world with its rivalries and camaraderies – and, as always, Chilli's presence had a calming effect on her.

There was a sudden shout at the far side of the dojo where a sparring bout was taking place and one of the fighters held his hand up against his nose, blood spurting crimson between his fingers.

'You must sometimes find this very odd, Chilli.'

He inclined his head enquiringly.

She gestured at the injured man. 'The idea that you have to injure your body in pursuit of excellence. What you teach is so different.'

'I teach martial arts, not fine arts.' His voice was mild. 'A sword is beautiful to look at but it is still a sword. It is made for combat. I've told you that often enough.'

'I know, but we practise *budo*. We strive for refinement of the spirit.'

'*Budo* is not an abstraction, Mia. Searching for the way is a physical thing. The fighting applications I teach you are real.'

His eyes travelled back to the injured fighter who was now allowing his bloody nose to be tended to by his sparring partner, who was making clucking noises like a worried hen.

'That's not my way, you're right. That's his way. But it, too, is valid. That man there knows what it feels like to confront his fears. In some ways he manages easily what you and I strive for through thousands of hours of practice: he goes directly to the goal. He lives now, he feels now. His experience is not filtered through the constant internal dialogue we have going on inside our minds. It is immediate.'

He looked back at her. 'By this time the fighting applications I have taught you are hardwired into your bones and your brain. If you are ever called to do so, you will be able to draw on them like a warrior draws his sword. No, you will become the sword.'

Mia didn't answer. In her mind came the memory of a man dressed in black, throwing her to the ground, placing his hands on her, leaving her terrified and helpless.

Chilli tapped her lightly on the arm. 'You should take a shower before you cool down.'

'I will.' She bowed to him.

He nodded and returned her bow. She watched as he moved away from her with a fluid shuffle that made it seem as though his feet barely touched the ground.

In the dressing room, Mia removed her gym bag from the locker and checked her mobile phone. She had one missed call: it was from Nick. The message was brief. He had seen Amy but didn't have much to report and was now heading for John Lennon Airport. He would call her when he arrived at Gatwick. She tried to return the call but only received his voice mail.

Well, no matter, she would see him in a few hours. Time for her to head home.

By the time she reached her house, the dusk had settled decisively into darkness. Mia turned the key and opened the front door. As she stepped inside, she stopped. Something was wrong. She couldn't say what it was, but the feeling was acute. She was sensing . . . rage?

Switching on the light in the lobby, she stood for a moment, listening. It was very quiet inside the house. The dark square of the door leading to the studio was to her right. It stood ajar. She was almost sure it had been fully open when she had left the house earlier in the day.

She took a few steps forward and placed her hand against the door and it opened silently. The light coming from behind her in the lobby cut into the dark studio and fell across the wooden floor in a sharply edged wedge shape.

The studio was empty. At the window the lace curtain billowed as a breeze pushed against it. The top page of the open appointment book flipped over lazily, as though touched by a ghostly hand.

Had she left the window open? She sometimes would: across the studio windows there were bars that kept out intruders. But had she done so today?

The window was almost closed, but not quite. As she stretched out her hand to the latch, she stopped. There was something stuck between the frame and the window but in the uncertain light she couldn't make out what it was. She brought her head down closer.

Sweetpea's body was squashed in the middle, her soft stomach creased grotesquely. The edge of the window had slammed into her side and had pinned her there. Her eyes were dead.

Oh, God. Mia brought her hand up to her mouth. Oh, God.

In the pocket of her jacket, her mobile pinged.

Her eyes still on Sweetpea, she fumbled with clumsy hands.

YOU FAILED OKIE. WILL YOU FAIL NICK?

CHAPTER FORTY-SEVEN

YOU FAILED OKIE. WILL YOU FAIL NICK?

Nick grimaced as he read the text on Mia's mobile phone. He had to admit, this was creepy.

Mia's eyes were fixed on the shoebox in which she had placed Sweetpea's body. 'Read the next message.' Her voice was thin. 'I asked him who he was and what he wanted.'

Nick placed his finger on the scroll button and clicked on the next entry.

MY NAME IS DRAGONFLY. I'LL BE WAITING FOR YOU AT THE RETREAT.

Dragonfly. Nick frowned. 'Can I use your computer?'

She gestured listlessly at the laptop. 'Why?'

'There's this member who leaves regular posts on the Kime discussion board. He calls himself Dragonfly. What are the chances this is him?'

Nick logged in and typed Dragonfly into the Kime search box. The screen blinked and opened on to Dragonfly's profile page.

It was still incomplete. It showed only the Chinese ideograms that identified Dragonfly's call sign and some bare bones personal information. Dragonfly was male. He was based in London. No age. No hobbies. He listed no musical preferences or favourite TV shows. He didn't give the name of his gym. Under fighting styles, he had entered 'Various'. He could just as easily be a cage fighter as a t'ai chi practitioner.

Mia placed her hand on Nick's shoulder and leant forward. 'I've seen those ideograms before.'

'Really?' Nick peered at the Chinese characters. 'These things always look the same to me. Do you know what they mean?'

'No. And often they look the same to me too . . . but every second vogue who comes in here wants one, so my eye is probably more attuned than yours.' She made a frustrated movement with her hand. 'I know I've seen these. I just can't think where.'

'So this could be our man.'

'And he was inside my house.'

Nick glanced at the shoebox and then quickly away again. 'Sweetpea's death could be an accident, Mia. The wind could have blown the window shut at exactly the wrong moment.'

'No.' She shook her head vehemently. 'I always make sure to tighten the latch very firmly on every window in the house – exactly because I was worried about something like this happening. And Sweetpea never stepped outside the sill. She just didn't.'

'Well, that's settled. We're getting you new locks tomorrow.'

'What's settled is that you're not fighting on Saturday.'

'OK, wait. Hold on—'

'Nick. The fight is three days away.' Her eyes were desperate. 'Don't be stupid.'

'Mia, just don't go to the ... Retreat ... or whatever exactly it is you do.'

'Don't you understand? He has targeted you!'

He placed his hands on her shoulders and looked into her eyes. 'Tomorrow is my last training session with Ash and JC. After that it is down time for me until the fight. Let me finish my training and then I'll concentrate on this, OK? And we'll figure it out. Together.'

'I'm scared.'

'Don't be.' He pulled her towards him.

'I can't lose you.'

He pressed his lips to her forehead. 'You won't.'

CHAPTER FORTY-EIGHT

Mia scrolled down the Kime discussion board. She was systematically reading every one of Dragonfly's posts, from his last to his first.

It was the custom among certain warrior tribes in Africa to eat the heart of a vanquished opponent in the hope of making the fallen warrior's courage their own. Eat his heart and his energy becomes yours ... Only warriors with indomitable spirit would be accorded this honour ...

Mia grimaced. If she had wondered if the writer was really the man they were looking for, she was no longer doubtful: this was him. And wasn't the name Dragonfly appropriate. She still remembered what Ash had told her about these insects. The ultimate predators, he had called them. Both lethal and beautiful.

Ash ... And suddenly she knew where she had seen those ideograms before.

In her mind's eye she is standing in the men's locker room at Scorpio. The cement floor shows damp footprints. Her breathing is furtive. She is watching a man: water is running down his lean body. Mingled with the admiration she feels for his physical beauty is the sense that something is happening – that this is a defining moment – which as yet eludes her understanding.

Until now.

Dragonfly. She knew who he was.

When she stretched out her hand to the phone, she noticed her fingers were trembling.

The door of Okie's locker stood open. It had not yet been assigned to someone else. Nick closed it gently.

'Good luck on Saturday, mate.' Dirk Dubois, another fighter, slapped him against the shoulder.

'Thanks.'

'Remember: no surrender, no retreat.' It was the fighter's mantra.

'You've got it.' Nick gathered up his shin-pads and gloves. It felt strange to think this would be his last training session. The next two days would be complete rest. On Saturday he would step into the ring and hope the sweat and concentration of the last three months would see him through.

As he walked out of the door and into the corridor leading to the dojo, he heard, faintly, the sound of his mobile going off inside his own locker. He had recently decided to change the tune from 'Eye of the Tiger' – the ring tone of choice for most fighters, which made things difficult when you were trying to determine whether it was your own phone ringing or that of one of the ten other guys who were also reaching for their mobile – to a rooster's crow. No mistake: it was definitely his phone that was ringing.

He hesitated. But he was already running late. Whoever it was would have to leave a message. He continued walking.

JC and Ash were waiting for him at the far side of the dojo.

Ash grinned at him. 'Closing orders, Mr Duffy.'

'You bet.' Nick smiled back.

'Three rounds of fists, followed by two rounds of groundwork?' Ash turned to JC for approval.

'Right.' JC nodded. 'But take it easy with Nick, especially on the mat. Lay off those armlocks. We need him in prime shape.'

'One prime fighter coming up.'

Nick closed the Velcro strap of his glove with his teeth and opened his mouth so JC could slip in his mouth guard. He turned to face Ash and said the words he had repeated so often over the past three months: 'Let's rock.'

Nick wasn't picking up his phone. Every time she called, Mia got his voice-mail message. And no one was picking up at the office either. She wasn't quite sure at what time Nick was training today but maybe she should head over to Scorpio and see if he was there.

She hesitated. One more time. She'd try one more time and then go and look for him.

Nick pulled off his head guard and Ash followed suit. They hugged, their arms slippery with sweat.

'Thanks.' Nick felt emotional. 'Thank you for everything, Ash.'

'Thanks for allowing me to go along for the ride.' Ash smiled. 'I live through you vicariously, you know.'

Some of the other fighters were coming up to Nick to wish him good luck. As he shook hands and traded friendly abuse, Nick thought how this was the best moment. He was in his fighting home, surrounded by mates who had watched him make the journey. His nerves were rock steady and he felt invincible. Another two days from now and it would be a different story, but right now it couldn't get any better.

His mood crashed the moment he opened his locker and took out his mobile phone. Twelve missed calls: all from Mia. Bloody hell, something must be seriously wrong. His heart beating fast, he pressed the reply button. The relief when he heard her voice was overwhelming.

'Are you all right?'

'I was just on my way over.' Her voice sounded unnaturally high. 'Get out of there. It's him.'

Nick was struggling to hear over the shouts of laughter and the sound of water running in the showers. 'Him? Who?'

'Ash. Ash is Dragonfly.'

'What are you talking about?' Nick looked over at Ash, who was rummaging inside his own bag.

'I remember where I saw those ideograms. They're tattoos. They're on his skin.'

'The ones you gave him?'

'No.'

He glanced at Ash again. 'Where are they then?'

A pause. 'On his bum.'

'Oh.' What he wanted to ask was how Mia knew the guy had a tat on his arse. Come to think of it, he himself had never had a glimpse of Ash's backside despite the fact that they had trained together for three months and had shared this changing room more times than he could remember.

'I'll explain later, Nicky. Just get out of there.'

'I'm on my way.'

He looked up to see Ash watching him. 'Everything OK?'

'Yes. Everything's fine.' He forced himself to keep his voice casual. 'So I'll see you at the fight.'

'I'll be there.'

'OK.' Nick nodded again and smiled as though he did not have a care in the world.

Once inside his car, he took out his phone again and dialled Coach Driver – Bill Muso's trainer in Edinburgh.

Coach Driver sounded rushed and Nick got straight to the point. 'Muso's training buddy. You said they were close.'

'Very much so. As I told you, the man left after Bill's death. He was that upset.'

'What was his name?'

'Robert. Robert Dell.'

'Oh.' Nick frowned.

'Anything else?'

'Could you describe him for me?'

'Tall guy. Fair-haired. Not bad-looking. Fit as hell.'

'And you don't know where I can find him?'

'Sorry.'

The next call Nick made was to Amy. As he listened to the phone ringing, he braced himself. When he had left her in Liverpool yesterday, she had been teary-eyed.

But she sounded more composed today and her voice lightened when he asked her if Valentine had worked with a training buddy for the last fight.

'Yes, he did. Chris and Valentine were really close, you know. Brothers.'

'Chris?'

'Yes. Chris Connor.'

'Is he still around?'

'No.' He heard her sigh. 'He just . . . left. I never heard from him again.'

'Was he blond, good-looking?'

'Yes, that's right. All my friends were drooling over him. You know . . .' She hesitated. 'You asked me about Mia, yesterday. Remember?'

He did indeed. It had been a calculated risk. He had worried how Amy would react to Mia's name but he had wanted to know exactly what Valentine had told her.

'Remember you asked me why Valentine hadn't told Mia he was fighting again?'

'Yes. You said you told him not to. Gave him an ultimatum.'

'I did. But Chris had a lot to do with it as well. He

warned Valentine that superstition has no place in a fighter's heart. That a fighter has to believe in his own abilities, not in some woman protecting him. A fighter has to make his own luck, he said.'

'I see.'

'Chris was right, wasn't he?'

Nick made a non-committal sound.

'Because after you left yesterday, I couldn't help thinking that we were wrong. We shouldn't have stopped him from telling her. It couldn't have hurt, could it?'

CHAPTER FORTY-NINE

It was raining: a quiet, insidious rain that misted her hair and silvered her raincoat. A fragrant hush hung over the street and she could smell the moisture in the air and the muddy scent of wet soil. A few houses in the street had light coming from the windows.

Mia moved from one leg to the other. She had been waiting for almost an hour. There was a bench only a few paces away but she did not want to run the risk of missing him. From here she had a clear view of the front door of the white stucco building with its wrought-ironwork and graceful pillars.

Ash had never invited her or Nick to his flat and it had never occurred to her that this might be unusual. When the three of them were together, they had somehow always gravitated to her place. Ash's apartment was less than three miles from her studio, but a world away. This was an upscale street in an upscale neighbourhood: quiet, green, plush. From here you could see the dome of the Albert Hall.

She glanced at her watch. He should have left by now. JC had a boxing class every Friday night at six and

Ash was a regular. But it was already a quarter to the hour.

A man and a woman walked past her. The woman was trying to worm her hand through the man's arm and the set of her head spoke of an eagerness to please. His spine remained rigid. The woman turned her head and looked into Mia's eyes. The subdued desperation of her gaze stayed with Mia as the couple walked away from her, disappearing round the corner.

The rain sifted down. The street remained empty. She glanced at her watch again. By this time Nick would have arrived at the sleep clinic at Exmare. It had come as a surprise to them that Ash had told Nick the truth about his former job. After all the aliases he had used they had fully expected the name Adrian Ashton to be fake and the details he had given them about his life as a researcher to be bogus as well. But no: Adrian Ashton had indeed worked at the Exmare Institute. Nick had spoken to one of Ash's former colleagues and she had agreed to meet him.

'Do you think it's worth talking to this woman?' Mia was dubious. 'She has nothing to do with fighting.'

Nick shook his head. 'I want to see where Ash worked and I want to talk to the people he worked with. He left under a cloud – he admitted as much. I want to know why.'

He grimaced suddenly and placed a hand on his back.

'What's wrong?' Mia looked at him apprehensively.

'I think I may have pulled a muscle when I grappled with the bastard yesterday.' Nick moved his shoulders. 'It's nothing, don't worry. It won't slow me up for the fight.'

Before he left, he hugged her hard. 'Stay safe, OK?'
'I will.'
'Don't do anything stupid. Keep away from Ash.'
'Yes.'

And she hadn't lied to Nick, she thought. She wasn't going near Ash. She was only going to take a look round his apartment.

The door opened and suddenly he was standing on the doorstep. Her stomach tightened. He was dressed casually in jeans and a dark all-weather jacket, and in his hand he carried a gym bag. His dark-blond hair was slightly tousled. He looked up and down the street and then turned left towards the Brompton Road.

She waited until he had fully disappeared from view before walking swiftly down the street. She had planned on pushing all the buttons at the door until someone buzzed her in – when people heard a female voice and saw an unthreatening woman on the spy camera they tended not to worry too much – but she got lucky. As she approached the front door it opened and a nanny and her charge emerged. The little boy had a bright-red umbrella, and Wellingtons that seemed too big for him. Mia held the door open for the nanny, who was struggling with a pram, and the woman thanked her.

There were five names listed next to the intercom. Adrian Ashton was in flat 4. Mia slipped into the building and the ornate door swung silently shut behind her.

It was dead quiet inside. An old-fashioned iron lift sat motionless on the ground floor, its doors open, but

Mia decided to use the stairs. They were carpeted in russet-gold and flanked by a highly polished and very elaborate banister. Light sconces lined the cream walls.

She walked slowly up the stairs, the thick carpet deadening her steps. There seemed to be only one apartment on every floor. On the landing leading to the fourth floor, she stopped for a moment and looked out of the window, feeling strangely removed from the textureless, slippery world outside. The pewter-coloured sky had turned a luminescent white. In the street below, the trees with their wet barks gleamed black.

She had noticed that Ash carried only one key on his key ring and it was no surprise, therefore, that the door leading to flat 4 showed only one lock. If it had been a Bramah lock, she would have had to turn round and go back. But it was nothing as ambitious. Danny had taught her how to do this one, eyes closed.

Danny Bright was a former client who had done time for burglary. Upon his release he vowed to turn over a new leaf and decided to get a tattoo to celebrate this life-changing decision. As he was low on funds, and unable to pay her, he had offered to teach her how to pick locks instead. She had agreed because it was sort of a cool skill to have. Today that skill was going to be essential.

Before she took out the pouch with picks from her pocket – a graduation present from Danny – she looked up at the ceiling to see if there were any security cameras. There were none.

She started working on the lock, forcing herself to stay

calm and not to rush. It was all to do with breathing and touch. If she became anxious, she'd lose it. Without warning, the door gave under the pressure of her hand. She stepped across the threshold, allowing the door to click shut behind her.

He had left the lamp on his desk burning and the light showed a room of elegant proportions. Tall sash windows looked out on to the street and the ceilings were high and airy. At the end of the passage leading off to her right she could see the edge of a bed peeping out from behind a door.

She stepped more fully into the living room. It was sparsely but luxuriously furnished in shades of charcoal-grey and moss-green. A deep leather sofa faced a fireplace that was filled with tubs of white hydrangeas. In front of one of the windows stood a highly polished knee-hole desk and on its gleaming surface was a closed laptop.

And there were books: one entire wall lined with tightly packed volumes. She tilted her head sideways to read some of the titles. Mixed in with books with in-explicable names like *Superconductivity at Room Temperature without Cooper Pairs* were books written in Chinese, the lettering delicate and mysterious. They were probably medical textbooks because when she opened them she saw they were filled with anatomical illustrations. There were also other, older books with weathered covers. Again, she wasn't able to read the text but she was almost sure she knew what they were. They were *bugei*, books on the warrior arts. They would contain information on fighting techniques that had largely disappeared over time – dropped from martial-arts styles because they were deemed too dangerous. She slipped one of the books from the shelves and touched the pages in awe.

There were several paintings on the walls but it was the exquisite gold, turquoise and red colours of a scroll painting that drew her attention. The scroll depicted monks with their heads slanted meekly sitting opposite a rotund, almond-eyed Buddha. She did not understand the symbolism of this particular scene but she knew what she was looking at. It was a Thangka painting. Travelling Tibetan monks used to roll them up and take them on their journeys as meditation tools. This one seemed to have something to do with medicine and healing. At the bottom of the frame were the words 'Mentsekhang/Lhasa' engraved in gold. But what made Mia's skin prickle was that Keepers used to carry these scrolls with them as well. An almost identical Thangka painting hung in one of the rooms inside the Retreat.

It did not feel like the home of a murderer. This was the home of an educated man with a sense of beauty. What exactly she had thought to find in Ash's apartment, she wasn't sure: she could only hope she would recognize it when she saw it. The man was a killer – but how did he kill? Somewhere in his home where he lived and felt safe, there should be something that would betray his secret.

The computer was of no use. When she switched it on,

her way was immediately barred by a password prompt and she had no choice but to log off again. But on the desk, next to the laptop, was a large, leather-bound portfolio trimmed with red stitching. The leather was creased and smudged as though it had absorbed the oils from many fingers over many years. She unhooked the leather thong that secured the two leaves and opened it.

She drew in her breath. The folder was filled with photographs of dead people: mummies, to be exact. The pictures were deeply unsettling – dried, monkey faces and once-plump bodies shrunk to skin, bone and left-over muscle. Some of the figures seemed racked with hilarity: bent over as if paralysed with laughter and teeth showing in grotesque smiles. Other corpses stared straight ahead, their mouths open and screaming.

And there were so many of them. She paged through the glossy pictures. One of the photographs was a long, wide-angled shot showing rows upon rows of bodies lining the walls, stretching into a far distance. How many bodies? There must have been thousands.

The very last picture in the folder was of a little girl who was sleeping. Her heart-shaped face was innocent and peaceful and the picture seemed completely out of place in this catalogue of horror. It was only when Mia looked closer that she realized she was looking at yet another mummified corpse. At the bottom of the picture was a label with the words 'Rosalia Lombardo, 1920'.

Rosalia. Such a pretty, feminine name. It fluttered in her mind – a tantalizing memory. Ash saying, '*The person who is responsible for who I am today is a girl. Her name is Rosalia.'* She had looked at him, not understanding, and he had smiled. *'Maybe I'll tell you about her someday.'*

He never had.

Mia stared at the picture of Rosalia Lombardo, a little girl who had inspired a man to become a killer, and she wondered why.

A hushed shuffle of footsteps sounded outside the door. Mia looked up sharply. There was another soft sound, as if a bag was dropped on to the thick carpet, and then came the unmistakable sound of a key inserted into the keyhole.

There was no place to hide in the living room. Without thinking, Mia slammed the folder shut and sprinted down the narrow corridor. From her peripheral vision she noticed a galley-sized kitchen and a bathroom leading off to her left. But she wanted to get as far away from the living room as possible. As she dashed into the bedroom at the very end of the passage, the front door started to open inwards.

There were only two obvious hiding places in here: inside the cupboard or behind the door. The cupboard was unknown territory and the last thing she wanted to do was to fight her way through jackets and shoes. She slipped behind the bedroom door and stood stock still.

The front door clicked shut. She heard the silver sound of a key dropped into a bowl, then quiet.

She was thinking furiously. Had she left any traces of her presence in the living room? She had switched off the laptop and closed it. The leather folder with pictures was probably not in exactly the same spot where he had left it, but near enough to make no difference. What else?

She went cold. The book on the lost warrior arts. She had not replaced it. She had left it on the seat of an upholstered chair next to the bookshelf so that she could have a last look at it before she left.

It was quiet. But after a few moments she heard another sound: he was at the desk and had switched on the computer. The sound she had heard was the opening sequence for Windows. Then came the light, irregular tap of computer keys.

The drumbeat of her heart was loud in her ears but she forced herself to calm down. If she kept giving off distress signals he would sense her presence. What she needed to do was to empty her mind and shut him out of her thoughts. Lifting her eyes, she looked out of the window on the opposite side of the room and recentred her focus.

The sky had turned to black. The leaves of a creeper brushed wetly against the pane. How long she stood there, she did not know. It was dark inside the room and the soft wash of light from the living room was far too faint for her to make out the time on her watch. But as she waited, the rain outside became sharper, drumming against the window, and the creeper shook in the wind. The room was filled with substantial shadows. She could identify the shape of a chair, and on the windowsill – black against the lesser blackness of the sky – was a vase, its lines as graceful as a woman's hips. On the bedside table stood a framed photograph, but in the gloom she was unable to see the picture inside.

Still she waited. Suddenly, the tap of keys stopped. A rustle of paper and then he was coming towards the bedroom. He had switched on the light in the passage and a burst of electric light spilt brightly into the bedroom. The photograph inside the frame on top of the bedside table was suddenly clearly visible and with a shock she realized she was looking at a picture of herself.

Just as his shadow fell over the threshold, the phone started ringing. He made a small noise under his breath — a soft, slightly annoyed puff of air — and she sensed him moving away. The ringing stopped and she heard his voice but the words were indistinct.

Her eyes were fixed on the picture in the frame. She had never seen it before: it had been taken without her knowledge. It was a close-up shot, he must have used a long-lens camera, and the photograph showed her in three-quarter profile. She was smiling and her one hand was brushing away the hair from her face. By some trick of light, it looked as though her hair was aglow — pure gold — and even her body seemed to shimmer round the edges. Her eyes seemed serene. She looked happy.

The sound of his voice stopped and her stomach clenched. But instead of walking into the bedroom, she heard him go into the bathroom, shutting the door firmly behind him.

She did not wait. Blessing the carpet for its

sound-deadening qualities, she forced herself to walk, not run, down the passage and into the living room. The book was where she had left it. She slid it back on to the shelf and made a beeline for the front door. With agonizing slowness, she opened the door and eased it shut behind her, trying to minimize the sound of the click. And then she was running, running down the stairs, out of the front door and into the black night and the rain and the wind.

On the opposite side of the street she stopped and turned round. Her eyes travelled up the side of the building to the graceful windows on the fourth floor. From here she could see the side of the bookcase and the Thangka scroll, its colours glowing like jewels. She stood there, half expecting to see his tall figure appear framed inside the window and silhouetted against the light. But the window remained empty and after a while she turned her back on it and started walking.

CHAPTER FIFTY

Alexa Longford was a good-looking, middle-aged woman whose hair was maybe dyed just a bit too red and who was relying a little too much on her Botox treatments. When she smiled at Nick, her expression stayed strangely enigmatic.

'What is it you do here exactly?' Nick asked as they walked to her office, passing by laboratories and messy work cubicles.

She gestured vaguely. 'The Exmare Institute is devoted to the study of chronobiology in general, but here, in this particular wing, we deal with sleep cycles. We're especially interested in how sleep patterns may be linked to disease.' She looked at Nick, her eyebrows raised. 'Nighttime can be perilous, you know.'

'In what way?'

'It's as though the body goes overboard as it tries to defend itself. Fevers spike because the body escalates its defences during darkness and this can lead to inflammation. Another example is the body closing down its airways at night. This keeps out foreign intruders but, as you can imagine, is very dangerous for people with breathing problems, which is why so many asthmatics die at nighttime. Most heart attacks and strokes take place in the early morning, but they brew at night. Why? We're trying to find out if some of these incidents correlate with sleep cycles.'

Nick glimpsed a long, hospital-like corridor through a glass-panelled door. The door had a big forbidding 'Keep Out' sign prominently displayed.

Longford noticed his interest. 'In there we run a lucid dreaming programme where we teach people how to take control of their dreams. Give them the ability to dream the dreams they want to, in effect.'

'That's possible?'

'Oh, yes. Stephen LaBerge managed to induce lucid dreaming under laboratory conditions at Stanford University in the eighties. Many psychotherapists now teach lucid dreaming to their patients as a way of helping them deal with past traumas.'

She suddenly turned a corner and gestured to an open doorway. 'In here.' Nick stepped into an office that was decorated in the determinedly feminine colours of peach and powder pink.

After they had both sat down, she said, 'You said you're a journalist and that you're doing an article on Adrian Ashton.'

'Yes. Thank you for agreeing to talk to me about him.'

'I'd rather you talked to me than some of the other people round here. He was not universally loved.'

'I gathered that. Did you know him well?'

316

'We were colleagues, as well as friends.'

'What did you think of him?'

'A brilliant mind. Absolutely first-rate.'

'I detect a "but" in your voice.'

Longford didn't answer. Pushing a stack of papers neatly to one side of her desk, she said, 'What exactly is it you want to know about Ash, Mr Duffy?'

'What was he working on? Why did he leave here on bad terms?'

'The answer to those two things are probably one and the same.' Longford paused. 'Mr Duffy, before we go on, you have to understand one thing. We're a research facility and the people who work here are scientists. We're supposed to explore new horizons. But the scientific community is not a lenient one and protocols are rigid. On the one hand, a good scientist is open to anything that comes his way. On the other hand, he should be ruthless about not giving credence to superstition and quackery. Science protects itself by sometimes weeding out new ideas that should probably have been allowed to flourish but, because they deviate so much from the wisdom of the great white fathers, they get rejected. Crucially, they don't get the grants they need.'

'The great white fathers?'

'Newton. Descartes. Darwin. Einstein. De Broglie. Schrödinger. Even in the twenty-first century, their laws and insights still rule the world of biology and classical physics. None of them ever questioned Descartes's edict that soul, mind and body are separate. But there are

Natasha Mostert

scientists out there who disagree. Ash was one of them. Some of his own ideas also jettisoned many of the sacred tenets of Western medicine. That never goes down well with your peers.'

'Did you agree with his ideas?'

'Truthfully? I don't know. But let me put it to you this way: Western medicine is a powerful tool for healing. But it still has not discovered the body's master computer. We know a great deal about the nuts and bolts of the body – bones, blood, enzymes, hormones. We value the brain and the heart above all else. But Western medicine has yet to discover the key to life itself. We still don't know why we fall ill. How we think. Why your pinkie develops as a finger and your big toe as a toe even though they share the same genes and proteins. How one cell becomes a fully developed human being. What happens to our consciousness when our bodies die. In other words: what is the organizing principle of it all.'

'And Ashton thought he knew?'

'He did.'

'He thought it was chi?'

'Yes. And he was obsessed with gaining physical control of it. Ash was inspired by Robert Becker's research on energy medicine and Fritz Albert Popp's experiments on biophoton emissions coming from humans. One of the things Popp studied was what kind of light is present in a person who is severely ill – like cancer patients – and in each instance he found that the biophoton emissions were off. They had lost their natural periodic rhythms and coherence. You can imagine the implications this might have for the field of medicine.'

'And Ashton?'

'Ash was fascinated by Popp's studies. Machines have been built that can measure human light emissions, you know, and Ash had his own light emissions studied and his periodic rhythms established. He called them his energy numbers, if I remember correctly. He spent years on this.'

'And?' Nick prodded.

'Well, what excited Ash in particular was that when Popp ran his tests on volunteers, he noted that their light emissions could be correlated by day and night and by week and by month – as though the body followed not only its own biorhythms, but also those of the world. Ash was excited. He interpreted Popp's research as our energy being in sync with the energy of the world around us. Being Ash, of course, he took the even more extreme view that this energy can be controlled and exchanged.'

'Exchanged? I don't follow.'

Longford cocked her head and looked at him quizzically. 'Ash believed that people can exchange their chi. Your energy can influence mine and my energy can influence yours – for better or for worse.'

'That sounds very New Age.'

'Ash looked at it scientifically. His theory was that we are all receivers and transmitters of energy in a quantum world.'

'Oh . . . right.'

She smiled faintly. 'According to quantum physics,

once subatomic waves or particles are in contact with each other, the actions of one will always have an impact on the actions of the other one. It doesn't matter if they separate and it doesn't matter how far they go in different directions. Physicists found this very upsetting at first, you understand. Even Einstein did not like this long-distance communication – he called it 'spooky'. But it has been verified numerous times: the universe has memory. We most certainly *do* live in an interconnected universe.'

Nick frowned. 'I'm sorry, I don't understand how this relates to people actually being able to exchange their energy with one another.'

Longford sighed. 'Well, this is where Ash broke ranks with other scientists and why his work was so contro-versial. Quantum physics, as it is understood today, is considered only relevant to dead matter at the micro scale . . . and definitely not to human bodies and consciousness. Ashton believed studies such as those by Popp demon-strate otherwise. He was convinced that our bodies also operate according to the laws of the quantum world. Why, he asked, should quantum physics only affect the small and the inanimate and not the large and the living? If the particles from which we are made exchange energy and retain memories, why would there be no con-sequences at the macro scale?' Longford looked at Nick as though expecting a response.

'And this put him at loggerheads with his colleagues?'

'Well, yes. Ash insisted that quantum theory could also be applied to biology: that human beings are a network of energy fields that interact with our chemical cellular systems. But what really set the cat among the pigeons was Ash's insistence that we are all plugged into a vast psi-space called the Zero Point Field, which allows us to interact and exchange our energy, even our consciousness.'

Nick said slowly, 'I can see that this idea might have created problems for him.'

'It was bad enough that Ash was going round saying quantum physics has effects in a single human being,' Longford continued. 'Imagine his colleagues' reaction when he suggested connections *between* humans.'

'Do you believe in the Zero Point Field yourself?'

'Of course.' Longford nodded emphatically. 'The Field itself is not a controversial concept. It is simply empty space – like the space between the stars.' Longford motioned vaguely in the direction of the ceiling. 'It is space with the lowest possible energy reading: almost nothing – only half a photon. But there are so many of these tiny electromagnetic fields that what people think of as an empty vacuum is really one infinitely large space filled with energy. Where Ash goes off the rails, according to his peers, is his insistence that the Zero Point Field provides the scientific explanation for chi and its link to human consciousness and the light shining from our own bodies. Chi, after all, is described by the Chinese as the energy of the universe, connecting to the energy within us. Just as the Zero Point Field is all-pervasive, so chi is all-pervasive. Ash even insisted that the Zero Point Field could explain paranormal activities like remote viewing and remote healing.'

Remote healing. Nick blinked.

'Mr Duffy?'

'I have a friend who . . . claims . . . to be a long-distance healer. She believes she can use her own vital energy to protect another person.'

Longford's gaze was keen. 'Ash would have been very interested in your friend. Ash believed there are those among us who are intuitives – people who have a great natural ability to tap into the psi-space. He called them gifted innocents. But even though these are individuals who are blessed with extraordinarily strong chi, Ash believed we all have this ability lying dormant within us.'

'Do you?'

She shrugged. 'Who knows? During the Aids epidemic in the eighties, a highly respected professional, Dr Elisabeth Targ, asked forty remote healers across the United States to take part in a study and they managed to improve the health of terminally ill patients – without ever being in contact with those patients. How to explain that study and many others like it? When you start thinking about these studies, then Ash's explanation that we are all receivers and transmitters of energy in a quantum world becomes compelling.'

'So Ash got into trouble because of his theories about psi-space.'

'And for claiming to have discovered a way to access it.'

'How?'

'Through dreams and meditation. What's more, he claimed he had managed to pull it off.'

'So he got fired because he was lying?'

'No — because he was not.'

CHAPTER FIFTY-ONE

'I don't understand.'

'Ash managed to access other people's dreams.'

'You're saying this actually happened?' Nick was incredulous.

Longford nodded. 'It appears so. As I said, we have a laboratory here where people are taught how to dream lucidly. All these students have dream diaries and when they wake up they write down what they experienced in their dreams. When we compared their notes with Ash's, they correlated. He saw what they saw . . . without ever being privy to their notebooks. Ash had no access to these students, so he could not have influenced them in any way. No subliminal suggestions. He never even spoke to them.'

'But that's fantastic.' Nick stared at Longford. 'You should have given him a prize. Not fired him.'

'We did not fire him. He just wasn't able to find funding.'

'Why?'

'The institute was worried about lawsuits. People complaining that their privacy had been violated. Or that they'd picked up health problems because he walked around inside their heads. And the institute was worried about the giggle factor. They didn't want to get the reputation that we're running a psychic hotline out here.'

'So he left.'

'Yes. And when he left, a lot of the energy disappeared from this place with him.' She smiled faintly. 'No pun intended.'

'Do you know what happened to him afterwards?'

'I heard he lived in Asia for many years. He never worked at any academic research facility again as far as I know, but I've heard rumours that he started a secret book on the Internet – a work in progress. It has a following among other Zero Point Field fanatics.'

'I wonder why he would choose to go on the Net rather than publish professionally.'

'Probably because he was never able to get published in a reputable journal again. Those science publications with their peer review systems are unforgiving, you know. Also, I heard his book is a mixture of personal philosophy, diary entries and science: in other words, it does not conform to classic scientific format. The name already gives you an indication – it is called *The Book of Light and Dust*. That is far too poetic a name for a straightforward scientific treatise.'

Nick reached for his pen. 'Can you give me the URL?'

'No. I've never been able to find it myself. It's all very secretive. You have to track it down and break all kinds of passwords and secret codes to gain access. You have to show yourself worthy – that kind of thing.'

Nick frowned. 'You'd think if he wants to go public with his ideas, he wouldn't make it so difficult to find.'

'He is probably no longer interested in a debate with classically trained scientists. But we scientists are narcissists, Mr Duffy.' Her voice was wry. 'We all want to leave a legacy. Ash is no different. He would want to be remembered . . . even if only by a small group of true believers.'

For a few minutes it was quiet between them. Then Nick said, 'He was never in touch with you again?'

'No.' For just a moment a great sadness came into her eyes. She had cared for him, Nick suddenly realized. This had not been a platonic relationship.

Longford spoke slowly. 'I can't believe it's already been thirteen years since the last time I saw him. By this time, Ash must be well into old age, so he may not be as passionate about all of this stuff as before. The fire burns out, you know.' She suddenly looked tired.

'Old age?' Nick was startled. 'The Adrian Ashton I'm talking about is in his mid-thirties.'

'No.' Longford's voice was firm. 'Ash was quite a bit older than me.'

Nick looked at her. She seemed to him to be in her fifties, but with women you could so easily be wrong . . .

As though reading his mind, Longford said tartly, 'I'm fifty-four, Mr Duffy.'

'There must be some mistake. We can't be talking about the same man. Do you have a photograph of him?'

She hesitated. 'Not any more.'

'Tall guy. Fair-haired. Good-looking.'

'Yes. That sounds like Ash. But he cannot be in his thirties, I assure you.' She was starting to look agitated. 'I'm sorry, Mr Duffy, but I have another appointment. I'll walk you outside.'

As they reached the door that gave access to the car park, Longford turned to Nick. 'Does he really look that young?'

Nick nodded.

'You know, he always said that if you managed to harness the energy of the Zero Point Field, not only would you be able to power up every car on the planet, but you would also be able to draw on its healing properties and live for ever. He was joking, of course.'

'Of course.'

'Some of us are fortunate. We keep our vitality instead of fizzling out. It's just luck. Ash was one of the most vital people I knew. It's no surprise he's ageing well.'

'You miss him, don't you?' After Nick spoke he was sorry. This woman would not wish to share something so personal with a stranger.

But to his surprise she nodded. 'I miss his sense of beauty. He was able to see beauty in the tiniest thing, you know. In my mind I always think of him as walking through a beautiful world shimmering with light and energy. When you were with him, he could make you see that world too.' She made an embarrassed gesture with her hand. 'I'm getting sentimental. I apologize.'

'Not at all. Thank you very much for your help.'

'If you see him again . . .' – she hesitated – 'tell him to come and visit. It would be good to catch up.'

'I will do that.'

She nodded and turned round to leave.

'Doctor Longford . . .'

She looked over her shoulder.

'Was Adrian Ashton a martial artist?' The answer to this, Nick thought, would go some way to establishing whether they were indeed talking about the same man.

'Oh, yes. It was his greatest passion. And he always said it might produce the key.'

'The key to what?'

But she had already turned round again and was walking away, looking straight ahead of her.

Keeping his eyes on her retreating figure, Nick took out his phone and pressed the speed-dial number for Flash. When Flash answered, he spoke briefly. 'It's Nick. Meet me at the office in two hours. And bring Mia with you.'

CHAPTER FIFTY-TWO

'*The Book of Light and Dust?* That's kind of a cool name.' Flash nodded appreciatively.

'Well, can you find it?' Nick was impatient. 'Longford says it's hidden somewhere on the Internet and isn't easily accessible. She made it sound as though you have to jump through hoops to get to it.'

'I can find it, yes. The question is: how long have I got?'

Mia spoke for the first time. 'Yesterday would be too late.'

'Hmm. Hmm. If it's an underground site, I won't find it by Googling it. I'm going to have to trawl through some shady areas. That's not so easy.' Flash thought for a moment. 'I might start with some of the chat rooms.'

'Chat rooms? Are you serious?'

'Of course. You can pick up a lot of gossip there.' Flash turned towards his computer and flexed his fingers. 'Let's see if I can get a lead on where the chatter's at. Pedal to the metal.'

For the next hour Mia and Nick watched as Flash sped from one site to another – a virtual acid trip through a formless, borderless world of faceless identities and made-up personas; a sprawling universe of off-the-wall ideas, bad grammar and lots of attitude.

The first clue was found in a chat room called #totalenergy.

Flash: Looking for The Book of Light and Dust. Anyone heard of it?

A reply appeared almost immediately.

Dark Decider: Why, dude?
Flash: Heard it was some radical chi trip.
Dark Decider: Radical is right. You don't want to mess with this shit, man.
Flash: Live dangerously. Ha. Ha.
Dark Decider: Eyeball?

Mia was shoulder-surfing. 'What does he mean?'

'At the moment everyone in the chat room can follow our conversation,' Flash explained. 'So he wants to go one-on-one. See?' A small window had opened on the screen in front of him.

Flash: You read the book already?
Dark Decider: No, man. Not me. But I hear you go to this board. BBS 3*32. Passcode: superc*hi. You find directions there.
Flash: Thanks for sharing.

Dark Decider: Peace, brother. Be safe.

The window disappeared.

'It's a bulletin board.' Flash's bony fingers were already moving again. 'These boards are unregulated, you know. Some scary stuff gets posted on them. Like how to blow up Big Ben.'

'Well, at least you have a lead,' Nick said hopefully.

But if Nick thought the end of the search was in sight, he was disappointed. The bulletin board supplied another URL and that site directed them to yet another location. Flash jumped from site to site. On some of them were helpful hyperlinks. On others there were barriers and Flash had to identify small hidden icons buried in the text or find steganographic visuals. He always found them, but it took time.

After another two hours Flash sat back and rubbed his neck. 'It's no use the two of you sitting here staring at me. You should shoot off. Don't you have a fight tomorrow?' He looked at Nick.

Nick nodded reluctantly. 'OK. But you call me immediately if you find it, all right?'

'Yeah. But don't hold your breath. This is going to be leisurely.'

Nick turned to look at Mia. Her eyes were exhausted. 'Let's go home.' He held out his hand.

After the after-hours quiet of the office building, the outside sounds and smells of the street were jarring — the whoosh of the cars, the stink of petrol, the thump of a boom box – everything seemed magnified. It had stopped raining. But there was still moisture in the air and the streetlights looked as though there were haloes round them.

Mia's mobile phone pinged. Nick watched as she read the message. The expression on her face did not change, but he felt suddenly apprehensive.

'Is everything all right? Who was that?'

'Only Lisa. She's just confirming she'll take my shift tomorrow so I can go to the fight.' Mia carefully closed the lid and slipped the mobile back into her bag. She said, 'Drop me off at my place. And then I want you to go home and sleep.'

'Aren't you coming with me?'

'No. You need rest and you need to get your focus back. You're determined to do this fight – so ... do it right. Push everything else out of your mind.'

'You're sure?'

'Yes.'

'Will I see you tomorrow morning? Before I leave for the weigh-in?'

'I hope so.'

Her eyes were huge in her small face. She had pulled her hair into a clumsy topknot and it made her cheekbones stand out sharply. She had lost weight, he realized.

She suddenly smiled, 'No retreat, no surrender.'

CHAPTER FIFTY-THREE

Mia struck a match and brought it to the wick. Cupping the candle with her hand, she placed it on the dressing table, where the flickering flame reflected glassily in the mirror. She stepped back, her eyes automatically searching the shadows for Sweetpea before she remembered.

The room was stuffy and she opened the window wide and leant out, elbows propped on the sill. She stared across the dark rooftops into the distance as though she might see his flat from here – the lovely moss-green room with its books, its soft rugs and paintings – and she wondered what he was doing right now, the man she would be meeting tonight.

Turning away from the window, she stopped in front of the dressing table once more. As she brought her hand up to undo her hair-clip, she paused. In that gesture, she suddenly saw Molly: the head slanted, the long neck, the pale, tapering fingers. But then she removed the clip and her hair curled round her face and she was Mia. No one here to rely on, except herself.

She kneeled in front of the trunk and took out the small

engraved tin box hiding underneath her clothes. Sitting down cross-legged, she placed the box with needles and moxa on her lap.

For a moment she closed her eyes. In her mind came thoughts of broken webs of light, of darkness and death and of time running out. She thought back to the text message she had received on her phone an hour ago.

MEET ME AT THE RETREAT. IF YOU BEAT ME NICK IS SAFE.

She opened her eyes and lifted the lid off the box. No more time to waste.

* * *

The track leading to the Retreat seemed narrower tonight and less even. She felt sharp pebbles bite into the soles of her feet.

The cry of a night bird brought her up sharply. The startled echo seemed to spin out into the woods and set her nerves on edge. Above her head, through a tracery of black branches, an army of restless clouds raced across the sky. A cratered moon glowed with preternatural brightness.

She pressed on. Not far to go now. Round the next bend in the track was the gate with its stiff catch and then the clearing with the house.

The gate was open.

The gate was never open.

Fear. It covered her mind, a sticky spider's web. It slowed her pace, dried her mouth. A gust of wind shook the trees and the rustle of leaves sounded like women sighing. *You die in here. You die out there.*

She should go back. Back to the house in London. She would lock the doors and close the windows. She would make herself hot tea and turn on the lights and all the shadows would leave.

I love you, Mia. You're my life. Nick smiling at her and his hands so gentle. Nick who would be sleeping right now, his heavy shoulders at rest. He would be gathering his strength, his lungs inhaling and exhaling cleanly; the energy inside his veins an insistent pulse.

She pushed the gate open even wider and shivered at the cold touch of the wrought iron against her palm. As she continued walking, the wind suddenly increased in strength and an acrid smell filled the air. She couldn't place it. It mingled uneasily with the scent of jasmine and the smell of rotting leaves. It made her feel even more anxious. The smell was unfamiliar, intrusive.

The last bend in the track was in front of her. On the other side was the Retreat. She turned the corner and stopped, feeling sick.

The Retreat was lit brightly by that toxic moon and it gaped, an empty burnt-out shell. The bamboo roof was completely gone and only a few beams thrust up into the sky. The windows stared, blind. She could see right through the charred frames to the swaying trees on the other side.

She had to force herself to place one leg in front of the other. Her chest felt tight. She walked across the clearing, her hands to her face as though they might shield her eyes from the devastation.

The stone steps were black where the fire had left its mark. Something glinted on the ground: the wind chime that used to hang at the entrance, the individual chimes now twisted and melted together, their voices stilled.

Slowly she stepped through the wreck of the door. Her eyes saw the destruction inside, but her brain refused to understand how beauty and elegance could be erased so thoroughly. Some things were too terrible to grasp.

It was almost all gone. The wall hangings, the wood panelling, the exquisite vases and polished hanbo staffs. At her feet was a half-burnt book, the pages charred and curling.

The various rooms were filled with ash. She hurried past the room of crickets, her gaze averted, not wanting to examine what she would find inside. The dojo was a black hole. The mirrors on the walls had buckled in the heat and her reflection seemed elongated and warped as though she were looking into the mirrors of a fun house.

Tears were running down her face. Her heart felt broken at the terrible loss: at the knowledge that the imprint of the women who had dwelled here had been burnt into oblivion and their true names erased.

A small sound came from behind her — like settling dust. She spun round, her eyes searching the layered darkness. But there was no one.

No one.

And that's when it struck her. He was not going to come. He was not going to give her the chance to win from him Nick's life.

'No!' She screamed but her voice had no power. 'Where are you? Show yourself!'

But she was alone. There was only the wind in the trees and a maimed moon slipping from the sky.

HEART

The starting point for developing *kiai* is to find *kokoro*,
or heart . . . 'indomitable spirit' and it simply means to
refuse to accept defeat.

Forrest E. Morgan, Maj. USAF,
Living the Martial Way

CHAPTER FIFTY-FOUR

The photograph of Molly and Juan on her bedside table was taken long before their death. The picture had rested, forgotten, in a shoebox along with a brace of other snapshots taken over the years. It was only several months after her parents' accident that Mia had discovered the picture. It had stood on her bedside table ever since.

Sometimes she would look at her mother's face and wonder about those last moments. What had gone through her mother's head as she had struggled against the current, her father's unconscious body a deadweight in her arms? Molly must have been so afraid. But what would have been the greater fear: her fear of drowning, or the fear that she might let go of her burden in order to swim unencumbered for the shore and safety?

Last night, as she had headed for the Retreat, Mia knew she had made the same choice as her mother. But whereas Molly had been given a fighting chance – pitting her own strength against the current – she, Mia, had not been given the opportunity of meeting the challenge head on. By not meeting her, Ash had denied her that. And she still was no closer to finding the answer to how he was planning to take Nick's life.

Mia turned away from the photograph and reached for her leather jacket. The fight was in a few short hours. She had done all she could for Nick; she could now only watch from a distance.

Poor Nick. She had pounded on his door at the crack of dawn this morning and had dragged him, sleepy and baffled, back to her studio. An hour later he had left her house with the Keeper's mark on his chest. Mixed into the alchemical blood marriage of skin and ink was her own chi. In the face of unknown danger it seemed feeble protection, but what else was there for her to do?

If only Nick would agree not to fight. She had tried to argue with him one last time, but to no avail. He had already entered that mental zone where fighters go in the final hours before they enter the ring, and his mind was closed to her.

Just as she was about to leave the room, the phone started ringing.

'Mia? Flash.' Without giving her time to respond, he continued, 'I found the book. It's massive big.'

Her fingers tightened round the receiver. 'What does it say?'

'Well, that's where it gets hairy. I found the site and, apart from the book itself, there's also some other stuff on that site, which looks like a bunch of scientific gobbledy-gook. But the actual *Book of Light and Dust*, I can't get into. It's password protected.'

'Can you crack it?'

'I don't know.' She heard him sigh. 'It's a fifteen-character-long password.'

She glanced at her watch: seven p.m. Nick's fight was at nine. On the bike it would take her about forty minutes – an hour if traffic was bad – to get to the Tavern. She could still make it easily, even if she stopped by the office first.

She reached for the keys. 'I'm coming over. I'll see you soon.'

Waiting was always the worst part. Nick moved restlessly on the bench.

He was alone in the changing room except for his reflection in the mirror that covered the wall opposite. The fluorescent lights made his skin look sallow and his new tattoo stood out like a black bruise on his chest. Two eyes: in one, a circle with three lines.

JC had been incensed when Nick arrived at the weigh-in earlier with the blood still bubbling from underneath the skin.

'You got the tat this morning? Are you crazy! You're not supposed to bleed before the fight, you idiot. What the hell were you and Mia thinking of?' JC's face was alarmingly red and he only calmed down once Nick stepped on to the scales. For once Nick had managed to nail his weight. In the past, much to JC's despair, he had often been forced to reach for a skipping rope to get rid of those two or three excess pounds that would follow him into fight days like a curse. No such problems today; in fact, he had weighed in slightly under.

Once again, he touched the black mark that sat on top of his heart. It would now be with him for as long as he was alive.

'I thought this was bad luck and against the rules,' he had asked Mia. 'Now that we're together.'

'Maybe rules were meant to be broken.' Her face was pale but determined.

Nick sighed. He had agreed to the tattoo simply because it had seemed like the easier request. He certainly wasn't going to cancel the fight as Mia wanted, so if giving him a tattoo helped her make peace with his decision, then he was happy to play along.

He wondered how she was coping. He would have called her but JC was a stickler: his fighters were never allowed phones in the changing room before a fight. Weeping wives and wide-eyed kiddies were banned as well. Nothing that could interfere with the focus of the fighter was permitted and no one except corners was allowed.

Nick moved his shoulders. He still had that strange little ache under the one shoulder-blade, which he had picked up during his final sparring session with Ash. It wasn't painful, but it was niggling. Nothing to be worried about, though, and he certainly wasn't going to mention it to JC.

Above the door was a big round clock with a bland white face and thick black arms. A thinner arm ticked down crimson seconds. Two more hours to go.

* * *

Flash's eyes were bloodshot and his hair lank. 'You and Nick owe me ten piña coladas.'

'Consider it done.'

He gestured at the computer. 'That's as far as I got.'

The screen showed an illustration: a book with its title written on the cover in flowing script.

Mia stared at the screen, her eyes burning. Somehow the image on the screen in front of her seemed less real than the phantom book of her dreams. But the title was unmistakable: *The Book of Light and Dust*.

Underneath the title was a large yin and yang symbol brilliantly coloured in saffron yellow and black, but as she watched, it slowly dissolved and in its place – like a ghostly hologram – appeared a face with empty eye sockets and a knowing smile. It had a rope round its neck.

'Creepy, huh?' Flash wrinkled his nose.

The desiccated face was dissolving, replaced by the floating yin and yang teardrops.

'I know what that is.'

Flash lifted a surprised eyebrow. 'What? The skeleton?'

'It's not a skeleton. It's a mummy.'

'Whatever.' Flash shrugged. 'It's dead anyway.'

'Can I try?' Mia leant over and placed her fingers on the keyboard. On the screen the mummy was coming into focus again.

At the bottom of the page was a small box: *Enter password*. Hesitantly she typed:

rosalia

She stopped and searched her brain for the sleeping girl's last name. Lombario? Lombaro?

lombardo

The screen flipped over.

'Wow. You go, girl.' Flash nodded, impressed. 'That's it. We're in.'

The body wears out and we are old ... We sleep less and we dream less. Light is turning to dust ...

'Check this out.' Flash was scrolling down the page and the screen in front of them was now covered with line drawings of bodies and body parts: feet, shoulders, backs, legs, a neck, the top of a head. The drawings were studded with black dots that were numbered and initialled, and these dots were connected to each other by crimson lines.

'What's going on here, then?'

'They're acupuncture points. Those red lines are meridians. See that?' Mia pointed at a line that ran down the midline of the body from the top of the head to the genitalia. 'That's the Du pulse – the directing vessel – which carries the downward flow of yang energy. There, at the back, is the Ren pulse, the conception vessel, which carries the yin flow of energy up the spinal column. These initials refer to the different meridians: LU is the Lung meridian, K is the Kidney meridian, H the Heart meridian and so forth. The numbers are specific acupoints on the meridians.'

'And this stuff about blacklight and whitelight?'

'I don't know.' She paused. 'But there's something weird going on here.'

An idea, as ephemeral as a cloud, as noxious as poison gas, seeped into her brain.

'Mia?'

She looked at Flash unseeingly.

'Mia, are you all right?'

'Chilli.' Her voice sounded strange to her ears. 'I have to show this to Chilli.'

Kenny Burton, Nick's opponent, walked past the open door of Nick's changing room, clutching an energy bar in his fist. For a moment their eyes met. Kenny had a stubby neck and a buffed-up six-pack like a member of the cast of *300*. His arms were thick and coiled. Usually, Nick had no fear of this kind of excessively muscle-bound fighter. Pumped-up muscles used oxygen and oxygen cut down on speed. A slow kickboxer was a doomed kickboxer. But he and JC had watched previous fight tapes and he knew this equation did not hold true for Burton. The guy was fast.

Kenny smiled at Nick, showing very pink gums. They had already done the staring-each-other-down routine at the weigh-in and no display of animosity was needed at this point. Despite the smile, Kenny was using his body language to intimidate. *I am strong. I'm stronger than you. I'm going to pulp you.* It was all there in the swagger of the hips and the set of the shoulders. Nick nodded and smiled back, keeping his eyes cool. *Yeah, right, tosser. Go and play with yourself.*

As Kenny moved out of sight, Nick forced himself to

relax. He placed his tongue on his hard palate and started to breathe evenly though his nose, the way Ash had taught him.

Ash. And Mia. Nick now accepted that the two of them inhabited a world that existed outside his own frame of reference. This morning Mia had told him that she had visited the Retreat the night before. She hadn't told him exactly what had happened while she was there and he hadn't asked. Frankly, he didn't want to know — didn't even want to think about it. He loved Mia more than anything, but all of this stuff was so strange. He was a grunt. Sweat, tears, blood and bruises in the real world: these were the things he understood and could wrap his head round. Besides, tonight he had more pressing dangers to deal with than the shadowy, undefined threat posed by Ash. The ring was a dangerous place. One blow could put him in a coma. The damage he sustained tonight could lead to the lobes of his brain separating and the slow onset of cotton mouth and dementia.

Bloody hell. What cheery thoughts. What a way to go, Duffy. Winding yourself up before a fight — bloody stupid. He breathed in deeply once more.

But even though he could feel his heart calming itself and his pulse slowing, one question refused to leave his mind.

Why? The question he and Mia had been unable to answer. Why had Ash gone to all the trouble of getting him into the best shape of his fighting career if his only goal was to kill him?

* * *

When Chilli opened the door to his flat, Mia hardly recognized her teacher. She was used to seeing him in a white martial-arts uniform but tonight he was dressed in a Hawaiian shirt and baggy shorts. She realized she had never seen his legs before. They were thin but muscular with deep-blue veins running down the calves. When he sat down in front of his computer, he slid a pair of old-fashioned cat's-eye glasses on to his nose.

His face became still as he scrolled from page to page. Once Mia tried to say something, but he waved her into silence.

He leant back into his chair, took off his glasses and rubbed his eyes. Replacing the glasses, he looked at Mia: 'What is it you want to know?'

'Is it what I think it is?'

'What do you think it is?'

'Death touch. This is a book on Dim-Mak.'

'Dim-Mak is not just about death, Mia. It is about healing, as well. Life and death. Yin and yang.'

'Light and Dust.'

Chilli nodded. 'It is about restoring chi as much as it is about draining it.'

'I thought Dim-Mak was lost.'

'It depends on what you mean by lost. The twelve Dim-Mak katas were always taught orally and it is true that things get lost in oral translation. The techniques also go back a very long time: the man who devised them was a doctor who lived towards the end of the southern Sung dynasty.'

'A doctor?'

'Yes, his name was Zhang Sangfeng.' Chilli grimaced. 'Admittedly, his methods were brutal. He experimented on live subjects – prisoners of war, criminals, animals – but it was the only way he could do his research. He discovered that if you strike certain points along the meridians, you could disrupt the flow of chi inside the body.'

'And cause death?'

'Again, it depends. There are many strikes. Sometimes a strike will cause excruciating pain, but the victim will stay alive. Other points are proper death point strikes and will shut down the body completely. Zhang went through a large number of live subjects to try and work out exactly where and in what combinations these points should be manipulated.'

Mia pointed at the computer. '*The Book of Light and Dust*: is that a translation? Was that written by Zhang?'

'Some of it, maybe.' Chilli squinted at the screen. 'But there is modern stuff in here as well – things that seem Western, in fact.' He shook his head. 'It's almost as though it is a combination of two disciplines. But, yes, many of the strikes described in here – Jade Pillow, Yin Dream and so on – are traditional Dim-Mak. The writer calls them Blacklight, but they are death touch.'

'And what are these? What are these abbreviations? DIR, SU, FRC. What do they mean?'

'They refer to direction, location and force. A Dim-Mak strike is very complex and involves the direction of the strike, the force used, which point is targeted and even at what time it is struck. The bladder meridian, for example, only becomes active between three p.m. and five p.m., so a strike involving this meridian would have to take place during this window of time.'

'So the traditional techniques are still out there — being used.'

Chilli shrugged. 'You can buy books detailing Dim-Mak techniques on Amazon. But in Ancient China, as you well know, warring families kept their martial-arts techniques secret. Zhang wove the death point strikes into formalized kata movements that masked their true purpose. The movements themselves were written down, but not what they meant. It was left to teachers to impart the real knowledge orally to trusted students or family members. As you can imagine, because such a limited number of people knew how to use them, many of the most potent techniques did, in fact, get lost over time.'

Mia flashed back on a memory. Ash standing behind Art, holding his arm and Art's head drooping in pain. 'I once saw . . . someone . . . press a point on a man's arm — right here — and the attacker became completely incapacitated.'

Chilli shook his head. 'That's not Dim-Mak. There are vulnerable places on the anatomy — the vagus nerve, the carotid artery and so on — that, if pressured, can produce incapacitation or unconsciousness in a victim. But that's not Dim-Mak. Dim-Mak works directly on acupoints, causing the organs to crash.'

'Like stopping someone's heart?'

'Oh, yes. Certainly.'

She was starting to feel sick. 'But you said it was about healing as well.'

'Absolutely. Dim-Mak is, at heart, medicinal. It was created by a doctor, remember. You cannot learn only one part of the system. Heart meridians, for example, are used primarily for healing. If you want to practise Dim-Mak, you have to know the healing as well as the destructive parts, otherwise you will fail. Dim-Mak is about balance: yin and yang. A Dim-Mak master would know how to use acupoints to cause death but he would also know how to use them to promote well-being. He would be a Qigong practitioner and a herbologist. And, most important, he would know antidote techniques.'

'Antidote?'

'He would know how to reverse a strike. You know how it is sometimes necessary to massage someone who has passed out in the dojo?'

Mia nodded. She had seen it happen more than once. Some fighter, usually a judo or ju-jitsu practitioner, would become unconscious but if you massaged his back and made him sit up straight, it usually did the trick and helped him revive.

'Well, Dim-Mak is a little like that. A reversal of the knockout.' Chilli gestured at the screen. 'Have you noticed how when the writer describes a *blacklight* technique he usually matches it with *whitelight*? That's the reversal strike.'

He turned to look her full in the face. His eyes were outsize behind his glasses. 'And now, why don't you tell me what this is all about? What's wrong, Mia?'

'I think . . .' She took a deep breath. 'I think Ash has used Dim-Mak on Nick. I think he wants Nick to die.'

CHAPTER FIFTY-FIVE

Nick caught a glimpse of his face in the mirror as he looked past JC's shoulder. It was glistening with Vaseline. JC finished taping his hands and the fight officials initialled the tapes and left the room.

Before shrugging into his gloves, Nick shadowboxed for a few seconds. His kicks were smooth, his punches fluid. He moved on air. In the ring it would be so different. In the ring, Burton would play havoc with his rhythm, smashing his fists through his guard, slamming his legs into his ribs. A battle of attrition. Ten rounds of pain and great exhaustion and the winner the one who could dig the deepest.

The ring. It was all he could think of now. Nothing mattered but the ring.

Dennis, his second corner man, helped him with his gloves and robe and then the three of them started walking down the concrete corridor towards the steel doors leading to the arena. Nick could hear his fight song starting up, the sound muted.

The doors opened. The roar of the crowd and the aural blast of the music swept over him like a wave. For one moment his eyes were blinded by the massive spotlights cutting like axes through the dusk.

He continued walking, looking straight ahead, but in his peripheral vision he could see faces. People were standing up, their heads craning on their necks to watch his progress. Their teeth gleamed phosphorescent white, their eyes were black smudges. Mia would be out there, somewhere. And Ash. These thoughts drifted through his mind but they did not touch him. He was only aware of the beat of his heart.

JC held the ropes for him and he clambered through. The canvas-covered planking felt hard and unyielding underneath his bare feet.

It was time.

The chimes of the grandfather clock in Chilli's entrance hall made Mia stare at her watch stupidly.

'Nick's fight. I'm going to miss it.' She felt curiously light-headed.

'Wait.' Chilli reached out his hand. He looked shell-shocked. 'These other fighters . . . and Okie . . . you said they died days after their fight?'

'Yes. Ash much have given them the strike before they went into their fights – during that final sparring session.'

'No.' Chilli was emphatic. 'Dim-Mak strikes are known to have a delayed effect, but the victim wouldn't be able to simply continue calmly with his life. That's the stuff of manga comics.'

'Are you sure?'

For a long moment, he did not answer.

'Are you *sure*?' she asked again.

When he spoke, his voice was wooden. 'There is a story that Zhang did attempt to devise a series of strikes that would be the assassin's perfect tool. The idea was that the victim would die unexpectedly many days later when the perpetrator was long gone. But Zhang never succeeded. He is reputed to have admitted that his under-standing of chi was not great enough, that it would be for someone else to discover – someone who had managed to take his research to the next level.'

Mia swallowed hard. 'But surely Nick would have felt the strike.'

'Not one strike. A series of strikes. Dim-Mak always requires both set-up and activation strikes.'

'OK, series of strikes, then. Nick would have felt them, right? I mean, wouldn't they have caused him severe pain?'

Chilli shook his head. 'A Dim-Mak master uses chi augmentation: he adds his own chi to the strike. Excessive kinetic force is not required. In fact, only light contact is needed. Nick might not even have registered the strikes particularly. He definitely would have felt *something*, but if they were grappling, for example, the strikes would have been masked by the rough and tumble of the train-ing. But I am convinced he would have collapsed – if not immediately afterwards, at least within hours.'

'Unless Ash managed to do it.'

'Do what?'

'Devise a delayed death touch.'

They stared at each other.

'It doesn't matter.' She spoke quickly. 'There are antidotes. *Whitelight*. As you said. We only need to find out which meridian Ash attacked to reverse the strike.'

Chilli didn't answer.

'Can't we? Chilli?'

'You can only reverse some strikes, Mia. If the *hara* is involved – and for a delayed strike it would be – then it is not possible to reverse the process. No *whitelight*.' He gestured at the screen. 'When you read the book, you'll notice that every now and then he mentions a strike that does not allow for a *whitelight* reversal. Besides, even if we could do a reversal, we wouldn't know which particular strike he used among the many in this book. It's futile.'

'How can you say that to me!' Her voice was rising.

'Mia—''

'You're saying Nick is already dead!' She was now shouting at him. She wanted to shake him. Smash his glasses from his face. He looked so calm; so unconcerned in the face of calamity.

Chilli tried to put his arms round her but she shook herself loose.

'I have to go to Nick. I have to take him to the hospital and warn the doctors.'

'Nick will check out healthy. What are you going to tell the doctors? That he is suffering from a fatal chi drain?'

She stopped, shocked. 'You're saying they won't believe me.'

'Doctors in this country don't work with chi, Mia. And even in China you would find it difficult to find someone who understands Dim-Mak this profoundly.'

'You're saying it's too late. You're saying Nick is already dying.'

He didn't answer. She couldn't bear the pity in his eyes.

'Where are you going?' He watched as she picked up her keys.

'To the fight. I promised Nick I'd be there. I can still catch the end.'

'Are you going to tell him? Mia, are you going to tell Nick?'

She turned to the door, feeling very tired. 'It wouldn't be of any use now, would it?'

Burton was a malicious fighter. Nick usually felt no anger towards his opponents but, when Burton dragged his glove across Nick's eye for the second time, he could feel the rage catching fire inside him. But the fight was going his way, which was probably why Burton was resorting to underhand tactics. Nick tucked his chin into his shoulder. Only two more rounds . . .

But then it happened. Burton lurched forward and slammed his head into Nick's face – whether deliberately was difficult to say. Nick blinked and shook his head. On Burton's jaw was a smudged crimson moon. With a feeling of surprise Nick realized he was looking at his own blood.

He was cut.

Fuck.

Despite the haze of blood everything seemed very clear: the enlarged pores on Burton's nose; the gleam of his eyeballs. Burton kept jabbing at his damaged eyebrow. Suddenly, with sickening speed, he turned at a complete right angle and whipped a sidekick straight into Nick's abdomen.

Nick gasped. His legs felt incredibly heavy. Desperately he tried to stay out of the reach of that punishing jab. For a moment he saw double: two Burtons throwing punches at his head. He just managed to rock back and block in time to escape a vicious spinning back kick.

If he could only last until the bell. If only JC did not throw in the towel. If only the referee did not stop the fight . . . He could still do it. *Never say die.*

Burton was dancing on the balls of his feet. He curled his lip and grinned behind the mouth guard. Kill time.

As if in slow-motion Nick saw Burton's right travelling towards his chin . . . felt his own knees flexing as he ducked, his head moving in the opposite direction of the punch, his bloodied eye still fixed on Burton's face. As if of its own volition, his left arm curled into a scything hook . . .

Nick broke Burton's cheekbone. He could feel the impact; feel it right through the glove, travelling up his arm and into his elbow, and he could see it in Burton's eyes.

Finish him. Nick slipped his shoulder and pivoted his hip . . .

* * *

From the back of the Tavern he watched as Nick droppe
his shoulder in a beautifully executed move, driving a le
into Burton's side with stunning ferocity. When Nick'
right fist slammed into Burton's jaw immediately after
wards, the moment looked stylized, choreographed – a
though Burton were playing along willingly, allowing hi
head to fly back violently, theatrically, for best effect.

With one breath, the crowd breathed out – a so
whoosh of air. *Aah.* Burton's legs gave way and he sagge
slowly, ever so slowly, towards the canvas. The crow
exploded.

Dragonfly threw his hands into the air and screamed i
ecstasy.

CHAPTER FIFTY-SIX

Pale light filtered through the shutters. There were still deep shadows in Nick's bedroom, but there was enough morning light for Mia to see Nick's jacket, slumped nervelessly over the back of a chair, and his boots lying sideways on the carpet where he had dropped them hours earlier.

Her eyes travelled slowly through the room, lingering on the photographs in their old-fashioned frames; on Nick's collection of toy locomotives, on a pair of deeply creased boxing gloves hanging from a hook on the wall. They were the first pair of boxing gloves Nick had ever worn in a proper ring fight. He had been only thirteen years old at the time and he had won. The gloves hung by the door and she knew that Nick touched them every morning for luck: a small, private ritual.

His arm was heavy across her breasts. Carefully Mia eased herself out from underneath and sat up straight, looking down at his sleeping body. He was lying on his stomach, arms and legs sprawling. His face was turned towards her, one cheek pressed into the pillow. The wide gash above his eye, which had so shocked her when she saw him immediately after the fight, had been neatly stitched up but the lid was swollen. He had also broken his small toe in the fifth round without even realizing it: the second time it had happened in his career. 'As long as it's not the nose,' he had joked afterwards in the changing room. 'The nose is sacrosanct.'

She had smiled with him, had pressed her face deeply against his chest. 'Did you see it, Mia? Did you see when the bastard tried that hook kick and I blocked him?' She had nodded, yes. And yes, too, to his excited recap of the knock-out punch. But she was lying, of course. She had not witnessed his triumph. She had arrived too late. She had only been in time to see the huge ungainly belt – garish as a child's toy – being strapped round his waist.

How peaceful he looked; how happy. The strong hands were propped up on the pillow – defenceless in sleep with the fingers loosely curled. The shadow of stubble darkened his jaw but his mouth was soft and relaxed and made him look so young.

But his skin . . . his skin seemed just slightly waxy . . . and those deep shadows under his eyes . . .

She breathed shallowly, trying not to succumb to the weight of emotion pressing on her crumbling heart. There would be time enough for tears later.

Slowly, slowly, she started to slide out of the bed. Nick mumbled, moved his head restlessly. She froze. He sighed and continued to breathe evenly.

Keeping her eyes on him, she stooped to pick up her clothes from the floor. She tiptoed into the living oom, closing the door of the bedroom softly behind her.

The curtains in the living room were open and she noticed that it was foggy outside, the mist pressing ghost-like against the windows. Winter had well and truly arrived.

His number was still on her speed dial. As the phone rang several times she wondered if he had already disappeared, but then there was a click and his voice came on the line.

She took a deep breath. 'Ash? If you have the time, why don't we finish that tattoo? Can you be at the studio in an hour?'

CHAPTER FIFTY-SEVEN

He pulled the front door of his apartment building shut and looked around him. It was still foggy, but the mist was thinning: it no longer obscured as much as transformed. Sharp edges seemed fluid, colours muted. In the garden square, the late-blooming oleander tree seemed marshmallow soft and the elegant white-pillared houses lining the street looked as though they were floating. He smiled in delight.

His whole life had been a search for beauty and the thrill of immediate sensation. Age was the enemy. Age dulled the ability for direct experience, the layering years forming an insensate carapace.

He glanced at his watch. He didn't want her to have to wait for him too long. It was a special day. This morning she would put the finishing touches to the love letter she had been writing on his body over so many weeks.

He started walking swiftly, enjoying the moistness in the air; the luminous, white light.

There was something about the light today that was dreadful. The light coming through the window of her studio was like the light you encounter in a nightmare – a kind of insane, colourless light that hurts your eyes. Mia pressed her forehead against the glass pane and squinted at the frail tendrils of swimming, shifting fog.

Her hands were cold. Her eyes felt dry and tearless. For a moment she thought of Nick, still sleeping in his warm bed where she had left him. It bothered her that she had difficulty envisaging his face. No matter how hard she concentrated, whenever she tried to visualize his features they would dissolve.

On the glass pane in front of her, her breath was condensing into a grey patch of moisture. With the tip of her finger she traced the outline of a word: *Dragonfly*.

She knew who he was now, his identity was clear, but as she stared at the watery letters she realized she was unable to think of him as the man who had become a part of her life during the days of summer. That man had been a friend; an almost lover. The man who would be hurrying towards her right this minute was an intruder and a destroyer. A killer.

He would be coming here, believing his identity still to be a secret. Good. Combat was about treachery and deceit as much as about courage and skill. His ignorance would be to her advantage.

The letters on the glass pane were disappearing, only the D still standing bold and strong. Shivering, she turned away.

It was chilly inside the room. She rubbed her arms, drawing comfort from the soft jersey fabric under her fingers and from the whiff of fugitive scent clinging to the fibres: Molly's perfume, faded but not gone.

Outside in the garden, the gate creaked.

She stiffened. Holding her breath, she waited. She had left the front door ajar for him.

There was the scrape of shoes at the threshold and she sensed him strongly. Suddenly he was standing inside the studio door, peering into the shadowed room.

'Mia?'

'Mia?'

There was no answer and if it weren't for the open front door he might have thought the house to be empty. But then he walked into the studio and in the split second before she stepped out of the shadows he sensed her presence. His sense of her was clear, unambiguous, dazzling: like flames chasing the night; like snow falling into black water. Beauty and darkness.

And then he saw her.

She was dressed in a black body stocking that clung to her like a second skin. It covered her arms down to the wrists, hugged her throat chastely. But the left side of her body was exposed, the suit cut away. She moved her arm and he caught a glimpse of the pale hollow of her armpit: of the lovely figure flowing in shades of blue and purple colour on to her hip. The Keeper's tattoo.

He stared, breathless.

She moved again, and again he had that tantalizing glimpse of skin.

'Let me look at you.' His voice was no more than a whisper.

She did not respond. Her eyes were watchful and her face was so pale. He was reminded of that moment when they had faced each other for the first time across a garden square filled with the sound of rustling leaves and the sigh of rain. Her eyes had looked into his unseeingly but she had had this same air of watchful stillness, as if sensing an energy disturbance and the gathering of forces. She had looked wild and beautiful and foreign.

'Please. Show her to me.'

For another moment she hesitated, but then she turned her body sideways and lifted her arm, allowing him to see the tattoo fully.

'Ah.' He felt the sweat burst through his skin. His excitement made him feel dizzy.

'Will you let me touch you?' He walked forward slowly and stretched out his hand. His fingertip brushed the incalculable softness of her skin. As his fingers traced the outline of the inked image, he felt the roundness of her breast, the surprising heat underneath her arm, the smooth coolness of her hip.

She let her arm fall to her side and turned to face him. As if of its own volition, his hand moved behind her head, his fingers burying themselves in her silky hair. Her eyes stared into his unblinkingly; her lips were slightly parted.

Light within, a golden pulse filling her veins. *What is the greatest desire?* With one hand he tilted her head up to his. His other moved across her shoulders, her breasts, her

hips, her stomach. She was completely quiescent under hi
fingers, her body still.

Her lips clung to his: soft, so soft . . .

Searing pain skewered through his body: a red flame
She had slammed the tips of her fingers into his side
angling upwards and underneath his ribs. Her finger
were rock hard and his surprised brain suddenly realize
that her hands were wrapped for combat. Gasping fo
breath, he doubled over. Without any hesitation, sh
swung her elbow viciously across his face. He managed t
slip his head to the side just in time to take the edge off th
strike, but the pain where her elbow slammed into hi
temple was still excruciating and it felt as though his ey
exploded. As he touched his fingers to his injured face, sh
moved cat-like past him.

He lowered his hand and straightened. She had place
distance between them but she was clearly not going any
where. She had adopted a fighter's stance: her intention
unmistakable. The slight figure behind her in the mirro
mimicked her movements like a malevolent ghost.

No! She knows! She knows who I am.

He blinked, his brain still fighting this sudden realiz
ation. For one horrifying, hallucinatory moment it seeme
to him as though her features were blurring and he saw th
faces of other women, other Keepers. A rank of warrior
marching through the veil of time.

Her face snapped back into focus. Her eyes were blac
as night, her mouth set.

* * *

He was recovering. The blank surprise had left his eyes. She knew she should move in immediately, but she had to know.

'Why?'

He gingerly touched his hand to his face.

'Tell me,' she said. 'You owe me that at least.'

He sighed and as he lowered his hand she saw blood on his fingers. Her elbow must have split the fragile skin above the eye.

'Do you know the story of the two kendo masters who were both skilled at catching birds with their bare hands?' His voice was casually conversational.

'What?' She stared at him, confused and hostile.

'One of them was the greater martial artist. He managed to catch the birds without harming them in the process. The other master always ended up with a dead bird inside his fist.' He shrugged. 'Like me.'

'What the hell are you talking about?'

'I didn't want those guys to die, Mia. I admired them greatly; they were my friends. In my heart I'm a thief, not a killer. If I could have stolen their chi from them without causing them harm, I would have. But I'm clumsy. When I touch . . . I kill.'

'And you don't care.'

'I do care. But in order for me to gain life, there has to be death. That's simply the way it is. I needed what they could give me.'

'Chi.'

'With you it is a healing touch. *Wai chi*. The chi

transfers from you to the other and it is nourishing. With me, it works the other way round. My touch draws thei chi to me. I need it – the way a patient needs a blood transfusion.'

'You're not a patient. You're a vampire!' She swallowed hard, tried to moderate her voice. 'Why fighters?'

'Fighters have chi like lightning. And the dojo is a contained, self-referential space. Like a laboratory.'

A laboratory. She felt like slapping him.

'Why these men in particular? Did you just throw a bunch of names into a hat?'

'Of course not.' He seemed genuinely affronted.

'So how do you decide?'

'You go after the ones with the biggest heart – they have the strongest chi. All fighters have courage. But I'm looking for someone who won't quit: the fighter who'l stagger out of his corner even though he is badly hurt and knows he has already lost.'

'Like Nick.'

He was quiet.

She felt a coldness in her stomach. 'You fattened up Nick, didn't you? Like a calf to the slaughter. You helped him gain his highest potential and then you moved in when his chi was at its strongest. During the fight, he was already dying. You had already taken from him what you needed during that last spar.'

Still he didn't respond.

'Nick is going to die, isn't he?'

'We are all dying.'

'Can you stop it? Can you reverse the strike?'

'*Dian Xue* cannot be reversed.'

Her heart shuddered and she breathed lightly, trying to control the pain.

'I can't let you leave here.' She spoke slowly. 'I can't allow you to go out and kill again.'

Snapping her arms into guard position, she turned her body sideways, minimizing the area open to attack. His face tautened and almost immediately his gestures followed hers and they started circling each other.

The floor space was limited. Before his arrival, she had pushed the two benches in the studio against the far wall to free up the room as much as possible, but this was still going to be close combat with little chance of escape.

Her heartbeat had speeded up tremendously, she could hear the blood rushing in her ears, but she was breathing cleanly through her nose and she was moving with intent. The previous time they had fought, she had allowed her thoughts and fears to interfere with her focus – *he's bigger than me ... I am afraid ... he's hurting me* – thoughts cluttering her mind, keeping her from attacking cleanly or defending with purpose. Her mind had turned against her body and had caused her movements to be hesitant.

Not this time. This time she would do as Chilli had taught her. Stay in the moment. Use his own power against him. And above all: stay off the ground. She did not have the grappling skills nor the upper-body strength to defeat him if he took her down.

He suddenly moved forward with that slithering,

breathtaking speed she remembered from their las
encounter and entered her zone. Entry and setup. Sh
recognized the technique: it was a fundamental attacl
movement – stepping in and following up with a short
distance, powerful straight punch and she could feel hi
internal energy projected at her with stunning intent. Sh
side-slipped but he kept up the attack, advancing immedi
ately once again. His fighting style was as before – linea
and highly aggressive. He was invading her spac
constantly, trying to get her off balance, his hands leadin¿
his movements: chopping, whipping, grabbing. This wa
yang energy – constantly advancing, never retreating.

If he was going linear, she would go circular. Her mis
take the last time had been to allow him to dictate he
rhythm. In response to his forward movements, she woul¿
use spinning motions, evading him. Fight like the wind
and get out of the way. He could not impose his power o¡
her if she did not accept it. Be like water and, if need be
yield. He grabbed her wrist, his fingers like steel. Instead
of trying to tug free, she slipped back round to his outside
using the motion of her pivoting body to free her hand.

But she was starting to feel overwhelmed by the con
tinuous pressure and when he made a sudden, viciou
sweep to her ankle her mind cringed. Suddenly all sh¿
could think of was of that moment during their las
encounter when he had almost snapped her Achilles hee
like a brittle twig.

No. She breathed in through her nose. Stay in th¿
moment.

She knew his weak spot. His right knee. For a moment she flashed back to the time she saw him stumble. *Keep it to yourself, OK? Don't tell Nick or he'll take advantage of me next time we spar.* As she had answered: *Your secret's safe with me.* She hadn't forgotten.

And suddenly, she had her chance. He struck at her, but she rocked back from the hips and he overreached, allowing himself to become unbalanced for just one split second. She felt the shift in his energy and stepped forward fluidly, blocking his attacking arm with her left. But unlike the last time she did not tense her arm, and even as she felt the force of their limbs connecting she allowed his energy to pass through her own body and across her shoulders, down her right arm and all the way into her right palm. As she pushed her palm towards his face, she visualized not the point of impact, but a point in space beyond his head.

The hilt of her palm smashed into his jaw. The power with which she connected surprised even herself. His head flipped back and he made a soft grunting sound. The next moment she kicked a roundhouse into his weak right knee, using her full body power, feeling the power surging from her hips, the energy travelling in a straight line from the grounded foot of her supporting leg.

He did not go down, but his leg swayed.

She went in low, slamming her shoulder into his solar plexus and hooking her foot round the ankle of his weakened leg. He went down like a tree.

She moved her foot until it hovered just above the

Adam's apple in his neck and he stiffened, his entire body
tense. If she were to project all her energy at him right
now, bringing the full weight of her leg down on his
throat, she would kill him. He stared up at her, eyes
rimmed with white.

Could she do it?

A memory, vivid as a wound, flashed into her brain.
Sun on her skin, a blue sky, glimmering wings skimming
luminous water. Her body shuddering with pain. His
hands cradling her bloody foot, then jerking the shard of
glass from the soft flesh. Tender violence.

She hesitated. With lightning speed he grabbed her
ankle and pulled her leg out from underneath her. She
slammed to the floor and the next instant he was on top of
her, crushing her body beneath his.

CHAPTER FIFTY-EIGHT

Touch a butterfly and you may kill it. The oils from your fingertips will loosen the fragile wing scales, damage the veins that circulate the blood and even the strong muscles of the butterfly's body will not be enough to compensate. He had been taught this lesson by his father after picking up a small tortoiseshell nymphalid and fatally damaging it with his fumbling little-boy fingers. He had felt sorry and distressed as he looked at the maimed insect crumpled in his palm. But even then, he recognized that if he ever found himself in a similar situation, he would reach for the butterfly again.

She was weeping. Her head was turned to the side and her eyes were closed, the long lashes forming perfect dark crescents but the tears pushing through unrelentingly. He touched her cheek that was glistening wet and in his mind came a refrain: *Don't cry, Mia. Don't cry. Don't cry.*

'Why?' Her voice was hoarse, barely audible. 'Why haven't you killed me long ago?'

If only you knew how close I've come. If only you knew how often. Draining you of your energy would be the biggest prize. I have never been more aware of it than right now, right this minute, as you lie beneath me and I sense the meridians inside your body: rivers of energy, rapids of light . . .

A wave of nausea suddenly swept over him and he clenched his jaw.

'Nick.' She looked up, the line of her brows pulled down in grief. 'Why Nick, not me? Why?' She suddenly screamed at him, pushing her palms futilely against his chest. 'Answer me!'

Such a temptation. I can't bear it.

She fell back again, her body sagging. 'I am so tired,' she said. 'So very tired.'

For a moment he closed his eyes and wondered at the breathtaking speed with which one can travel from happiness to despair. Less than an hour ago he had walked towards her with a hopeful heart and the world had seemed right in every way. The man who had set out this morning had been happy. The man who had set out this morning had been *deluded*. For so long he had lied to himself that delusion had become truth; truth, delusion. He had convinced himself he would be able to defy his own nature and keep his hunger in check, but the feel of her light-pulsing body beneath his made him realize he was still that boy with the grasping, destructive fingers. A destroyer. A killer. She would never be safe from him.

There was a metallic taste in his mouth. He couldn't risk the feel of her soft body any longer. Pushing himself away from her, he got to his feet. She slowly followed suit, moving hesitantly as though she was hurting.

They faced each other.

'Nick is fine.'

'What?' She stared at him, her face slack. 'What did ou say?'

'Nick is fine.' He realized his hands were shaking.

'You never gave him *blacklight*.' Her voice was a hisper. He could see she was not giving herself per- ission to hope yet.

'No.' He smiled mirthlessly.' I had every intention: it as all set up for that last spar. And then . . . I didn't.'

It was dead quiet in the room. Her face was a mask of ock. No joy, only disbelief.

'This has been the best summer of my life. You, me, ick. I think . . . I think I had this sentimental dream . . . e three of us living together for the longest time.' He rugged. 'Stupid. I wouldn't really have been able to are you with Nick. When I found out the two of you re lovers I felt such anger.'

He stopped. Cold sweat burst from his pores.

'You know he will never really accept you for who you e, Mia. Nick is not your true mate. He will always be comfortable with your world. There's a part of you he esn't know. Sadder, still: he doesn't *want* to know.'

The nausea gripped him again. '*I* know you.'

But the way I want to love you is the way I want to rt you. Time to face the truth: I can never trust myself ound you, sweet Mia. Keeper. Your very name spells nptation. One day I will touch you and I will kill you.

He looked into her vulnerable face and the knowledge

of his own weakness filled him with such despair, he cou
hardly breathe.

'What do we do now?' Her voice was hesitant.

He did not answer. In his mind came glimpses
journeys still to be travelled and a stir of echoes urgi
him onwards. It was all ahead in the future, waiti
for him: moments of passion, visions of beauty, glimme
ing hours strung together like a tightrope without end. I
saw himself walking that tightrope with the hour gla
frozen in time, the flow of sand arrested. How could
deny himself? It was his destiny.

Her eyes were questioning; her mouth so defenceles

Destinies can be altered. But it requires sacrifice. *Ti*
to be a hero, Ashton.

He stepped forward and took her hand. For just
moment she resisted, but then she allowed him to gui
her fingers and press them gently to his body.

'We are transceivers and transmitters of energy, M
You and I both. All that separates us is intent. *You w*
have to change your intent.'

At first her eyes remained confused, but then he saw
them slow comprehension and felt her fingers jerk agaii
his hand. 'No.' She took a step back, straining against t
pressure of his fingers. 'I can't.'

'A minute ago, you were ready to kill me.'

'But I couldn't do it! And that was combat, this is not
am a Keeper. We exchange energy for healing, not
destroying.'

'You are not only a Keeper of Light. You are alsc

eeper of Dust. *Fa chi* is both yin and yang. Black and
hite.'

'No!'

'I am not asking you to kill. I'm asking you to restore
. *balance.*'

Her face was deeply flushed, emotion staining her
eekbones like paint.

'Do it for Nick. Because I will be coming for him, Mia.
stayed my hand once, but one day – tomorrow, the day
ter, next year – I won't be able to help myself. It is only
matter of time.'

'I will protect Nick.'

'How many fighters can you protect? What about all
e others who will cross my path? They will never be safe
om me.'

You will never be safe from me.

He looked into her stricken eyes and he wondered if
ere was anything more painful than losing what had
ver truly been yours.

'Do it. Before I change my mind.'

the end, it did not take so very long after all. Barely an
our. Not long, she thought, to reverse the journey of a
etime.

He was staring at his reflection. She watched, numbly,
he stretched out his hand towards his mirrored image
d stared with sick amazement at the ink marks on his
in. During the past hour she had obliterated each of the
yphs and ideograms she had so painstakingly

transferred to his body over the summer and had fill
them in with black ink. They sat on his flesh like blin
malignant warts. Blocked. Across his energy numbe
were tattooed two eyes. In one eye, a circle with thr
lines. Energy exchanged; energy reversed.

The ultimate death touch.

For a moment she closed her eyes, unable to watch t
helpless horror on his face.

She opened her eyes to find that he had turned aw
from the mirror. The disbelief had left his face and I
features were now in eerie repose: that beautiful face wi
its strong planes and angles, the wide, sensual mouth, t
slightly hawkish nose and graceful brows. He was butto
ing his shirt with unhurried, precise fingers as thou₃
nothing was wrong, as though this had just been anoth
of their sessions together.

He looked up and his eyes were a clear, light gr₄
'Here is where I leave you.'

She didn't answer, couldn't. She tasted salt in h
mouth, felt tears on her cheek.

At the door he turned to look at her. And then, u
expectedly, he smiled and it was the same secretive sm
she remembered from when he had first walked throu₃
that very same door months ago: a smile that said, *I kn₄
you.*

'Goodbye, Mia. Have a good life.'

And then he was gone.

CHAPTER FIFTY-NINE

Fight Right Magazine

28 March

Nick Duffy loses shot at UK title in titanic battle
REPORTED BY LEE JAMES

On one of the coldest nights of the year the action inside the ring was red hot as Nick Duffy failed in his bid to capture the WKA British Kickboxing title in the light-heavyweight division. He was stopped in the ninth by his opponent, Raoul du Preez, who fired a surprise roundhouse kick at Duffy's head.

Six months ago, Duffy won the Southern Regional belt against Kenny Burton and last night it looked as though he would take home the British championship as well. It was a glorious battle and it brought the crowd to their feet. For nine gruelling rounds, Duffy never eased the pressure, locking his opponent in against the ropes and battering him with a flurry of combinations: attack kickboxing at its purest.

The judges' scorecards had put Duffy ahead for the first eight rounds before he went down in the ninth. To have victory snatched from you in the blink of an eye is enough to break any fighter's heart, but Duffy seemed to take his defeat in his stride. He was even philosophical about his broken nose: 'It had to happen some time. And the woman in my life says it's an improvement.'

DUST

We die only once and for such a long time.

Molière

EPILOGUE

The snow underneath his feet was virgin white. It was still very early in the morning and the light was just arting to touch the sky.

He folded his arms across his chest as though trying to eep the warmth inside. He was so very cold. The breath aving his lips was a cloud in the icy air. He stopped and oked back over his shoulder at his footprints in the ow: the imprints of his right foot seemed deeper than e left, as though he was suffering from an injury that used him to labour as he walked.

The cold. He had problems coping with the cold.

But these days he could not cope with hot weather ther. For a moment he thought back on the recent onths he had spent in Thailand. Every morning he had alked past the steaming rice paddies and past the shrines here garlands of flowers oozed sickly sweet perfume, d it had been a struggle to breathe. Sometimes he had ade the journey to the open-air camp where the Muay hai fighters were training; their sleek, strong bodies orking out for hours in the heat. They had paid no tention to him, this *farang*, foreigner, who at first looked on with longing but who could then no longer find within him any desire.

Greater than the vitality oozing from his body was the vitality oozing from his mind. In Thailand he had been content to spend most of his time sleeping on the veranda of his house, dozing next to his song birds in their bamboo cage, singing their hearts out day after day. He'd sleep oblivious to the aching blue of the sky above him, to the beauty of the glimmering wings of the dragonflies flitting across swampy water at the bottom of the garden.

A month ago, he decided the time had come to return home.

The catacombs would not be open to the public for another two hours but the Capuchin monks knew him well by this time. His donations were generous and in return they allowed him inside long before the tourist buses arrived.

So cold. The place was dim with shadows and his foot-steps echoed flatly. The mummies stared down at him with their ruined faces.

His little princess was waiting for him. He placed his hands on the case in which she lay and the glass surface was chill against his fingers. Her face was peaceful and unchanging – forever young.

Turning away from her, he sat down heavily on a wooden bench. The icy stone of the floor seeped into the soles of his feet. His joints ached.

He was turning into a living Deadman. He could feel it. He could see it. When he looked into the mirror, he

otice the greying of his skin and the lilac veins under-
eath his eyes. The flesh at his jaw was slackening and his
air was thinning and growing coarse. He'd open his shirt
nd stare at his reflection. He'd stare at the black ink
arks on his skin: a visible curse, an open wound draining
is chi from his *hara* in a slow – such a slow – drip.

He no longer tested his light emissions: he knew they
ere incoherent and his energy numbers off. His periodic
ythms were unstable.

Why live if you don't feel alive? He was reaching out
his own death, longing for it, but when would it come?
eeks, months . . . years from now?

Who was thinking these thoughts? Was it him? Or his
eadman? In his dreams he still desired; in his dreams his
i was flowing through his body like liquid lightning. He
as whole again when he slept.

A stale ray of sunshine fell through a window up high,
d on to the bench on which he was sitting. Dust motes
eamed in the light. He closed his eyes and leant back
ainst the wooden bench. On his eyelids, the sun lay
ftly.

An old man slumbering, searching for dreams. His
outh was half open and his breath passed his lips
allowly. All sensation in his body was converging into
at small space behind his eyes and then – there she was,
olding out her hand to him. Her hair was a cloud of gold
d her slim, strong body seemed etched with light.

Oh! He felt his heart contract. And even though he was
leep, he knew there were tears oozing from underneath

his eyelids. He was so happy to see her. And as he looked at her lovely face he remembered a time and a place where everything made sense.

She asked him a question and it was the same question she always asked: 'What is the greatest desire?'

He opened his lips, but the words would not come. She turned her head and her hand fell by her side. But as she walked away, leaving him in the cold with his dreams and his memories, he whispered:

'To *love* for ever. *That* is the answer.'

THE END

FIGHTING FOR PEACE

Shortly after finishing *The Keeper* I happened to come across a BBC News article about a group of Afghan women who are being taught how to box. These ladies are sponsored by a peace organization that is endeavouring to make the women feel more empowered and in charge of their lives. What I found especially poignant is that the gym in which they train is located in a football stadium that was used in the past by the Taliban for public executions, including the killing of women.

I know how liberated I feel when I am in the dojo, and can only imagine how much more so it must be for these women who lead restricted lives and who are still coming to terms with a terrible period in Afghan history. The photographs that accompany the article tell the story. One picture shows a girl, her hands encased in boxing gloves, an expression of utter delight on her face. Another picture of two women sparring. One of them has her hair upswept and gathered with a comb and she looks beautiful and feminine, but also strong and determined. You look at these pictures and you sense the joy and energy in the room.

I immediately knew I wanted to be a part of this projec in some way and have decided that a percentage of th income I derive from *The Keeper* will go towards fundin CPAU Fighting for Peace. The organization responsibl for the programme is Cooperation for Peace and Unit and the inspirational people in charge have ambitiou hearts. Not only would they like to enlarge the currer programme but they are even hoping to bring a team c Afghan lady boxers to London in 2012 if female boxing granted Olympic status. Any readers who would like t know more about Fighting for Peace or how they ca contribute, please visit www.cpau.org.af/CPAU_Fighting for_Peace/CFFP.html

NOTE

was working on the final chapters of *The Keeper* when I
roke my ankle. It happened while I was sparring with my
ickboxing instructor and managed – much to the surprise
f both of us – to sweep his leg out from underneath him.
Iy ankle remained entangled with his and when we both
it the mat it snapped. For the next eight weeks I would be
Crutches Tiger, Hidden Dragon.

Being able to laugh in a lopsided way at my misfortune
ould not take away from the fact that the fracture was
ainful, required surgery and would keep me from train-
ig for six months. I've had accidents in the past as well –
ruised ribs, a cracked nose and a broken little toe – but
iis was the first time a few uneasy questions started to
attle around in my mind. What was it that so attracted me
> combat? Why do I like to punch and be punched? What
ind of person does that make me?

I still don't have the answers. All I know is that when I
ain I am happy, and am acutely aware of my own vital
iergy. I could therefore not think of a better milieu for a
ook that deals with the concept of chi. However, I know
iere will be readers to whom the idea of physically

challenging someone, even in a controlled environment,
unacceptable and they may have difficulty understandin
Nick Duffy and the world in which he lives. I have com
plete respect for this point of view. But I think Joyce Card
Oates, in her book *On Boxing*, may have said it best:

*Of course it is primitive, too, as birth, death and erotic lov
might be said to be primitive, and forces our relucta
acknowledgement that the most profound experiences of ou
lives are physical events – though we believe ourselves to b
and surely are, essentially spiritual beings.*

Tattoos, quantum physics, sweaty men and chi:
started writing *The Keeper* with a number of highly hap
hazard ideas in my head. Some of these ideas had bee
germinating for a while. When I researched the topic
'remote viewing' for my previous book, *Season of th
Witch*, I became interested in the concept of psi-space an
read up on Hall Putoff's work at Stanford Researc
Institute and his enthusiasm for the Zero Point Field.
chance reading of Lynne McTaggart's *The Field*, in whic
she offers a compelling argument for the concept of a
interconnected universe, further inspired me, specificall
her chapter on Fritz-Albert Popp and his research int
biophotonics. Her second book, *The Intention Experimen
was invaluable to my understanding of remote healin
My imagination was also kicked into overdrive by Robe
O. Becker's intriguing book *The Body Electric*, which dea
with organ regeneration and bioelectronics. As for Reik

is worth remembering that, though Usui Mikao (865–1926) is considered its founder, the origin of healing through universal energy dates back to before the time f Christ and Sammasambuddha. *Fa gung* – the transmission of chi in meditation – is a very old concept.

Dim-Mak – death touch – is a staple of manga and martial-arts films and spans the spectrum with characters hose heads explode as in *Fist of the North Star* to Quentin Tarantino's vengeful Bride in *Kill Bill*. However, he concept itself is a highly complicated one, as I discovered when I started researching the subject. For those eaders interested in reading an actual Book of Light and Dust, I recommend A. Flane Walker and Richard . Bauer's *The Ancient Art of Life and Death*, which also eatures a highly informative section on acupuncture and aditional Chinese medicine. Another excellent work is *he Encyclopedia of Dim-Mak*, by Erle Montaigue and Vally Simpson.

Increasing your chi sensitivity is central to the iscipline of martial arts. For a beautifully written xposition of this journey I highly recommend Kenji okitsu's *Ki and the Way of the Martial Arts*.

The phrase 'stepping out' is my own, as is the concept f 'the Keeper', but I was inspired and enchanted by the any myths and legends that feature battle-scarred arriors who are protected – or cursed – by beautiful, owerful women.

ACKNOWLEDGEMENTS

am privileged to belong to two great dojos: KX Gym UK, and Tim Izli's Cobra Gym — the fighting home of a umber of talented fighters, many of them title-winners. ome of these men and women have trained alongside me, parred with me and have patiently answered my never-nding questions as I followed them from fight to fight. In o particular order, I would like to thank: Tim Izli, Scott oulton, Victor Espinosa, Mati Parks, Frankie Dervish, arah Skelt, Jaime Bodkin, Aaron Deere, Dave Laurent nd the magnificent Errol 'Classy' Christie — a great ghter and a fighting great. Thanks to Cengiz 'Hawk')ervis — Cengiz, it all started with you! Special thanks to hensoy Dervish: *Shen Chi Do* master and the man with ıe stupendous, flying kicks. I have attended his Monday vening class for the past six years and cannot imagine arting my week any other way. I am hugely indebted to arlos 'Lionheart' Andrade, former WKA European ght-heavyweight kickboxing champion. He is teacher, iend and the father of my adorable goddaughter. His ıg-heart fighting style gave me the idea for this book. I

would also like to thank fitness guru and tattoo enthusias
Gideon Remfry for his assistance and for introducing m
to the very cool Mr Alex Binnie of 'Into You Tattoo'. A
Alex never read the manuscript, any errors are, of course
my responsibility alone.

Many thanks to my editor, Selina Walker, and the res
of the team at Transworld Publishers who work so har
on my behalf.

My agent, Jonny Geller, is unfailingly unflappable an
professional and I am terrifically privileged to have him i
my corner.

I depend on a group of friends whose judgement I trus
implicitly to be my first readers. Thanks to Rochell
Colfer, Ksana Golod, Catherine Gull, Dianne Hofmey
Sonja Lewis, Karen McMurray, Niki Muller and m
mother-in-law, Joan Mostert, for their input and encour
agement. Thanks to Valerie Salembier, a lady wit
exquisite taste, for her comments. Special thanks t
Gaynor Rupert: I wouldn't dream any more of turning i
my manuscript without the benefit of her meticulou
feedback. Thanks to my brother, Frans, who has th
unenviable task of ensuring his sister does not embarras
herself too much when it comes to the scientifi
aspects of her books. As I do not always follow his soun
advice, he should in no way be held responsible for m
more extreme flights of fancy. Stefan, my oldes
brother, reminds me to think visually and is responsibl
for my inspired website. My mother, Hantie, is my touch

one. I have never met anyone more creative or imagina-
ve.

Finally, there is Frederick, my deeply wonderful
usband. I am so blessed to have him in my life.

SEASON OF THE WITCH

By Natasha Mostert

CAN YOU REALLY enter someone's mind – and find pure evil?

Gabriel Blackstone has an unusual talent. A computer hacker by trade, he is also able to enter the minds of others.

But he uses his gift only reluctantly – until he is contacted by an ex-lover who begs him to find her stepson, last seen months earlier in the company of two sisters.

And so Gabriel visits Monk House, a place where time seems to stand still, and where the rooms are dominated by a coded symbol of a cross and circle.

As winter closes in, Gabriel becomes increasingly bewitched by the house, and by its owners, the beautiful and mysterious Monk sisters. But even as he falls in love, he knows that one of them is a deadly killer.

But which one? And what is the secret they are so determined to protect?

'A mesmerising thriller – this woman will haunt your days
and keep you awake at night'
MO HAYDER

'Vividly and evocatively written . . . enthralled me right to the end'
THE TIMES

9780553818505